MW00753263

BAJA FLORIDA

Also by Bob Morris

A Deadly Silver Sea
Bermuda Schwartz
Jamaica Me Dead
Bahamarama

BAJA FLORIDA

Bob Morris

Minotaur Books ✹ New York

This is a work of fiction. All of the characters, organizations, and events portrayed in this novel are either products of the author's imagination or are used fictitiously.

BAJA FLORIDA. Copyright © 2009 by Bob Morris. All rights reserved. Printed in the United States of America. For information, address St. Martin's Press, 175 Fifth Avenue, New York, N.Y. 10010.

www.minotaurbooks.com

Library of Congress Cataloging-in-Publication Data

Morris, Bob, 1950–
  Baja Florida / Bob Morris. — 1st ed.
      p. cm.
  ISBN 978-0-312-37726-7
  1. Chasteen, Zack (Fictitious character)—Fiction.   2. Americans—
Bahamas—Fiction.   3. Bahamas—Fiction.   I. Title.
  PS3613.O75555B38 2010
  813'.6—dc22

                                                              2009034522

First Edition: January 2010

10 9 8 7 6 5 4 3 2 1

For Debbie, who has yet to see
the flash of green

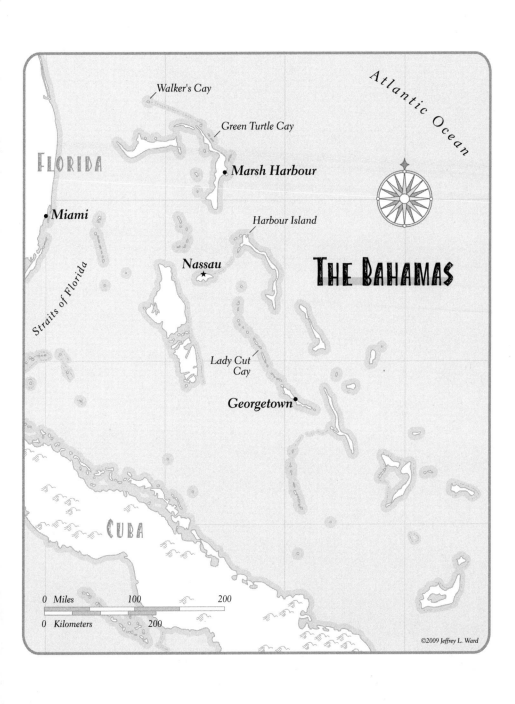

Walker's Cay

Green Turtle Cay

FLORIDA

• Marsh Harbour

• Miami

Harbour Island

Straits of Florida

Nassau

THE BAHAMAS

Lady Cut
Cay

Georgetown•

CUBA

Atlantic Ocean

0 Miles   100   200
0 Kilometers   200

©2009 Jeffrey L. Ward

BAJA FLORIDA

"You screwed up. She's like in a coma or something."

"She'll come out of it."

"You keep saying that. She'll come out of it, she'll come out of it . . ."

"She drank water this morning. She drank some of that juice. What was it . . ."

"Mango nectar. It's healthy."

"Yeah, that. Someone in a coma they wouldn't sit up and open their mouth and drink it."

"She drank it and then she passed out again. How much of that stuff did you give her anyway?"

"Not nearly as much as the other two."

"Jesus, I hope not. The other two, it dropped them like bags of rocks."

"Yeah, they never even knew what was happening."

"You think anyone will find them?"

"You kidding? A thousand feet of water? Out in the middle of nowhere?"

"What about the boat? What if someone comes looking for it?"

"The boat's taken care of. Not our problem anymore."

"But what if something goes wrong? What if . . ."

"Look, stop worrying, will you? You're driving me nuts."

"But my mind won't stop. I can't think about anything else."

"Here's something else."

"What?"

"Think about the money."

1

I was sitting on the front porch enjoying the breeze off Redfish Lagoon when I heard the crunch of tires on our shell driveway.

Oyster shells mostly. Early-warning devices. Not as annoying as barking dogs. Cheaper than closed-circuit cameras.

Small craters and washouts riddled the driveway. Dodging the holes demanded considerable zigzagging. A poor man's security system. One does not approach Chasteen's Palm Tree Nursery unannounced or at a high rate of speed.

It was too early in the afternoon for Barbara and Shula to be returning home.

I wasn't expecting any deliveries.

And the nice people from Jehovah's Witnesses had long since stopped dropping by to chat. Had something to do with the time I opened the door wearing nothing but my Zackness. An innocent lapse on my part after a long night involving Guayanese rum.

No telling who might be heading down the driveway.

An actual paying customer would be nice. They'd been scarce lately. But customers, at least the regular ones, usually got in touch first to make sure I had what they were looking for and to check on prices.

So who could it be?

Tourists sometimes pulled in thinking this was part of Coronado National Seashore. A forgivable mistake seeing as how fifty-seven thousand acres of park surrounded us on three sides, running all the way east to the Atlantic Ocean and along sixteen miles of undeveloped coastline, an oxymoron anymore in Florida.

The federal government would love nothing more than to gobble up our measly thirty acres and add it to their holdings. To his last dying day my grandfather succeeded in fighting them off. The courts ruled that as long as Chasteen's Palm Tree Nursery remains a viable business then Chasteens can continue to live here.

I make some money selling palm trees. Make some money doing other things, too. Just call me Mr. Viable.

The crunching got closer.

And the breeze blew a little harder.

It was coming out of the northwest, carrying with it the lagoon's rich estuarial aroma. Lots of folks, they take a whiff and say it stinks. But it stinks good. The primal stink of Florida—muck and mangrove and all manner of briny things.

A black limo rolled to a stop at the end of the driveway.

We don't get many limos, black or otherwise, in LaDonna, Florida, population four human beings, twenty thousand palm trees, and fifty gazillion mosquitoes, more during the rainy season.

Down by the lagoon, a contingent of carpenters, dry-wall guys, electricians, and what-all was adding a second and third story to the boathouse. Barbara's new office, the galactic headquarters of Orb Communications.

When it was done she could finally stop commuting to Winter Park and back, two hours round-trip, which meant taking Shula with her because the whole breast-feeding thing was still going on.

Barbara had tried the alternative—breast pump and bottles and leaving Shula at home with me.

"It's just not working, Zack," she said after a week of trying it.

"Am I doing something wrong?"

"No, not at all. It's not you. It's me. The pump, the bottles—it's all just such an aggravation. Plus . . ."

"Plus what?"

"Plus, I just can't bear being away from her."

I couldn't bear being away from either one of them, but since Barbara couldn't just close up shop, and since I was the dispensable part of the feeding equation . . .

The addition to the boathouse couldn't get finished fast enough. The two women in my life, I was ready to have them here with me all the time.

The hammering and sawing and what-all stopped. Eyes turned to the limo.

No one got out.

I could see the driver behind the windshield. Big guy in a chauffeur's hat. The other windows were tinted and I couldn't see anything behind them.

I took my feet off the porch rail but I didn't get up from the chair. A plantation chair with long arms and a rattan back and a plump, soft cushion to sit on. Not the kind of chair one abandons without considerable regret.

It was April and a waxing crescent moon. Shrimp had been running in the lagoon—browns and whites. We don't get the pinks up here. You find them more offshore and down in the Keys.

The prime falling tide was still hours away, but already several small boats had claimed their positions along the channel as it funneled around the puzzlement of islands behind our house. Last run of the season, probably. The shrimp were smaller now, but still plenty sweet.

Maybe, come dark, I'd go out on the end of the dock and try to net a few. Shrimp and grits for breakfast the next morning. Yeah, that would be just fine. Toss in some chunks of Spanish ham first and sauté the shrimp with that. Even finer.

The driver's door opened on the limo. The driver got out.

White guy. Black suit, black shirt, black shoes. Not quite as big as he looked through the windshield but big enough.

He eyed me on the porch, straightened his hat, started walking my way.

I put my feet back on the porch rail.

The driver stopped by the steps.

"Zack Chasteen?"

"You're looking at me."

"Mr. Ryser is waiting in the car."

The driver read the look on my face.

He said, "You weren't expecting us?"

I shook my head.

He said, "Mr. Ryser called twice earlier today. Left a message both times to let you know he'd be dropping by."

"Didn't hear the phone and I'm bad about checking messages," I said. "You're telling me Mickey Ryser is in that car?"

The driver nodded.

"He'd like to see you."

I had to laugh.

Mickey Ryser. In a limo.

Not that he couldn't afford it. He could buy a fleet of them if he wanted. But it wasn't his style.

Mickey's last visit, he'd been on a Harley Fat Boy with a flames-of-hell paint job. Time before that, behind the wheel of a vintage Porsche 356 D Roadster, silver as I remember.

Mickey Ryser. It had been a while.

"How about you tell Mr. Mickey Ryser he can drag himself out of that fancy car and join me on the porch," I said. "Meanwhile, I'll grab us a coupla beers."

I got up from the chair.

The driver hadn't moved.

"Please, Mr. Chasteen. If you'll come with me."

Something about the way he said it . . .

As if on cue, the breeze laid. Everything got still.

I stepped off the porch and followed him to the limo.

2

A back door of the limo opened as we approached.

A woman stepped out. A stout black woman in a crisp white uniform. A dainty white nurse's cap on her head. The hat looked peculiar, like a tiny bird had made a nest in her hair and abandoned it for something better. She nodded me inside the limo.

I heard Mickey Ryser before I saw him: a gurgling sound, like a straw siphoning the last of a Big Gulp.

Came from a tube running into Mickey's nose, a tube attached to a green oxygen tank. More tubes running into his arms. Attached to plastic IV bags filled with clear liquids and dangling from the rail of a stretcher.

One of the limo's seats had been removed to make room for the stretcher. Mickey Ryser lay atop it, the head of the stretcher cranked up so that we were eye to eye when I squeezed inside and sat down on the remaining seat.

My face gave me away again.

"Aw, c'mon, Zack. I don't look that bad, do I?"

But yeah, he did. Shrunken and gray, eyes big in their sockets. Way too much hollow in his cheeks.

He wore what he always wore—a vintage and gloriously tacky tropical shirt over khaki shorts. This particular shirt was a hideous red with grinning purple monkeys drinking out of big yellow coconuts. A valiant effort at jauntiness on Mickey Ryser's part, but not enough to hide the fact that he was little more than a cadaver in clothes.

"Good to see you, man," I said.

He stuck out a hand and I gripped it and we held on to each other until it got awkward and then we let go.

Mickey coughed. And then he coughed some more.

The short, stout black woman got back into the limo and knelt by the stretcher. She poured Mickey a cup of water, held it while he drank, and toweled off what dribbled down his chin.

"Zack, meet Octavia," Mickey said. "She calls herself a nurse. Mostly she just sits on her wide black Jamaican ass and watches TV."

Octavia took a playful swat at him.

"Bettah hold dat tongue, mon. Else you be finding someone else to look after your awful white self."

"Me and Octavia, we have a rapport," Mickey said.

"Hunh," Octavia said. "What you and me have is daily combat."

She fluffed his pillow, straightened his shirt, made a fuss over him. Then she sat down beside me.

Mickey said, "Spent the last week in Gainesville, at Shands Hospital. Heading down to Miami now. Got a plane chartered to take me to my place in Exuma."

"Didn't know you had a place in Exuma."

"Bought it a year or so ago, right after . . ." He looked himself over. "Right after all this started."

"Whereabouts in Exuma?"

"About twelve miles north of George Town. Little speck of a place called Lady Cut Cay."

"You bought a whole island?"

"Not like it's all that big. But it's got a grass landing strip. Protected harbor with a new dock. Little bit of elevation with a house up top looking out on everything. Used to belong to some actor bought it for him and his wife to go on their honeymoon. Then they split up. It's beat-all beautiful, Zack. And the sunsets, they're something else. Saw the flash of green three times last month."

"Sounds nice."

"It is nice, Zack. That's why I bought it," Mickey said. "Man needs a nice place to die."

I didn't say anything.

"Don't mean to get all heavy on you. But there's no other way to tell it."

"How long?"

"Days, weeks. Who the hell knows?"

I looked at Octavia. She looked out the door. We were quiet for a while.

Finally, Mickey said, "What you thinking?"

"I'm thinking you should have gotten in touch before now."

"Why? So we could have a pity party on the telephone? You know me better than that, Zack. I don't go for that moping-around crap. Been too busy planning my wake. Gonna have it in Miami. At Vizcaya Mansion. A real blowout. Loud band. Lots of booze. Fireworks. The whole bit."

"I'll be there."

"Damn right you will. I've got you down for the eulogy. Make me look good, you hear?"

"That'll take considerable lying."

"Why I picked you," he said.

We laughed. Then we stopped. And we sat there for a while saying nothing. My throat got tight. Octavia shuffled in her seat.

"Need to get me some air," she said. She stepped outside and joined the driver, who was leaning against the front of the limo.

Mickey looked at me.

"Hell of a thing, isn't it?"

"Yeah," I said. "It is."

"I'm good with it though. I've made my peace, settled up all my accounts. Except for one thing."

I looked at him, waiting.

"Need a favor, Zack. A big favor."

"All you gotta do is ask, Mickey. You know that."

He grinned.

"In that case," he said, "make it two big favors."

3

So," Barbara said. "It's his dying wish."

"Two wishes."

"To take his boat out for a last ride."

"And to be with his daughter," I said.

"The boat's in Nassau?"

"Yeah, but it's more yacht than boat. A sixty-eight-foot Trumpy. One of the last Trumpys ever built. Mickey bought it a few years back and dropped a bundle restoring it. It was getting some engine work done up in Nassau, only it took longer than he planned. Mickey had a crew lined up to deliver it to his place in Exuma, but they bailed on him."

"What about the daughter?"

"It's complicated," I said.

We were in the kitchen. Barbara sipped chardonnay and played with Shula while I finished making dinner. Sautéed snapper with sweet plantains on top. Grilled romaine with blue cheese, lots of it. Cuban bread, homemade from the James Beard recipe. You roll the dough into a loaf, cut three slashes across the top, brush it with ice water, then put it in a cold oven with a pan of hot water underneath it. Bake at 350 degrees for forty minutes. Comes out nice and crusty. Then you slather an ungodly amount of butter on it. And everything is right with the world.

The last bit of daylight was seeping from the sky. Redfish Lagoon basked in the afterglow, its waters gone purplish now. We had the windows open and the no-see-ums were coming in through the screens.

They didn't seem to be bothering Barbara or Shula. But I was slapping my ankles and scratching at my head and cussing all of insectdom.

Barbara poured a bit more chardonnay, her two-glass limit. I opened another beer. Shula slurped juice from her brand-new sippy cup. The family happy hour. Life was good. Except for the damn no-see-ums. And the news about Mickey Ryser.

Barbara said, "He seems so young."

"Seven years older than me."

"Tell me again how the two of you met."

"It was right after my parents died."

"What were you, six?"

"Yeah, almost," I said. "A couple of weeks after the funeral, Mickey showed up here at the house and asked if I wanted to learn how to surf."

"Just out of the blue?"

"That's the way it seemed then, but looking back on it now it was probably my grandfather's idea. Most likely, Mickey saw the chance to make a little money and he grabbed it. He was a hustler, even back then. Had to be."

"Why's that?"

"His family. It was all screwed up. Mickey's dad was long gone. His mom came and went. Mickey and his sisters lived with an aunt. Trailer park, down by Edgewater. They didn't have much. Anything Mickey ever got, he got for himself."

"So your grandfather paid him to look after you?"

"Yeah, only I didn't figure that out until years later. It wasn't like he was a babysitter. More like . . ."

"A friend?"

"A brother," I said. "The big brother I never had."

"So he taught you how to surf?"

"He taught me everything," I said.

Not to take anything away from my grandfather, who did his best to raise me after my folks were gone, but my life would surely have assumed a different trajectory had it not been for Mickey Ryser.

By the time I met him, Mickey had already won the first of several Eastern Surfing Association championships. The classic Florida beach kid—long sun-bleached hair, seldom seen wearing much other than a pair of board shorts. In and out of trouble, but nothing all that bad. Cherry bombs in the grumpy neighbor's mailbox. Driving a car without a permit. Stealing beer from the 7-Eleven on a dare from some older kids.

Mickey Ryser was fearless, the coolest guy in Minorca Beach. And I wanted to be just like him.

He taught me how to surf. He taught me how to throw a baseball. He taught me how to tackle with my shoulders instead of my arms. He also taught me a bunch of other things essential to a young man's adolescent development—how to cuss, how to blow smoke rings, how to act around girls.

Yes, Mickey Ryser was always there for me.

Even in high school, when he had a car, along with social opportunities that were not enhanced by hanging out with a punk like me, he found the time. After graduating, he went to work at the local surf shop. He claimed he couldn't afford college. But although he never said as much, I later came to understand that one reason he didn't want to leave town was me. He wanted to make sure I was going to be alright.

"So how did he make all his money?" Barbara asked.

I pulled the bread out of the oven. It needed to rest a couple of minutes.

"Let's just say he parlayed an unexpected windfall to his advantage," I said.

I never heard the story straight from Mickey's mouth, but substantial rumor had it that he'd gone surfing early one morning at Coronado Inlet and chanced upon a half-dozen bales of pot that had been tossed overboard by some luckless smuggler. Square grouper. The catch of the day along the Florida coast back then.

Mickey wasn't a doper, at least no more than anyone else in those days, but he wasn't one to turn his back on opportunity either. He sold the pot, bought the surf shop. Then he just kept buying and buying. Mickey was smart about real estate. Smart about business, too.

By the time I was playing ball at Florida, Mickey was flush enough to pony up the sizable donation it took to be a Bull Gator. Private parking privileges, seats on the fifty-yard line. He brought my grandfather to all the games.

After I signed with the Dolphins, Mickey decided he might as well buy a place in Miami, too. He was into all sorts of things by then. Apartment buildings in Atlanta. A car dealership in Fort Myers. A horse farm south of Gainesville. Over the years we saw less and less of each other. Still, we were forever connected.

"So tell me about the daughter," Barbara said.

"Her name's Jen," I said. "Mickey hasn't seen her in a long time. Since she was a kid. More than twenty years ago."

We both looked at Shula. Still slurping from her sippy cup. Still adorable.

"Can't imagine," Barbara said.

"Me neither."

I put dinner on the table. Another masterful presentation from Chef Chasteen. Barbara was digging in before I sat down. An enthusiastic eater, Barbara. High on the list of the many things I loved about her.

"Mickey's first wife—her name was Molly—she won sole custody of Jen when the two of them split up. She didn't make it easy for Mickey to see their daughter. She moved them around a lot, never told Mickey where they were."

"He didn't have to pay child support?"

"I don't know all the details, but Molly had plenty of money of her own—her family was well off, owned timberland and pulp mills—and apparently she was fed up, wanted a clean break, nothing more to do with him. Can't say that I really blamed her."

"Why's that?"

"Mickey was a wild man back then. He had more money than he knew what to do with and he was barely thirty. He had no business getting married, no business having kids. We all have times in our lives when we wish we could claim do-overs. That's one of his."

"Still, Zack, there are ways, legal ways, for a father to occasionally visit his children. If he really wants to. I mean, how could he go that long without seeing his daughter? It's unthinkable."

"You're absolutely right. I know Mickey regrets the way he's handled things. Especially now."

"This Jen, she's his only child?"

"As far as I know."

"So she stands to inherit something when he dies?"

"Mickey and I didn't talk about that. But Mickey being Mickey, yes, I'm certain he plans to take care of her."

"What about the mother?"

"Molly died six months ago. Car accident. Mickey heard about it and that's when he found Jen and reached out to her."

"Did she reach back?"

"The two of them have been talking, yes."

"Does she know he's dying?"

"Can't tell you that. All I know is that the last time Mickey heard from her—about a month ago—she said she was planning to visit him and would be there within a couple of weeks. She had been living in Charleston, going to college, and had just bought a sailboat. She and some friends planned to head south, do some island-hopping, their big post-graduation adventure before finding jobs and making their ways in the real world."

"Putting off the inevitable."

"Which, ultimately and in the very broadest sense, is the lifework of us all."

"Whoa," Barbara said. "You getting philosophical on me, Chasteen?"

"Fatherhood has brought out the profundity in me."

We worked on our food. It was easy work. I thought about another beer. I thought maybe I'd forgo the beer in favor of an after-dinner rum. Another example of me, the deep thinker.

"Here's what I don't get," Barbara said. "Why would he ask you to track down his daughter? I mean, there are people who do that sort of thing for a living. Professionals."

"I told him that. He did everything he could to find her. But he didn't really have a lot to go on. The only phone number he had for her was a landline and it has been disconnected. Didn't know the names of Jen's friends, the ones who were going with her. Didn't even know the name of her boat or where she was keeping it in Charleston. He tried to go through Bahamian authorities, just to see if she had passed through customs and immigration. Got nowhere on that front. Just before he went into the hospital, he hired a private detective in Miami. Sent him a ten-thousand-dollar retainer. Hasn't heard a word since."

"And time is running out for him."

"Yeah, I'm afraid it is."

"So, Chasteen to the rescue."

"Appears that way."

"You find the girl, get the yacht, and grant Mickey Ryser his dying wish."

"Simple as that," I said.

She came out of it in stages. Sleeping, waking. Sleeping, waking. Not certain where one ended and the other began.

Her mouth was dry, crusty around the corners of her lips. Like when she was sixteen and had knee surgery after her cleats caught on the lacrosse field. Torn ACL. The anesthesiologist stuck a needle in her arm and told her to count backward from hundred. She'd made it to ninety-four.

And when she'd woken up it was like this. Woozy, nothing making sense. She half expected to see her mother standing at her bedside. She had always been there for her. Always.

She strained to see. Everything was black.

She tried to put thoughts together, hold on to something.

She hurt all over. Especially along the top of her back, the left side, by the shoulder blade. She remembered: A storm. Running to the foredeck, falling. And blood. Lots of blood.

And who was it? Will. Yes, Will. Dr. Will. Helping her down below, cleaning the wound, making her drink Absolut straight from the bottle as he stitched her up. And Pete, always the joker, saying, "Just like the cowboys would have done it. Here, pardner, take a belt of cranberry vodka."

But that had been on the crossing, not long after they left Charleston. And other days had followed that.

And what? Then what?

The last thing she recalled: On the boat. Night. All of them sitting in the cockpit, having a good time. And then . . . and then things fell apart.

What she thought was: Something happened, something bad, and now I'm at the hospital.

Only . . .

She couldn't see. Something was wrapped around her eyes.

A bandanna? What? Duct tape . . .

Must pull it off.

But she couldn't. Her hands, tied behind her. Her feet, they were tied, too.

That's when she screamed.

4

The deal that Barbara and I have going is that I do the grocery shopping and the cooking, and she does the cleaning up afterward. Which can be considerable. My *mise en place* is better described as me really messing up the place.

So when we were done with dinner, I got out of the way and headed down to the boathouse with Shula. She was strapped in a baby sling, a papoose-style contraption that let her ride on my chest so she could face out and see everything I saw.

Time was when I would spot a father hauling his child around in a baby sling and think: *No way on God's good earth will you ever catch me wearing one of those things.*

Then Shula came along. And I got soft in the head.

My office, such as it was, occupied the first floor of the boathouse. I stepped inside, flipped on the light, looked around: Sofa, desk, refrigerator, rods and reels, cast nets, tackle boxes, outboard motor propellers, gas cans, motor oil, nautical charts, a couple of crab traps, scuba tanks, assorted flotsam and jetsam that I couldn't remember exactly how it got there or what I needed it for.

There wasn't any work that really needed doing in my office, but it gave me a sense of accomplishment to visit it occasionally, put in an appearance, let it know who was the boss.

Before long, I'd have company on the two floors above me. I wasn't sure exactly how many people would be making the move to the new

Orb Communications headquarters. As many as twenty perhaps. Editors, an art director, and a couple of designers. Some accounting people, the circulation director, and an IT guy. Barbara ran a pretty bare-bones operation. The ad reps were scattered all over the place and telecommuted mostly. Barbara farmed out the HR work.

Compared to the rest of the magazine business, which was in a fiery tailspin, Barbara's publications were holding their own. The flagship, *Tropics,* was a few pages thinner than in previous years, but circulation was steady and a loyal core of advertisers remained on board. Barbara had steered the company more in the direction of custom publishing for niche audiences. Quarterly in-room magazines for boutique hotel chains. Slick biannual publications for some high-end resorts and a couple of cruise lines. A few months before Shula's birth, she had made a trip back to London, met with some old college friends now in high places, and landed lucrative contracts for publishing the annual reports of several international corporations. She called it bottom-feeding, but it bulked up the cash flow. And there was enough hope in the future to constitute a capital investment in a new office atop the boathouse.

Not all the staff was happy about leaving Winter Park. For those who'd be moving to Minorca Beach, Barbara was helping absorb the relocation costs. And for those who would be making the haul back and forth, she was leasing a couple of vehicles for carpooling and giving plenty of flex time. She was good to her people.

I was good to my people, too. I told him he had put in a long, hard day and it was time to knock off for the night.

"Thanks, boss," I said.

Then I flipped off the office light, locked the door.

I walked Shula and me out on the dock and sat us down at the end, feet dangling over the water.

Shula cooed and made her little-girl, gurgly sounds. Whatever she was saying, it was brilliant.

I cooed back and made gurgly sounds of my own. Yeah, totally soft in the head.

I sipped from the glass of rum I'd brought from the house. Flor de Caña. From Nicaragua. The twelve-year-old old stuff. My go-to brand of late. I sampled some more.

Drinking while daddying. Call the authorities.

The big lights that hung out over the end of the dock illuminated the water and I could spot shrimp after shrimp working their way in the falling tide. My Oak Hill Sock was close at hand. It's a tight-mesh dip net on a twelve-foot aluminum pole. The net funnels at the end and hangs down like a long tube sock. The shrimp stay put in there so you don't have to empty the net every time you catch one.

It was a pretty good run, a regular freeway full of shrimp, free for the plucking. There was lots of activity on the boats in the channel. But tonight I figured I'd let the shrimp live. Plenty of fun just to sit there and watch them.

Shrimp don't exactly swim. It's more like they do abdominal crunches in the water. They draw their tails toward their heads and then snap straight and it propels them along.

Which, thanks to the way shrimp are built, means they move through life ass-backward, never knowing exactly where they're going or what they might be getting themselves into.

Not that the metaphor for my life was identical to that of a lowly crustacean's, but there you have it.

I leaned over and nuzzled Shula. Gave her lots of kisses, rubbed my nose along the back of her neck. There's no smell quite like baby smell. Maybe it's the innocence seeping out.

Shula crooked her head and looked up at me. In her growing inventory of expressions, she was giving me a new one. It was a look that said: *Something's going on, I know it. What's bugging you anyway?*

Women. You can't hide anything from them.

I held Shula close and we sat like that until she dozed off and I heard footsteps on the dock and Barbara sat down beside us. She put a hand on my knee and leaned against me, her head on my shoulder.

A mullet leaped and belly-flopped back into the water. Country music played from one of the boats in the channel. Barbara pointed at something in the night sky.

"Look," she said. "A falling star."

"Lightning bug."

"Mmmm, you're right."

"Don't sound so disappointed. Better to see lightning bugs these days than falling stars."

"Oh yeah?"

"Yeah. Lightning bugs are becoming extinct. Their numbers are down something like forty percent over the last decade. I read it somewhere."

"Hmmm," Barbara said.

"Urban sprawl. Fewer and fewer places where it gets truly dark any-more. Makes it tough for male lightning bugs to find female lightning bugs. Bottom line: No lightning bug babies."

"I'm intimately familiar with how that works," Barbara said.

"Meanwhile, there are more and more falling stars. Only most of them aren't really falling stars but what astronomers call orbital debris—space junk and chunks of dead planets. World's going to hell, the universe is crumbling around us."

Barbara looked at me.

"In a bit of a funk, are we?"

I shrugged.

"It's not like you, Zack."

I shrugged again.

Barbara sat up with a start, pointed overhead.

"Look, there goes another one," she said. "Maybe that's the male lightning bug about to find his honey."

"Maybe," I said.

She snuggled beside me, tickled my ribs.

"You think when lightning bugs do it they shoot off sparks?"

I laughed.

"Hope so," I said.

"You leave tomorrow?"

I nodded.

"Boggy going with you?"

I nodded again.

"Well, that makes me feel a little better."

"Just a little?"

"A lot actually. Nothing the two of you can't handle."

"Figure we'll head down to Miami first, have a few words with this de-tective who's giving Mickey the runaround. Any luck, he'll have some kind of a lead on where we might find Jen Ryser."

"How old is she? Twenty-two, twenty-three?"

"Something like that," I said.

"You know how it is when you're that age, Zack. Out spreading your wings, having a good time, oblivious to the rest of the world. You'll find her and be back home before we even knew you were gone."

"Doesn't make leaving any easier," I said.

She looked at me.

"And since when did you become Mr. Homebody? You haven't been anywhere in nearly six months, since Shula was born. Not like you to stay put for that long."

"Guess I'm becoming domesticated."

"You say it as if it were an infectious disease."

"No, it's not like that at all. But . . ."

"But, but, but . . ." She shook her head. "Darling, you are a wonderful husband and an absolutely perfect and doting father, but you will never be wholly domesticated. It is not in your nature. So don't be frightened that it might be happening to you. It's a biological impossibility. And I love you ever the more for it."

I started to say something, but she put up a hand to silence me.

"Please, I know that the gentleman in you feels it necessary to protest, feels it necessary to make me think that you are perfectly content to sit on your porch and oversee the construction and keep an eye on your business and . . ."

"Hasn't been much business, lately."

"My point exactly," Barbara said. "Inertia does not become you, Zack Chasteen. You are a creature of motion. Deep down inside you've been craving for something to come along that would require you to haul yourself out of house-husbandry and hit the road. That opportunity has now presented itself and you need not feel the least bit guilty about it."

As always, she'd pegged me.

Barbara said, "Thing about us, Zack, we get along together. And we get along apart. Not everyone can say that."

"I like the together better."

"Me, too. But sometimes we need the apart to fully appreciate the together."

"You saying you'll be glad to get rid of me?"

"No, I'm not saying that at all. But . . ."

"But what?"

She curled up against me.

"I won't mind having the bed all to myself when you're gone."

"Is the bed really that crowded with me in it?"

She looked up. Something about her eyes. They swallowed me.

"Perhaps I'm mistaken," she said. "Perhaps further research is required."

"Perhaps we should go hop in that bed and conduct research of a collaborative nature."

She gave my leg a squeeze.

"Perhaps, my ass," she said.

Breathe in, breathe out. Stay calm. Try to figure out what's going on . . .

She lay on her side. Thin mattress on a narrow bed. Her legs hanging over the edge of it. Coarse blanket against her cheek.

She was on a boat. She knew that much.

She could feel it rocking gently, side to side. Like it was anchored somewhere. No slap-slap-slap of forward motion.

Not her boat. Because there was the odor of old bilge and diesel and mildew, and her boat, it didn't smell like that.

She was a fanatic about keeping her boat tidy. When they were provisioning, getting ready to leave Charleston, Karen had made fun of all the cleaning supplies she'd bought at Harris Teeter.

"Ya know, Jen, they do *sell Clorox in the islands. And an entire case of teak oil? You think there's going to be a worldwide shortage while we're gone or something?"*

Her boat didn't sound like this boat either. Her boat, she knew its creaks and groans. She'd lived on it for two months before they left, fell asleep each night listening to the clang of the halyards, the whine of the stays.

Her boat, it spoke to her. This boat did not.

She heard: Footsteps, from somewhere above, getting closer. A door sliding open.

A voice: "Well, well. If it's not Sleeping Beauty."

Another voice: "Damn, it stinks down here. Look what she did to the blanket. What a mess."

"The back of her T-shirt, it's all bloody."

"Too bad Dr. Boy isn't here to take care of her."

She recognized the voices.

"We need to get her out of those clothes, wash her down."

"You'll like that, won't you?"

"Just shut up and help me."

"We'll have to untie her first."

"You untie her. I'll hold her. She's not going to put up a fight. Are you, Jen? Just be a good girl."

She said, "Where are my friends?"

"Don't you worry about them, Jen. You just do what we tell you."

She felt his hands upon her shoulders.

She tensed.

The other one untied her legs, her arms.

She waited.

Hands, his hands, pulling her T-shirt over her head and off.

Other hands unbuttoning her shorts . . .

She waited.

Yanking her shorts down . . .

And then she rolled, pulling both of them with her onto the floor. Landing a knee, hard, into the one beneath her. Her elbows jabbing ribs, soft flesh, anything.

Her blows had little strength behind them. Still, weak as she was, she managed to break free, scramble blindly across the floor.

They were on her in an instant, pinning her down.

"Bitch!"

A hard fist into the side of her head. Again and again.

Darkness . . .

5

Boggy and I were on the road by 6:00 A.M. I had a thermos of Café Bustelo. Boggy had a thermos of God-only-knows-what. He poured some in his cup. It made the car smell like something that might get stuck on the bottom of your shoe and you wouldn't bother scraping it off, you'd just throw the shoe away.

"What is that stuff?"

"*Maja acu*," Boggy said. "Is Taino for 'Big Eye Tea.'"

"Big Eye as in wakes you up?"

"No, more like Big Eye as in helps you see."

"See what?"

"See what you would not see if you did not drink it."

"It legal?"

"By whose law?"

"By the law of any highway patrolman who might pull me over, ask what's in there, and then haul the both of us to jail."

Boggy drained the cup. Then he drained the rest of the thermos.

"We're good," he said.

He closed his eyes and for the rest of the drive to Miami he just sat there seeing whatever the hell he saw—a short dark man with long black hair and the visage of some ancient stone-faced tiki god.

I saw U.S. 1 going south in the early morning. Tiny pockets of it were still distinctly Florida—tidal creeks and salt marshes, mom 'n' pop motels and bait shacks, houses built to fit a place, not to make a statement about net worth.

But more and more it was just a slice of anywhere. The same restaurant that would serve me the same hamburger in Omaha. The same motel that would offer me the same thin mattress in Dubuque. The same gated developments with the same insipid names—Oak Run, Pine Glen, Quail Hollow—that substituted nomenclature for what they had stripped from nature.

I recalled a sign I had seen at Minorca Beach, just north of our place. Most of Minorca County allows people to drive cars on the beach, a long-standing tradition in this part of Florida, dating back to the days when the first stock car races were held on the hard-packed sands at Daytona. A big part of me knows that driving cars on the beach doesn't make a lick of sense. Not good for loggerhead hatchlings that get squashed under steel-belted radials. Not good for sunbathers on beach blankets who get mistaken for speed bumps. But this is Florida and good sense is not an abundant natural resource. All fourteen million of us want a place where we can plant an umbrella and a chaise lounge and enjoy our little place in the sun. Yes, the beach belongs to everyone. And the notion that access to it is the exclusive domain of those who can afford to own pricey oceanfront homes doesn't sit right with me either.

Recently, driving had been outlawed along a five-mile stretch of south Minorca Beach. In addition to putting up Day-Glo barricades to divert traffic, the county had erected a pair of giant signs that read "Natural Area Ahead." It was like planting wildflowers in the median of the interstate and calling it a "Wildlife Refuge." No matter that beyond the pair of giant signs the five-mile stretch was zero-lot lined with ticky-tacky condos built where soaring dunes once stood. No matter that the beach itself was actually fill that had been pumped in from offshore by huge dredges after the last hurricane and would likely disappear with the next big blow. No matter that the endemic coastal vegetation—sea oats, scrub oaks, and spartina grass—had been replaced by sod lawns, hibiscus hedges, and other exotic flora that needed constant irrigation from an increasingly tapped-out aquifer. No matter that the most abundant fauna was flocks of squawking seagulls that subsisted on a diet of Cheetos and discarded fried chicken. It was, by official proclamation and garish signage, a "Natural Area." And it irked me. It irked me because it bespoke an insidious mentality, one that had crept in to diminish our understanding of nature in its most precious and bona-fide form. It made us increasingly numb to venal encroachment and blind to greed masquerading as progress.

But simmer down, Chasteen. You're getting older. You're a husband and a father. By all rights, your mellow years are well upon you. The rage? Let it go, man, let it go.

Besides, generations of Floridians have been raging and to what good? The thirty percent of us who vote still elect county commissioners who buddy-up to developers and lack the foresight of a flea. And the legislature, populated largely by realtors who fancy themselves statesmen, provides ongoing evidence that everything all the other states think about us yahoos down here might well be true: It's not the heat, it's the stupidity.

Perhaps it really is better just to marvel over the ongoing spectacle of Florida, do what you can to save your little part of it, and hope for the best.

If we've succeeded at nothing else, then at least we have succeeded in out-weirding California. Really, there ought to be a cable news channel that is all Florida, all the time. Chronically botched elections, astronaut/hitwomen wearing adult diapers, and Burmese pythons taking over the Everglades. Condo commandos, world-record shark attacks, and a critical mass of trailer trash.

Our peculiar peninsula is the original Dysfunction Junction. Give the U.S.A. a good shake and all the loose parts roll down our way.

Yes, the road to hell passes straight through Florida. Grab a chaise lounge, kick back, and enjoy the parade.

6

Around Titusville I pulled onto I-95 and slid into the southward flow. Traffic started jamming when we hit Delray Beach a couple of hours later, became a total snakepit in Fort Lauderdale, and by the time the interstate folded into Dixie Highway south of downtown Miami, I was ready to get where we were going.

The detective's name was Delgado. Abel Delgado. Mickey Ryser told me he'd been referred to him by a friend of a friend, someone who worked for the Metro Dade Police Department. Delgado had left the force and set up shop for himself. I'd called his office twice on the drive down. Each time I'd gotten a voice on the answering machine—Delgado's, I supposed; monotone, like he was reading from a script—followed by a beep. Then the call disconnected like it does when the answering machine is full.

I'd been expecting a shabby storefront in a run-down strip mall some-where. But the address was Coral Gables, a shiny, five-story office build-ing on Ponce de Leon. Nice neighborhood with soaring palms—Cuban Royals, *Roystonia regia*—lining the street.

I found shade under a banyan tree at a corner of the parking lot. Boggy was in the exact position as when we'd left home hours earlier. Sitting up straight in the passenger seat, hands clasped in his lap, eyes closed.

I gave him a shake. One eye eased open and considered me.

"We're here," I said.

The eye closed. Boggy didn't budge.

Fine, then. I'd go it alone.

I got out of the car and went inside the building. A receptionist's desk sat in the middle of the lobby, sans the receptionist. Near the elevator, a directory listed who was where, and I picked out Delgado Investigations, Suite 121.

I walked down a hall and found Suite 121 at the end of it, past the law office of Andrew Strecker, Esq., and a real estate appraisal firm. I tried the door. Locked. I knocked. No answer. I knocked again. Same thing.

I looked at my watch. Ten o'clock. No reason a private detective should keep regular office hours.

I walked back to the car. I gave Boggy another shake. This time I kept shaking until both his eyes opened.

"Nap time's over."

"Wasn't napping," he said.

"You hungry?"

"No."

"Good. You can watch me eat."

A few minutes later we were sitting at Lario's, just south of Sunset. There are more authentic Cuban joints than Lario's in Miami, places where you order at a walk-up window and eat at the counter next to old men smoking fat cigars and old women studying scratch-off lottery tickets, sometimes vice versa.

But Lario's had a patio and I liked sitting there. The view was nothing special—a Winn-Dixie across the street—but the human scenery was always worth taking in. Not the fashionista South Beach scene, but the ebb and flow of a neighborhood. Good-looking moms with their good-looking kids. Guys with slicked-back hair who might be mobsters. Or who might just as easily be deposed Central American dictators. U.M. coeds who might moonlight at Club Platinum. Young men in dark suits doing deals. Old men in guayaberas dreaming of deals they once did.

When the waiter appeared, I ordered a *cortadito*, Cuban toast, and a chorizo omelet with pica de gallo. Boggy said he'd have the same thing.

"Thought you weren't hungry."

"I'm not," Boggy said.

"Just being sociable?"

He looked at me. Like I should know better.

The waiter brought the *cortaditos* and the toast, and we broke off hunks of toast and dipped them in the coffee and didn't talk.

A man sitting at the table next to us was going on about the Heat and how with a stud like Dwyane Wade why couldn't they do any better than they did. The guys sitting at the table on the other side were talking about all the grouper they'd caught in the Dry Tortugas over the weekend. Then again, they could have been talking about the Heat, too. My Spanish pretty much sucks.

The waiter brought our omelets and we ate them. I ordered another *cortadito*, sucked it down, and paid the bill.

We drove back to the office on Ponce de Leon. This time Boggy deigned to accompany me inside.

It was still short of noon. Still no receptionist at the receptionist's desk. Still no answer to my knocking on the door of Suite 101.

Maybe the neighbors knew something. No one home at the real estate appraisal firm. But the door to the law firm of Andrew Strecker, Esq., opened and we stepped inside.

A woman sat behind a desk in the anteroom. Mid-thirties, pretty enough. More than pretty enough, actually. One of those women it took you a second glance to see all the pretty.

She looked me up and down without passing judgment. She looked at Boggy and her eyes lingered longer and she smiled. That's the way it always is. Women see Boggy and they want to hug him. Sometimes they wind up doing more than that. Beats hell out of me.

"Help you?" she said.

"Actually, we're looking for the guy at the end of the hall. Abel Delgado."

It didn't register. Then she brightened.

"Oh, the detective you mean?"

"Yes, him. Any idea when he usually comes in?"

She shook her head.

"Afraid I can't help you. I've never even laid eyes on him." She shrugged an apology. "But then, I've only been working here a couple weeks. Just a sec . . ."

She punched the intercom button on her phone.

"Mr. Strecker?"

A voice said, "Yeah, Maria, what is it?"

"Men here are asking about the office down the hall."

"They want to rent it, tell them to call the leasing agent."

"I don't think they want to rent it." She looked at me. "Do you?"

"No, just looking for Abel Delgado," I said.

"They're just looking for Abel Delgado," she repeated into the intercom.

A pause, then: "Oh, looking for Abel Delgado. Hold on . . ."

"He'll be right with you," Maria said.

She nodded to a pair of chairs. We didn't take her up on sitting down. She didn't seem offended. She studied Boggy and smiled some more.

A few seconds later, Strecker stepped into the anteroom. Younger than his secretary. Not long out of law school. Tall with shaggy blondish hair.

"Sorry," he said. "I thought you were interested in the office next door. Closed up shop. Appraisal business isn't what it used to be."

"We're looking for Abel Delgado," I said.

I figured if I said it enough it might finally sink in with someone.

Strecker thought about it.

"May I ask what for?"

"Yes," I said.

He waited. Then he got it. He looked away, coughed.

"Reason I ask," Strecker said, "is because I represent Mr. Delgado in . . . in his personal matters. And if this pertains to that, then . . ."

"This pertains to ten thousand dollars he took from a friend of mine as a retainer to locate his daughter. Thing is, my friend has had exactly no luck contacting Mr. Delgado to find out what he has done to earn the money and find the daughter. And now it has become a personal matter. For me."

"Oh, I see," said Strecker. He seemed to be eyeing us for the ball-peen hammers we might have brought along to use on Delgado's kneecaps. Guess I couldn't blame him for thinking that, this being Miami and two guys walking into his office looking like Boggy and me. "I'm afraid I can't help you with that."

"You got any idea what time Delgado might show up at his office?"

Strecker shook his head.

"No," he said.

"What time does he usually show up when he shows up?"

"No special time really," Strecker said. "Early. Late. All hours. It depends."

"When was the last time you saw him?"

"I don't know. A week ago. Maybe longer."

"Know where he lives?"

"Yes," Strecker said.

I waited. Then I got it. Touché.

"Gentlemen," Strecker said.

He turned and went back to wherever he came from.

I tipped my head to Maria.

"Thanks for your time."

She looked over her shoulder to make sure Strecker was long gone.

"Hang on," she said.

She turned to her computer, tapped on the keyboard, squinted at the screen. She wrote something on a piece of paper, folded it over, and handed it to me.

"Try this," she said.

"Appreciate that."

She smiled. This time it wasn't all for Boggy.

"Hope you find the guy's daughter," she said.

The next time it was just him and he didn't untie her.

He pulled her upright on the bed. He sat beside her. They had found her a clean pair of panties and put them on her and that's all she wore now.

He touched the back of her shoulder. She flinched.

"Looks infected," he said. "I'll get something for it."

He ran his fingers down her cheek, put a hand on her thigh.

Her stomach tightened.

He moved his hand between her legs. She tried to squirm away but he held her there.

He brought his face close to hers and spoke in a whisper.

"Sweet, sweet Jen . . ."

"I need to pee."

He jerked his hand away and moved back from her. He helped her up from the bed. He loosened her feet just enough so she could hobble. He left the blind-fold on and her arms bound behind her as he walked her away from the bed. She was a little wobbly and she had to lean into him to keep her balance.

She heard a hatch door slide open. He pulled her panties down to her knees and turned her around. She bumped her head against the top of the door frame. The ceiling was low and she imagined that, tall as he was, he was having to stoop not to scrape against it.

He said, "OK, sit."

He helped her ease down onto the toilet. It sat low on the floor. A chemical toilet, not one that flushed into a holding tank. It told her that the boat she was on wasn't all that big.

He said, "OK, go."

"Can you shut the door?"

"Nope."

The head was cramped. Her shoulders brushed against the walls as she positioned herself atop the toilet. When she was done, she said, "Can you undo my hands?"

"What for?"

"So I can clean myself."

"Down there?"

"Yes."

"All you did was pee, right?"

"Yes."

"So drip dry."

She sat there, and after a moment she said, "I'm thirsty. I need something to drink."

He stepped away and she heard water running from a faucet. She looked up and had a slight sensation of light. Maybe there was a small hatch above her or a ventilation shaft. She could feel air coming from above.

He returned and touched a cup to her lips. He put a hand behind her head, helping her as she drank. She emptied the cup.

"More," she said.

He snickered.

"Oh, Jen, I love it when you say that."

She spit at him. And she kept spitting, bracing for the blow she knew would come. But nothing happened. He stepped away. She sat still and heard the water running and he came back with another cup. She emptied it, too, and when she was done he helped her to her feet, pulled up her panties, and walked her back to the bed.

"You hungry?"

She was weak and hollow and she did not feel like eating. Most of all, she did not want to take anything more from him. She could not bear to feel his touch against her skin. But she knew she could not let herself slip away.

"Yes," she said. "I could eat something."

She heard him rustling around and when he returned to the bed he fed her saltines and chunks of cheese. There were pieces of apple, too.

She ate slowly at first, tentatively, and then as her stomach stopped protesting, she began to devour the food, waiting anxiously for him to offer her another bite. She told herself: Stop it. You're eating from his hand. Don't let it be like this.

But she was so, so empty. So hungry . . .

"That's all," he said, patting her head. "Good girl. You get a gold star."

"Can you at least take off the blindfold? It's not like I don't know who you are."

"No, I don't think so. You misbehaved."

"Just take off the blindfold. Please. I won't try anything. I promise."

"Is it getting to you, Jen?"

"Please . . ."

"Because it would get to me. Can't see anything. Don't know where you are. Don't know what's going to happen next. Yeah, it would really get to me."

He got up from the bed. She heard him pacing. And then he stopped. Jen could tell he was standing there, watching her.

"Seeing you like this, all tied up, feisty, it kinda gets me off. You know what I mean?"

She didn't say anything.

"Gets me off a whole lot more than when we were together."

He stepped close, right in front of her, talking down to her.

"I'm not saying I didn't like doing you, Jen. Not the best I ever had. But not bad. I know you liked it. You liked it a lot, didn't you? I made you scream, didn't I, Jen? You loved it, didn't you? Didn't you?"

He moved in closer, brushed the front of his pants against her face, then thrust himself hard against her. She fell back onto the bed, trying to get away from him.

He stayed where he was, standing above her. She could hear him breathing.

She said, "What do you want?"

"What do you think we want, Jen?"

"Just tell me, alright? Just tell me . . ."

He laughed.

"It's easy, Jen. Real easy," he said. "We want it all."

7

The address Maria gave me belonged to a house way out near the Red-lands. Forty-five minutes west to Homestead and then north, along the edge of the Everglades, an edge that kept getting pushed back and back and back. Zero-lot line homes and spec developments gave way to plant nurseries, small farms, and houses that sat on five-acre tracts.

I drove down a long lime-rock driveway that led to a small concrete-block house. Might have once been a bright shade of yellow, now faded to a cheerless off-white. Brown minivan parked outside, cardboard duct-taped where a rear window used to be. Mango and avocado seedlings studded the backyard, but it looked like whoever planted them had given up on the trees ever bearing fruit. The garage was crammed full of boxes and furniture—the belongings of people who were either moving out or who had never really moved in.

I got out of the car. Boggy stayed put. Still doing his not-really-napping thing.

"You coming?"

No answer.

"Good thing I brought you along," I said.

I walked up to the house and rang the doorbell. Inside, a dog barked. Tiny dog by the sound of it.

A woman's voice said, "Tico, stop it. Stop it right now . . ."

The door opened. A reddish brown furball lunged forward and froze at the threshold yapping away.

"Tico, I told you . . ."

The woman was short and just this side of plump. She wore a baggy T-shirt and baggy sweatpants, thinking maybe the plumpness wouldn't show. She gave the dog the side of her foot, not so hard as to hurt it, but hard enough to make it scoot out of the doorway and stop yapping.

The woman carried a child on one hip, a little boy about two. Behind her I could see a little girl, maybe four, sitting on a sofa watching TV. It was turned up too loud.

The woman wore the wary look of someone who every time she opens the door expects to get more bad news. Still, she forced a smile. Not much hope in it, but at least a try. Who knew? I might be that Publishers Clearing House guy.

"Yes?"

"Looking for Abel Delgado."

The little bit of hope vanished. The woman looked at the ground by my feet.

"Are you Mrs. Delgado?"

She looked at me.

"For now," she said.

She turned and put the little boy in a playpen. She told the little girl to look after her brother while Mommy went outside for a minute.

She stood on the top step, gathering her frizzy brown hair in a ponytail and wrapping a pink scrunchy around it.

"I don't like to talk about Abel in front of the kids." She shrugged. "I mean, he's still their father no matter what."

I nodded.

"I served him the papers three months ago. Told him to move out. Finally had to get a restraining order. I don't know where he has been staying since then. Divorce isn't official yet. He and his lawyer have been postponing things. Abel keeps saying he wants to give it another try." She shook her head. "I'm about tried out."

"When was the last time you heard from him?"

She tilted her head, eyes narrowed.

"You a cop or something?"

"Do I look like a cop?"

She gave me the once-over.

"Better shape than most of them."

I smiled.

"I'll take my compliments where I can get them."

"Not that big a compliment," she said. "Most cops I know are lard asses. Abel, he used to be a cop."

"I'm not a cop."

"So what are you then?"

"Just someone who wants to find your ex-husband."

"He owe you money?"

"Nope."

She gave it some consideration. I gave her another smile.

"Because if Abel owes you money it is really not in my best interest to help you find him. You understand? Because if you get money from him then that is less money he has to give me and the kids. And I could use whatever he's got right now. He's paying the mortage and far as I know that's current. But I've got other bills long past due. Lots of them. Plus we have to eat."

Tears puddling in her eyes.

"His idea to quit the department, go out on his own. There went the health insurance. There went a regular paycheck. His idea to rent space in some fancy office building he couldn't afford. But that's Abel. He says it's thinking big. I say it's getting in over his head. And where has it gotten us? Where?"

She was sobbing now. She sat down on the steps and buried her face in her arms.

The little girl appeared behind a screen window and looked out at her mother.

"It's OK," I told the little girl. "You can go sit down."

But she kept standing there, her eyes going back and forth between her mother and me.

The woman wiped her face with the back of a hand, tried to compose herself.

"Sorry," she said.

"It's alright."

"Sometimes it just gets more than I can take and I explode."

"Good to do that," I said.

She let out some air.

"Look, Mrs. Delgado, I don't want any money from your husband. I just want some information. He's been looking for the daughter of a friend of mine and I need to find out what he knows about her. That's all."

She looked up at me.

"The rich girl?" she said.

"Excuse me?"

"The last time I spoke with Abel, he called to say some rich girl's father had hired him to look for her. He sounded all excited about it. He said . . ."

She stopped.

"He said what?"

She looked away.

"He just said when it was all over he'd have money and everything would be good again."

"When was this?"

"I don't know, two or three days ago."

"You know where he was calling from?"

"Some bar in the Bahamas. He'd been drinking. That was part of the problem. He'd been drinking. A lot."

"He say where in the Bahamas?"

She shrugged.

"Might have, I don't know. Just the Bahamas. That's the part I re-member. We were supposed to go on a cruise there last fall. Didn't hap-pen."

"You have a cell-phone number for him?"

"Yes."

She recited it and I jotted it down.

"Mommy . . ."

The little girl was still at the window.

"Yes, honey. What is it?"

"Ricky spit up, Mommy."

"OK, honey. I'll be right there."

She pulled herself to her feet.

"Duty calls," she said.

I reached in my wallet, pulled out three hundred-dollar bills. I handed them to her. She looked at the money, then at me.

"What's this for?"

I gave her my card.

"If you hear from your husband again, give me a call."

"I can't take this money."

"Sure you can," I said. "Thanks for your help, Mrs. Delgado."

She looked at the money. She looked at me. She stuck out a hand.

"I'm Gloria," she said.

8

We needed a place to spend the night, so I got us a two-bedroom suite at the Mutiny Hotel. Came with a balcony looking out on the bay and the boats anchored around Dinner Key.

There are swanker hotels in Coconut Grove. But the Mutiny enjoys a notoriety that trumps its five-star neighbors and endears it to me.

Back in the day, it was the hangout for the *Miami Vice* crowd before there was a *Miami Vice*. Bad hair, pastel sport coats, cocaine cowboys, and plenty of stories about guests finding bundles of twenties stashed under mattresses by previous tenants who were either too fried to notice or in one giant hurry to get the hell out of Dodge City on the Biscayne.

A little ahead of my time. Still, I felt a certain kinship to the era if only for the fact that I occasionally found myself in the position of having to stash money in places where I hoped it wouldn't be found. The money had come my way via circumstances that, while wholly honorable, were not, by strict definition, legal. Money acquired for services rendered. Money that would take some explaining. Far be it from me to strain the resources of the good and overburdened people who work for the IRS. Better that they should pursue those who acquire their money by dishonorable means. So, to make it easier on both of us, my mattress of choice was currently a bank in Bermuda. A nice little pile of money. I didn't play with it. No sheltered investments or real estate schemes. Just money sitting around, drawing very little interest, but there if I needed it. I thought about it sometimes, fondly, but not so much that it consumed me. Otherwise, it was money not worth having.

No sooner had the bellboy delivered us to our suite than Boggy went into his room and closed the door. Mr. Sociable.

Another way the Mutiny endeared itself to me: It didn't have minibars. I hate minibars. Minibars are the scourge of a gracious hotel experience. The very name—minibar—diminishes the entire expansive notion of imbibing.

So I happily called room service and ordered two bottles of Heineken, cashew nuts, and some extra sharp cheddar cheese. After it was delivered—with a proper flourish, on a tray, with a starched white napkin and a tiny orchid in a bud vase—I sat on the balcony and snacked and drank beer and tried to sort out where things stood.

I needed to get Boggy and myself to the Bahamas, find Jen Ryser, put us all on her father's yacht in Nassau and take us down to Lady Cut Cay. A straightforward enough proposition.

Getting to the Bahamas was the easy part. A pilot buddy, Charlie Callahan, was on standby, just waiting for my call. And I'd already contacted the shipyard in Nassau. Mickey Ryser's yacht was ready to go.

But where, oh where, could Jen Ryser be?

To find someone, it helps if you actually know a little something about that someone. And I knew precious little about Jen Ryser. Not much other than her name, really. I knew that she had graduated from the College of Charleston, bought a sailboat, enlisted some friends to join her on a cruise through the islands, and set off first for the Bahamas. I didn't know exactly where in the Bahamas. I didn't know what kind of sailboat it was, nor its name. I didn't know how many friends were on board, nor their names. I didn't even know what Jen Ryser looked like or how to describe her to anyone who might have seen her. I didn't have a photograph of her. That's because Mickey Ryser didn't have a photograph of her. He hadn't laid eyes on her in more than twenty years. He didn't know what color her hair was, what color her eyes were, how tall she was, how much she weighed. She was just a voice on the phone to him. And he to her. And it was up to me to connect the two of them after all these years so they could have their father-and-daughter reunion. And then Mickey was going to die.

I opened the second Heineken, finished off the cashews.

I called around and got the number for the main Bahamas customs and immigration office in Nassau. I spoke to a clerk and then the clerk's supervisor and then the supervisor's supervisor, all of whom told me what I already knew: Under no circumstances could they give out information about who had entered the country to private citizens such as myself.

"I could have lied and told you I was Homeland Security," I told the supervisor's supervisor.

"Good day, sir," she told me.

I called the U.S. Embassy in Nassau. I eventually spoke with a young man who tried his best not to sound bored as he asked me questions.

"Has the person you are looking for officially been declared missing?"

"No," I said.

"Have you specific reason or evidence to suspect foul play?"

"No," I said.

"Are you among this person's immediate family?"

"No," I said. "But I represent the father."

"Are you an attorney?"

"No," I said. "Just a friend."

"Hmm, I see," said the young man.

Cut to the chase: Not a damn thing he could or would do for me.

I thought maybe I should double my plan of attack. Maybe I should also set my sights on finding Abel Delgado. Maybe I could throw some green incentive at Strecker, the kid lawyer, and get him to help me locate his client.

Gloria Delgado telling me, *"He said when it was all over he'd have money . . ."*

That could mean Delgado had succeeded in finding Jen Ryser and was trying to leverage it for more serious coinage. Or it could just as easily mean that he was barhopping his way around the Bahamas and living life large until the ten-thousand-dollar retainer was all gone. At which point, he would call Mickey Ryser and try to extract a little more. Meanwhile, his soon-to-be-ex-wife and his two kids were sitting in a crummy crackerbox house way out in the Redlands, watching TV on a sofa with no idea where life was leading them.

I sipped Heineken. I ate the last slice of cheese.

I thought about the Bahamas.

It might seem like a small place, just specks on the map. In total land area, it's only about the size of dinky little Connecticut. But that land is spread out over more than three thousand islands, cays, and islets, only about seventy of which are inhabited. And the entire archipelago, stem to stern, stretches nearly eight hundred miles, like the drive from San Francisco to Seattle.

Baja Florida, I call it.

Once you're over the border, no one asks too many questions. A little money, you can hole up, be anyone you want to be.

Drift here, drift there. A lot of territory.

And plenty of places to hide.

"She musta really got you worked up, huh?"

"You complaining?"

"Not at all. I've been itching for you, baby. It's been too long."

"Just a couple of weeks."

"But all that time I had to watch the two of you, going on like you did. You know what that was like?"

"I had to do some watching, too."

"Yeah, but you could tell I wasn't enjoying it."

"You faked it pretty good then."

"We both did."

"That's what we do."

"Still . . ."

"Still what?"

"I don't know. I just keep thinking maybe we should have kept it simple. Like before. Take the boat, get some money, disappear. Now we've got her to worry about."

"Opportunity comes along, you grab it."

"Maybe we tried to grab too much. Maybe we should just get rid of her."

"Trust me, it'll work."

"What makes you so sure?"

"Because I've got confidence in you."

"Yeah?"

"You and me, we're a team. We're gonna pull this off."

"And then what?"

"You know. We talked about it."

"Tell me again. I like to hear you say it."

"And then we're set. We can live the life. Do anything we want to do, go anywhere we want to go."

"Argentina?"

"If you want. Yeah, sure. Argentina."

"Money can go a long way there."

"What I've heard, too."

"South Africa. I always wanted to go on a safari. Wouldn't that be cool?"

"Yeah, wherever."

"You don't like South Africa?"

"Let's get this over with first, OK? Then we can talk about the rest. Lots of things still have to fall in place."

"We need some food, some other stuff."

"I'll go into town this evening."

"Can I come, too?"

"No, you're staying here."

"But I'm going crazy, just sitting around."

"We can't leave her here alone, you know that."

"How long will you be gone?"

"I don't know. Not long. I need to find an ATM, see if the bank card works."

"What if it doesn't?"

"Then she's got a problem. A big problem . . ."

9

Boggy emerged from his room about 5:00 P.M. and announced that he was hungry. We walked down Bayshore to Scotty's Landing. We snagged a table near the seawall. A waiter finally made it our way. I ordered a cheeseburger.

"Same for me," Boggy told the waiter. "But I'll start off with two dozen oysters. And a big glass of chocolate milk."

The waiter wrote it all down and stepped away.

"Chocolate milk and oysters?"

"Such cravings are typical at the end of a long journey," Boggy said.

"Wasn't such a long journey. We left home this morning, drove three hundred miles, and here we are in Miami."

"That was a temporal journey," Boggy said. "I am talking about a journey of a different sort."

"Did you go somewhere I don't know about?"

He just looked at me.

"Oh yeah, right," I said. "One of your *spiritual* journeys. Off in la-la land. You sucked down that mojo yucko stuff . . ."

"*Maja acu,*" Boggy corrected me. "It transports those who drink it to a different plane."

"Cuckoo Kool-Aid."

"The journey, it was long and difficult."

"But now you're back?"

"Yes, now I am back."

"Well, glad to hear it because, frankly, my strange brown friend, you've been a pain in my ass all day. Like some kind of zombie, like you weren't really here."

"Yes, and for that I am sorry, Zachary. Under ideal conditions, I would drink the *maja acu* while I am alone and not inflict others with the burden of the journey. But time is critical. We have only a week."

"Only a week for what?"

"Until the full moon."

"And that matters why?"

"The naming ceremony, Zachary. That is when your daughter will meet her spirit guide and be shown the path of her life."

Ever since Shula's birth, Boggy had been going on and on about how, when the appropriate time came along, he would conduct the ancient ritual that would bestow upon Shula her official Taino name.

Boggy's full name is Cachique Baugtanaxata, which in Taino-speak means "Chief of the Cenote." Cenotes are freshwater sinkholes that descend through layers of limestone and connect to the underground aquifer. The ancient Tainos, who once lived throughout the Caribbean, believed cenotes were portals to the spirit world and their shamans often conducted ceremonies and made offerings at such sites.

According to experts in such matters, the Taino were extinct by the early 1600s. Yet, despite overwhelming historical evidence to the contrary, Boggy contends he is full-blooded Taino, the last of a long line of shamans, someone who can trace his lineage back thousands of years.

I've long since learned not to argue the topic with him. Besides, his juju, wherever it comes from, has gotten me out of numerous jams.

And there was little doubt of his devotion to Shula. Boggy doted over her, was always strapping Shula into her sling and taking her for walks, telling her the Taino words for different plants and animals. It had gotten to the point that Barbara and I often joked that we had to vie with Boggy for time with our daughter.

"So," I said, "on this little trip you took, you discovered Shula's true Taino name?"

"Yes, Guamikeni," Boggy said.

That's his name for me. It means "lord of land and sea." It's what the Taino called Christopher Columbus after they were there to greet him when he landed on San Salvador. At first I was flattered that Boggy would give me such an illustrious title. I thought it demonstrated the great respect he had for me. Then it sunk in: Columbus and those who followed him brought the disease and violent colonization that wiped out the Tainos. Boggy was just being a smart-ass, displaying what I could only assume was the Taino penchant for mordant humor.

"And what would Shula's Taino name be?" I asked him.

"Not now," he said. "It will be revealed at the naming ceremony. Eight days from now."

"What if we aren't back from the Bahamas by then?"

"We must be back by then, Zachary. We have no choice."

"Look, there's a full moon every month. It doesn't have to be this particular full moon, does it?"

Our waiter arrived with Boggy's appetizer and set it down in front of him. Boggy opened a bottle of hot sauce and splashed it on the oysters.

"It must be this full moon and no other," Boggy said. "It is a moment in time that will never come again. If your daughter is not united at that precise moment with her spirit guide, she will be forever lost."

He slurped an oyster from its shell, washed it down with chocolate milk.

"Ya know, sometimes," I said, "you really creep me out."

10

By the time we finished eating it was barely seven o'clock. Boggy went back to our room at the Mutiny. Said he needed some real sleep.

It was way too early for me to turn in. I called the number for Abel Delgado that his wife had given me. No answer, no voice mail, no nothing. I asked the valet to bring the car. Time to pay one more visit to Delgado's office.

It had been several days since Gloria Delgado had heard from her husband. Maybe he had returned home. Maybe I'd find him toiling away at his desk, doing whatever it is private investigators do when they aren't out investigating.

It was worth a shot anyway. I didn't want to head for the Bahamas the next morning looking for Delgado only to discover he was back in Miami.

The main entrance to the office building was locked. I hung back and waited, trying not to make it look like I was hanging back and waiting. Tougher than it sounds. After a few minutes, a couple of guys in suits left the building and I slipped in behind them.

I headed down the hall. A trash can propped open the door to Suite 121. The light was on inside.

A woman in a blue housekeeper's uniform was vacuuming around the chairs in the small waiting area, oblivious to me standing in the doorway. Beyond her, the door to Delgado's office was open and I could see his cluttered desk.

"Excuse me . . ."

The woman jumped and spun around, a hand to her chest. She was short, Hispanic, in her fifties.

I smiled. She didn't. She switched off the vacuum cleaner.

"Sorry," I said, moving past her to the office. "Didn't mean to scare you."

I went behind Delgado's desk and sat down in his chair. I began flipping through stacks of paper and looking at notepads.

The woman studied me, uncertain.

"I'll just be a second," I said. "Happened to be in the neighborhood and thought I'd pick up a couple of things. Don't let me interrupt you."

"*Que, senor?*" she said.

"*Un momento,*" I said. "No problemo."

The only other thing I remembered from high school Spanish was "*Yo tiene catarro,*" but I didn't think she cared whether or not I had a cold.

The woman backed out of the office and disappeared down the hall.

The papers on Delgado's desk were mostly bills. Nothing I found made any reference to Jen Ryser.

A red light flashed on Delgado's answering machine. I pressed PLAY. The digital voice first announced that the mailbox was full and then told me it had twenty-two new messages.

I sat back and listened. Calls from credit card companies. Calls from Gloria Delgado. A call from Mickey Ryser. A call from Abel Delgado's bank.

As the messages played, I went through the desk drawers. Found some framed photographs. One showed Abel and Gloria Delgado on their wedding day. She looked about thirty pounds lighter and a whole lot happier than when I'd seen her earlier. He looked considerably older than I had imagined him, in his forties, with a thick neck, black hair spiked with gel, and a much grimmer expression than the situation called for. Tough cop with a pretty young bride. Another picture showed the Delgado family a few years later. Gloria held the little boy, who looked no more than a month or two old. The little girl sat on her daddy's lap. Abel Delgado didn't look any happier in that photo than he did on his wedding day.

Then a woman's voice came on the answering machine:

"Yes, Mr. Delgado. This is Helen Miller with H.M. Associates in Charleston, calling about that young woman you are looking for, the one with the sailboat. Got something if you want to give me a call."

I grabbed a pen and scribbled down the number she read off. There were only two more messages after that and none of them meant anything to me.

I used Delgado's phone to call the number in Charleston. Helen Miller answered on the third ring.

"Abel Delgado's office returning your call," I said, which was kinda not a lie. "Got a message saying you had some information for us regarding Jennifer Ryser."

"Oh yeah, right. I'm in my car right now, don't have the case file in front of me," Helen Miller said. She had a nice voice. Smoky, with a pleasant low-country lilt to it. "But I can give you the gist of it."

"I need all the gist I can get," I said.

Helen Miller laughed. She had a nice laugh to go with the nice voice. It made me wonder what she looked like. A little innocent wondering never hurt anyone.

"Took me a while to search the state's boat registration data base, but I finally found a vessel registered to a Jennifer Ryser of Mt. Pleasant. Bought brand-new about five months ago. Paid cash. A Beneteau 54."

"Nice boat," I said.

"Yeah, about nine hundred thousand dollars' worth of nice, according to the state sales tax receipt. You want the boat's name?"

"You bet."

"*Chasin' Molly*," she said.

Molly, after Jen's mother. A fitting moniker for the boat. Spirits in the wind.

"You find out anything else?"

"Nope, that's all you asked me to find out."

"Oh yeah. Right . . ."

"Is this Abel Delgado? You don't sound like the same guy I spoke to."

"I'm an associate. My name's Clete," I said. "Clete Boyer."

"Like the baseball player?"

"Yeah, like him."

"My father was a Yankees fan."

Just my luck.

"Ol' Uncle Clete," I said. "Quite a guy. My mother's favorite brother. That's why she named me after him."

A pause on the other end of the line. Then:

"So how come if your mother was Clete Boyer's sister, then your name is Boyer? Didn't she have a married name?"

"My mother was a very progressive woman. Way ahead of her time."

"Oh, really?" Helen Miller didn't sound very convinced. "Look, I've got about three hours in this. I'll send an invoice."

"That'll be fine. And, please, go ahead and add an extra hundred dollars to it. I appreciate how quickly you got back to us about this matter."

"Very generous of you, Mr. Boyer."

"That's the way we do things here at Delgado Investigations," I said. "And if you've got the time, then I'd really appreciate it if you could look into a few other matters as well."

"Be glad to," she said.

I was giving her the details when the maid returned to the office. She hadn't returned alone. She'd brought along a guy in a blue uniform who looked like he might be her supervisor.

The supervisor started to say something. I held up a finger and cut him off.

"Hold on," I told him. "I'm busy here."

I finished telling Helen Miller what I needed to know and how she could reach me. I hung up the phone, stood up from the desk, and started walking out of the office.

The supervisor moved to block my way.

"Look," I said. "I really don't appreciate you barging in here while I'm on the phone with a client. Mr. Delgado will hear about this."

The supervisor look startled but he recovered quickly.

"Who are you? What are you doing here?"

He got in my face. I got in his.

"Well, I'm damn sure not Clete Boyer, I'll tell you that. And don't let anyone tell you differently," I said. "I have never played third base for the New York Yankees. Neither has my mother. As far as I know I don't have an uncle. And even if I did my mother wouldn't have named me after him. Do you understand?"

He shook his head, thoroughly confused.

"No, I don't understand at all."

"Good," I said. "Keep it that way."

I brushed past him and out the door.

11

Knowing the name of the boat wasn't much of a start, but it was a toe-hold. On the drive back to the Mutiny, I called Lynfield Pederson.

"You better tell me what you need to tell me and tell me quick," Pederson said. "Because I am due at my mother-in-law's house for dinner in exactly five minutes."

"Nice talking to you, too, Lynfield."

"Chicken 'n' dumplings."

"What about them?"

"That's what she's making," Pederson said. "And believe me when I tell you that she is putting dinner on the table right this very minute. That woman will not hold a meal for me or anyone else. Doreen is already over there."

"How is Doreen?"

"She's just fine. I'll tell her you asked. But let me warn you about something, Chasteen."

"What's that?"

"I do not look kindly upon anyone who causes me to eat my chicken 'n' dumplings cold."

I'd first met Lynfield Pederson years ago when we both played ball at Florida. He was a walk-on freshman when I was a senior and he never let me forget the fact that he had once knocked me on my can during a scrimmage before the Auburn game. The block had helped win him a spot on the traveling squad and ultimately a full scholarship.

After a few years of police work in Florida, he returned to the Bahamas and eventually landed the position as superintendent of the Royal Bahamian Police for the Eleuthera district. It included Harbour Island, where he was born. Aside from the fact that he once briefly considered me the prime suspect in a murder that took place there a few years earlier, he was as astute a lawman as I'd ever encountered. And that was not damning by faint praise.

Harbour Island sits about halfway between the Abacos and Lady Cut Cay, a popular hopping-off point for cruisers heading south. I told Pederson I was looking for a boat called *Chasin' Molly*, hoping he could spread the word down his way and maybe turn up something.

"You thinking bad thoughts?" he asked.

"Don't want to, but no one knows for sure where the boat is. Girl's father is getting anxious."

"And he's a friend."

"A good one."

"Well, boats like that, they have been known to get stolen," Pederson said.

"Even with lawmen like you riding the range?"

"Shit, I'm so shorthanded I can't keep up with niggah cutting niggah, much less look after stupid, rich white folk passing through on fancy-ass boats."

"Least you got priorities."

"I'm just saying . . ."

"Know of any boat thieves working the waters?"

Pederson snorted.

"You talking the Bahamas, man. Been boat thieves working these waters for nearly four hundred years, back to when they'd build bonfires on the beach and lure in passing ships and run 'em aground in the shallows."

"How they do it nowadays?"

"Well, boats get stolen nowadays, it's generally two types. Got your go-fast boats—the Cigarettes and Donzis and all that. People steal those kinda boats—hot wire them and haul ass—they're doing business the next day. Running dope, running people, running guns. Running whatever it is needs running and that people will pay lots of money for. Boats like that they're disposable. Boats like that they don't try to sell them. They just sink them or burn them up and go steal another one," Pederson said. "But boats like the one you're talking about, that's a whole different thing. Different kind of people working that. They got a system, a network. They're organized."

"You talking Mafia organized?"

"Wouldn't go so far as to say that. But there are some slick operations and they are plenty bad-ass. Because there's some big money to be made by stealing big boats. The Bahamas is just one part of it, like a passing-through spot. They steal the boats somewhere else. Florida, mostly. Florida's got a shitload of boats and absentee owners and no one always around keeping an eye on things. On up through Georgia and the Carolinas, same thing. Way I hear it, they got crews. Some of them get paid for being spotters. They check out the marinas, backyard docks, that kind of thing, and find a likely target. Then someone else comes along, someone who knows boats, and they do the stealing. They get over here with it and deliver it to someone else who can make it disappear," Pederson said. "You know how they got chop shops for cars?"

"Steal a car, disassemble it, sell the parts . . ."

"Yeah, well, they got the same thing for boats. Only boats like the one you're talking about, they don't have to worry about taking them apart and getting rid of the pieces. All they gotta do is maybe repaint them, slap a new name on the transom, jimmy-up the paperwork, and send them on down the line. Puerto Rico, the DR, Venezuela. Hell, they caught this one crew, working out of Cartagena, they had thirty-forty yachts loaded on a cargo ship. Were gonna haul them to Hong Kong, sell them to some rich Chinese assholes. Plenty of demand for fancy boats, especially if they can be had for a good price. And people don't pay nearly as much attention to where a boat comes from as they do a car," Pederson said. "Plus, there's this other thing."

"What's that?"

"People who get their boats stolen, it's not like they do a whole lot of squawking. People who can afford to go out and buy new boats like that, they got 'em insured. Gets stolen, they just gonna collect their money and buy another one. They ain't going to a lot of trouble to track it down. That's the way it works."

"But what about the insurance companies? They send out investigators, right?"

"Yeah, they do. They certainly do. And we see them from time to time. Mostly they're just interested in doing their paperwork, filing a report, dragging it out so they can get themselves a little vacation time in the islands. Every now and then, though, you get an investigator who actually wants to do some investigating. Wants to marshal the troops, work hand in hand with the local authorities to find the culprits and bring them to justice."

"Something in the air. Smells like cynicism."

"Like I said, sometimes it's hard to work up a lot of enthusiasm on behalf of stupid, rich white people with fancy-ass boats."

"So Bahamian cops, they turn a blind eye to boat thieves."

"Did I say that?"

"Hey look, I'm trying here."

"What I'm saying, what I meant to say, there's thieves. And then there's some that's worse than thieves."

"How's that?"

"Thieves just steal things," he said. "They don't kill people."

We let it sit there for a moment.

"You've had some of that down your way?"

"No, not here exactly. But plenty of other places. And over to Nassau, there was a pretty ugly incident not long back. Involved a Canadian couple. They'd spent a few years cruising around the Caribbean on their yacht, you know, living the dream. But they were getting up there in age and they needed to sell it. So they advertised it and this fellow, he was American I think, he kept dropping by the marina to take a look at the boat. Got chummy with the couple. Took the boat out with them a time or two. Kept dickering with them over the price. Finally, they settled on a number—this boat, it was worth a few hundred thousand—and he gave them some money as a deposit. I don't know how much exactly. Not much. Say ten grand or something. And he asked them to get the papers ready—registration, a bill of sale, and everything—and he'd come around the next day, they'd do the deal.

"So he shows up and he's got these two other fellows with him. He says, 'These are my partners in the boat. They just flew in this morning. They want to see how it runs and then we'll do all the paperwork.' He even brought along a bottle of champagne to celebrate. So they took out the boat, got a few miles offshore, and this fellow says, 'OK, give me my ten grand back.' And the man, the boat's owner, says, 'Why, don't you want the boat anymore?' And this fellow says, 'Yeah, I still want it. But I want it for free.' And him and his two buddies proceed to beat hell out of the man and his wife.

"Still, the old man, he refused to sign over the bill of sale. So this fellow and his buddies they get out the anchor and the anchor chain and they lash the couple to the anchor. And then they say, 'We're gonna throw you overboard unless you sign over that bill of sale.' So the man, he signed it."

"And then what?"

"And then they threw them overboard anyway. Took the yacht down to St. Martin and sold it there, two months later."

"Jesus . . ."

"Joseph, Mary, and all the saints, too," Pederson said. "Finally caught the bastards who did it. But there are plenty more out there just like them."

"Not easy, though, stealing a big boat like that."

"No, not like stealing a car. Not like stealing some go-fast boat either. Can't go a hundred miles an hour and get the hell away with it and disappear. Takes some time to dispose of. Which means disposing of anyone who might miss it right away. And making sure they aren't missed right away either," Pederson said. "That couple that got thrown overboard, it was almost a month before their family back in Canada got worried about them."

"Because they were accustomed to not hearing from them for long stretches of time."

"Uh-huh," Pederson said. "That's the way it is in the islands with people on boats. That's why they come down here—to be out of touch."

"Sell the house, quit work, tell friends and family they'll hear from them when they hear from them."

"No clock, no commitments . . ."

"No worries, mon."

"Yeah, uh-huh, that's just exactly how it is, Chasteen. Shit," Pederson said. "If there wasn't a ton of worry in this world, then I wouldn't have myself a job."

"What took you so long? I thought you'd be back a couple of hours ago."

"Took me a while to find an ATM that had any money."

"The ATMs are out of money?"

"Yeah, I talked to this guy at a convenience store and he said it happens all the time. Especially in the evenings. And especially when there are lots of Americans on the island like now. He said the ATMs get refilled in the morning and if you want to get money then you better do it before noon."

"But the bank card worked?"

"Yeah, it worked just fine. She gave us the right pin number."

"How much did you get?"

"A hundred."

"That's all?"

"Yeah, I just wanted to see if it worked. It gave me the balance. Take a look at this."

"Holy shit. Even more than we thought."

"Lots more."

"Holy fucking shit."

"Yeah, I figure tomorrow, first thing in the morning, you can go into town and get a couple thousand."

"But what if the ATMs are still out of money?"

"You aren't going to use the ATM. They max out at five hundred. So you're going to walk inside the bank, hand the teller the card, and tell her you want to make a withdrawal."

"But what if the teller asks for ID?"

"Well, she's goddam sure gonna ask for ID, you can count on that. So you show it to her. You've got the passport. You've got the driver's license. You've got all the ID they could possibly want."

"You think it will work?"

"Yeah, it will work. It's not like you're dealing with Homeland Security. It's a fucking Bahamian bank teller. She's going to look at the photo and see a white girl with lots of blond hair. And then she's going to look at you."

"I'll wear my hair down, like in the photo."

"Yeah, and smile like she's smiling. The smile helps."

"Maybe I should wear sunglasses or something."

"No sunglasses. That could make them suspicious. Just go in there with your hair down and smiling and, trust me, everything's going to work just fine."

"And there's no way they can trace this?"

"Who's they?"

"I don't know, the bank, the cops, whoever. They see we're taking money here and somewhere else down the line and they can find us."

"Yeah, they can trace it. But who's looking? No one. Not yet anyway. I figure we've got a week at least."

"What then?"

"Then everything's going to fall in place. Just like we planned it."

12

By ten o'clock the next morning we were taking off from Fort Lauderdale Executive Airport in Charlie Callahan's brand-new seaplane.

"Not just any seaplane either, Zack-o. A Maule-MT-7-420. Only a dozen like it in the world," Charlie said. "Rolls-Royce engine. Seriously overpowered. Off the water in four seconds if it's just my skinny ass on board. I can land it in less than a foot of water. Or put it down on the runway. Just about anywhere you want to go, this puppy can take us."

I said, "How long to Walker's Cay?"

"No more than an hour. Just hold on to your dipstick and leave the flying to us."

The plane was a four-seater. I sat up front with Charlie. Boggy sat in the back.

Charlie wore his pilot's "uniform"—flip-flops, a pair of faded Madras shorts, and a T-shirt that said, "Hell yes, I'm the pilot. Got a problem with that?" For extra flourish, his T-shirt boasted Army surplus gold-braid epaulets. His hair had gone to gray but he still had plenty of it—a gnarly mane of dreadlocks that descended halfway down his back.

When I first started playing for the Dolphins, Charlie was the team pilot. But an incident involving two Dolphins cheerleaders, a boa constrictor, and Dolphins owner Joe Robbie's private cabin on the plane—I was never quite clear about the details—got him booted from that gig.

After that, the legend of Charlie Callahan only grew. According to some stories he was running guns to Nicaragua. Others had it that he was doing everything from flying dope out of Colombia to delivering mercenaries to sub-Saharan Africa. I don't know if any of it was true, but whatever he was up to it probably wasn't missionary work.

When he finally resurfaced, he had enough money to buy a small fleet of planes and start Sorry Charlie's Island Charters. Reputation and appearance worked in Charlie's behalf, an effective if inadvertent marketing plan. His well-heeled clients liked the idea that they were flying with a Genuine Colorful Character. It gave them stories to tell. And Charlie had all the work he wanted.

All I knew was that Charlie was a steady hand, a good man in a tight spot, and if someone had to fly me around the Bahamas looking for Jen Ryser or Abel Delgado or whoever I could find first, then I wanted it to be him.

Fifteen minutes out of Fort Lauderdale and Florida's armored coastline was just a glimmer on the horizon. Below us, the Big Blue River— aka the Gulf Stream—churned northward on its way to make the British Isles a slightly more habitable place.

Every now and then, I'd spot a patch of white on the water and make out the lines of a sailboat. Sometimes I'd spot a patch of white and think it was a sailboat, only it would turn out to be a trawler or a fishing boat or the froth from a big breaker.

It is devilishly hard to spot boats on the water when you're flying at safe altitude. Harder still to determine exactly what kind of boats they might be. And damn near impossible to pick out a name like *Chasin' Molly* on the transom.

With its big jib flying, a Beneteau 54 would offer a highly visible profile. But on any given day there are hundreds of pleasure boats cruising the Gulf Stream. By the time you reach the protected waters of the Bahamas, the hundreds become thousands. Combine them with thousands more that are moored at marinas, tied up at docks, or tucked away in coves and, well, no way we could just bop around on Charlie's seaplane and count on finding the boat we were looking for.

So I had devised a plan. Not much of a plan but the best plan I could come up with considering what little we had to go on.

There are more than thirty official ports of entry in the Bahamas. Upon reaching Bahamian waters, foreign vessels must make it their first order of business to clear customs and immigration at one of these ports.

Since the bureaucrats in Nassau were showing me no love, I had opted for a grassroots approach. Pick the most likely port where Jen Ryser might have entered the Bahamas, win over the local authorities with my great charm, and hope they would bend regulations, give me the information I was looking for, and let me know if I was on the right track.

In the Seventh Edition of Chasteen's Complete and Unabridged Dictionary, the synonym for "my great charm" is "bribe money." And I had a pocketful of that.

Jen Ryser and crew had set out from Charleston. I was betting they had chosen the quickest route—a straight shot to the Abacos, the chain of islands at the upper tip of the Bahamas.

The Abacos offer several ports of entry. Most cruisers head straight for Marsh Harbour, the sailing hub of the Bahamas, with plenty of marinas and places for provisioning.

But Walker's Cay is the northernmost port in the Abacos, and although its luster has diminished in recent years, some boats choose it for clearing customs. Besides, I am nothing if not methodical. I liked the idea of starting at the top of the Bahamas and working our way down. So Walker's Cay would be our first stop.

This is not to say my brilliant plan didn't have plenty of holes in it.

According to Helen Miller's snooping around, Jen Ryser had bought *Chasin' Molly* only a few months earlier. Chances were this was her first significant outing in the boat. No matter how seasoned a sailor she might be, maybe she wasn't comfortable with the notion of immediately setting out on a four-hundred-mile open-water crossing. Maybe she had taken a more prudent route, stuck close to shore, run all the way down to Miami, made the fifty-mile crossing to Bimini and cleared customs there. That would put her closer to Exuma and Mickey Ryser's place on Lady Cut Cay.

The previous few weeks had brought some rough weather. Late-season blows out of the northeast. Maybe Jen and her crew had stuck to the safe confines of the Intracoastal Waterway, or The Ditch as it's popularly known. A boring haul, but it comes with one redeeming factor—numerous rowdy watering holes along the way, from Savannah down to Lauderdale. These were kids not long out of college. Maybe the idea of leisurely barhopping their way south appealed to them more than dealing with heavy seas.

Or maybe, after so many years of not knowing her father, Jen Ryser had decided against paying him a visit. Maybe she still bore him a grudge.

Maybe she had just said to hell with it. Maybe she had bypassed the Bahamas altogether and was now cruising the Virgin Islands, heading for more distant ports.

So many maybes.

So little time to find Jen Ryser before her father's ship set sail.

They both came in and fed her breakfast. After that, they left and closed the hatch behind them, and she could hear them talking from up above, on the deck.

"Where should I go to?"

"I saw a Scotia Bank near the dock. Try it."

Moments later she heard him call out: "Straight there and back, you got that?"

Jen waited a few minutes. No more talking. It was just him and her on the boat now. How to make that work to her advantage?

She yelled up to him: "Hey, down here. I need some help."

"What is it?"

"I have to use the head."

He took his sweet time getting there. Finally, the hatch slid open.

He said, "You just went a little while ago."

"Yeah, but I started my period."

A groan of disgust.

"So what do you want me to do about it?"

"My backpack," she said. "There's a little purse in a side pocket. Cloth with a paisley print. It's got some tampons. Just open it and get me one."

Another groan.

Guys. They could be so squeamish about this kind of thing. Exactly what Jen was counting on.

"Here," he said, putting the backpack on her lap. "You get it."

"You need to untie my hands."

He paused, thinking about it.

"OK, but no funny stuff. You understand?"

"Uh-huh," she said. "How about the blindfold, too?"

"No, that's staying on."

After her hands were free, Jen rummaged around in the backpack and felt the cloth purse. She felt the other thing she was looking for, too. But she knew he was standing right there, watching her.

"Can you get me some water?"

She heard him step away, and she quickly stuck her Leatherman into the little cloth purse. The only time she had ever really used it was for the corkscrew. But it was like one of those Transformer robots. It could turn into almost any kind of tool—chisel, file, needle-nose pliers. Eighty-seven different uses. Or some such thing.

He came back with the water. She drank from the cup.

He said, "You get what you need?"

Jen held up the paisley purse so he could see it.

"Right here," she said.

He pulled her up from the bed, loosened the rope around her feet just enough so she could walk. He guided her to the head and backed her inside.

"Close the door," she said.

And this time he did as she asked.

Her hands immediately went for the blindfold. She didn't pull it all the way off. Just enough to peek over the top.

She saw: A narrow stall, white fiberglass walls. Not much in there except for the toilet. One shelf with cans of Comet and Lysol and some rolls of toilet paper. Not even a sink.

In the ceiling above the toilet—a Plexiglas vent, about eighteen inches square, the kind that can pop up to let in air or seal tight in a storm. It was up.

She stood atop the toilet and did her best to peek out the vent. The opening was only about five inches high. It gave her a glimpse of the boat: Bigger than she thought, thirty-four feet at least, its deck pale blue. A sleek sportfisherman with a pair of fighting chairs near the transom and a ladder that led to the flying bridge.

She turned atop the toilet, looking beyond the boat in all directions and saw: Open water. More open water. A scattering of boats at their mooring buoys, the closest maybe two hundred yards away. And a mangrove shoreline, at least a half mile in the distance, with a long dock, a few houses tucked here and there, a couple of spindly radio towers, and the flickering image of cars passing on a road behind the mangroves.

Her spirits lifted. All this time she had thought they were at some remote location, an uninhabited cay, a hidden cove. Yet, here were cars and boats and houses—other people, the chance for escape.

She pushed against the vent. It wouldn't open any farther. Its top was fastened to the base on aluminum hinges. The hinges were attached to the base by rivets. Easy enough to work loose.

A knock on the door.

"You done in there?"

She stepped down from the toilet.

"Just a second," she said.

She pulled the Leatherman from the purse. It had several types of blades—a hacksaw, a file, a basic knife. None of them more than a couple inches long. Capable of doing some damage, but only if her first strike was directly on target—the middle of his forehead, an eye. If she missed or if the blade was deflected or any number of other misfires, then that was it. He'd be all over her. She didn't have a chance of fighting him off.

Better to use the Leatherman to undo the hinges on the vent. The vent was narrow but she felt sure she could squeeze through. But where to hide the Leatherman? She looked around. The only place was behind the toilet. She tucked it away.

She sat down on the toilet. She put the blindfold back in place.

Another knock on the door.

"All done," she said.

13

Charlie brought the plane in low and made a quick loop around Walker's Cay before putting down.

Over the centuries, all kinds of characters have dropped anchor at Walker's Cay. Ponce de Leon visited the island during his search for the Fountain of Youth. Confederate blockade runners sought haven in the Civil War. And a long procession of treasure salvors have scoured the nearby shoals for sunken ships and hoards of gold.

A fellow by the name of Bob Abplanalp bought the entire seventy-acre island back in the 1960s after he made the first of many, many millions from his most famous invention—the aerosol nozzle, the little thing that goes "sssssssst" on top of a spray can. Abplanalp was drawn here mainly for the fishing. More than a dozen world record catches have come from waters within just a few minutes of Walker's Cay.

Abplanalp spruced up the place, built the Walker's Cay Hotel & Marina, and turned it into a favorite haunt not only for sportfishermen but those who wanted to kick back and enjoy themselves well removed from the public eye. One of Abplanalp's pals, Richard Nixon, made several trips to Walker's during his presidency.

After Bob Abplanalp died, his family continued to run their little fiefdom as it had always been run, a gracious, low-key hideout for those who could afford it. Then came 2004 and the double whammy of hurricanes Frances and Jeanne. Walker's Cay never recovered. The island was up for sale. Reported asking price—$20 million.

In pre-Barbara days, I tallied my share of good times at Walker's Cay. I'd caught bonefish in the flats, lost marlin in the deep water, and bunked down with more than one temporary sweetheart in a cottage overlooking the green-and-turquoise waters.

Broke my heart to see the place now.

Docks where sleek boats once lined up gunwale to gunwale during big money fishing tournaments had long since surrendered to the sea. Weeds and creeping vines had taken over paths that once wound through well-manicured grounds. A big portion of the roof on the resort's main house had collapsed. And none of the cottages were without broken windows or crumbling porches.

But the runway was clear, the asphalt in fairly good repair. And the blue, yellow, and black Bahamian flag fluttered above the glorified shack that passed for the customs house.

Charlie apologized for the slightly bumpy landing.

"Still getting used to the way this baby handles," he said.

Our greeting party consisted of a half-dozen or so land crabs. The black variety, not the white. They observed us defiantly from the edge of the runway, their crimson claws raised, ready to repel any attack.

Land crabs are a delicacy in the Bahamas. Andros Island, to the south, has vast crab colonies in its piney wood interior, and Androsian bush cowboys round them up by the thousands each May for the annual Crab Fest. I attended it one year with Barbara, who was a judge in the culinary competition. Crab 'n' rice. Stuffed crab backs. Crab dumplings. Spicy crab soup with whole scotch bonnets floating in the bowl.

The crabs must have noticed the gustatory gleam in my eyes. They skittered into the high grass as we walked from the plane.

A short, stocky fiftyish man appeared in the doorway of the customs office. He had the fair features and sun-blotched skin common among many white Bahamians. They trace their lineage to British Loyalists who fled the colonies during the American Revolution.

The man was smoothing back his reddish hair and tucking the tail of his white shirt into his black pants, doing his best to look official. He put on a pair of glasses and peered out at us.

"Catch you napping, Mr. Bethel?" Charlie said.

"You supposed to radio, say you coming in."

"Tried that. Didn't get an answer."

"Shoulda kept trying," Mr. Bethel said.

He turned away from the door. By the time we stepped inside he was sitting behind a gray metal desk. A boxy old computer occupied one end of the desk. Next to it a worn, black ledger book. And next to it, an assortment of rubber stamps and ink pads.

On the wall behind him was a framed photograph of the prime minister of the Bahamas, a nautical chart of the Abacos, and a framed print of Queen Elizabeth that might have been hanging there since shortly after her coronation. Poor gal looked old even back then.

"How's your family, Mr. Bethel?" Charlie asked. "They doing alright?"

"They doing."

A real bundle of good cheer and hospitality, Mr. Bethel.

He stuck out a hand. Charlie gave him our passports and papers. For the next several minutes no one said anything as Mr. Bethel dutifully eyed everything there was to eye and then eyed it again. Occasionally, he would reach for a rubber stamp, ink it up, and give one of the documents an authoritative pounding.

On the immigration papers, the line where it asks the purpose of your visit, Boggy and I had each checked the box for business rather than vacation. Mr. Bethel looked at me over the top of his glasses.

"You Mr. Chasteen?"

I nodded.

He looked at Boggy's passport, then at Boggy.

"And you're Mr. Boggatonna . . ."

He gave up.

"Baugtanaxata," Boggy said.

Mr. Bethel studied both of us some more. He looked at our papers again.

"What is the nature of your business in the Bahamas?"

I said, "We're looking for someone."

Mr. Bethel absorbed the information. It seemed to sour his stomach.

"That's your business? Looking for someone?"

"On this trip it is," I said.

"And this someone you're looking for, you think they're here on Walker's?"

"No, but I'm thinking maybe they passed through here. Thought you might help me."

"Help you how?"

"Find out if the person we are looking for cleared customs here." I nodded at the computer. "Might be in your records somewhere."

"What's this person's name?"

"Jennifer Ryser. R-y-s-e-r. She'd be in her early twenties. Would have arrived within the last month or so on a boat called the *Chasin' Molly*. Nice boat, a fifty-four-footer."

If it registered with Mr. Bethel, he didn't show it.

"The immigration registry is a restricted government document and not open to public inspection," he said.

"Yes, sir. I know and respect that," I said. "I was just hoping you might see fit to make an exception in this case."

"And why would I do that?"

"This girl we're looking for, her father is dying. It's urgent that we find her and take her to him."

"You need to go through Nassau," he said.

"Tried that," I said.

Mr. Bethel studied my face for a long moment. Then he went back to examining our papers. He stamped our passports and handed them to us.

He looked at his watch.

He said, "About this time each day I step outside, walk down to where the docks used to be, and have a smoke."

He opened a desk drawer, pulled out a pack of Marlboro Lights.

He said, "Sometimes I have a couple of smokes. Depends. But I'm never gone more than half an hour."

He stood up from the desk.

I reached for my wallet. I plucked out a hundred-dollar bill and slipped it under one of the ink pads.

Mr. Bethel looked at it. Just the slightest hint of regret in his eyes.

"You can put that back in your wallet," he said.

I gave him a look: You sure?

He said, "I didn't know that's why he was looking for that young woman."

"He?"

"Man came through here day before yesterday," Mr. Bethel said. He glanced at the hundred again. "Wasn't quite so generous."

"This man, he was looking for the same person?"

Mr. Bethel nodded.

"Only, he didn't know the name of the boat she was on."

"You remember his name?"

"Don't recall."

"His name somewhere in your records?"

Mr. Bethel shook his head.

"No, he cleared customs at the airport in Marsh Harbour. Came up here by boat."

"What did he look like?"

"Big, tough-looking. Said he was some kind of cop."

"He say he was a cop? Or did he say he was a detective?"

"What's the difference? He looked like whatever he said he was."

Mr. Bethel shook loose a cigarette, stuck it in his mouth, and headed for the door. He turned around just before he reached it.

"That computer, the government sent it up here almost seven years ago now. I haven't ever turned it on, not once," he said. "Like doing things the old way."

He glanced at the black ledger book. Then he stepped out the door.

14

It didn't take me long to find what I was looking for. Only a few entries had been made in the ledger book since Jen Ryser's arrival.

I went down the list of names of those aboard the *Chasin' Molly*. Charlie looked over my shoulder. Boggy wasn't interested. He left the office to wander around outside.

"According to this they arrived eight days ago."

"Six of them on board," Charlie said.

Jen's name was at the top, listed as captain/owner. It showed her date of birth—she was twenty-two—and listed her passport number.

I found a pencil and paper in one of the desk drawers and wrote down names and pertinent information for the five other people on board: Justin Hatchitt, 28; Torrey Kealing, 25; Karen Breakell, 23; Will Moody, 22; and Pete Crumrine, 22.

Below the list of names, Mr. Bethel had duly noted that Jen Ryser paid $300 in cash for a cruising permit good for three months, including departure tax.

And below that was the notation: "Benelli: M4-L38777634 and M4-L38777704 (4 boxes/24 per)."

I said, "Who's Benelli?"

"Not a who, it's a what," Charlie said. "Shotgun. Italian made. Kind of a chi-chi designer gun. Run about two thousand dollars each and up."

I looked at Charlie.

"How do you know these things?"

He shrugged.

"Some things need knowing," he said.

"So they have one of these Benellis on board?"

"Two of them, actually."

"And that's legal?"

Charlie nodded.

"It's OK to bring guns into the Bahamas on a boat, but you have to declare them, give the serial number, and show exactly how much ammunition you have on board. You also have to keep any weapons under lock and key at all times. If authorities board the vessel somewhere down the line, they can ask you to produce the ammunition. And if it's not all there, then you better have a good explanation."

I looked at him.

"You got a gun on the plane?"

"Zack-o, please. If I had a gun, I would have declared it, wouldn't I?"

I waited.

"Like I told you, some things need knowing," he said. "And some don't."

I don't like guns. I don't carry any guns on my boats. But I could understand why some people did, especially young women setting out on long cruises.

I scanned other pages in the ledger, but there was nothing that jumped out or looked as if it would be helpful in leading me to Jen Ryser.

I put the ledger back where it had been sitting on Mr. Bethel's desk. We stepped outside.

Charlie looked down the runway, toward a sprinkling of small islands across a channel to the east.

"I'm thinking we ought to hop over to Miner Cay," Charlie said.

"See if Cutie knows anything?"

Charlie nodded.

"Cutie knows all," he said.

I looked around but Mr. Bethel was nowhere to be seen. I didn't think it would hurt his feelings if we didn't give him a formal good-bye.

Heading for the plane, we spotted Boggy in a ditch that ran the length of the runway. It looked as if the ditch had been backhoed fairly recently, probably to help drain the runway.

The walls of the ditch exposed layers of crumbly shell and soft limestone. The bottom of the ditch was mud soup. Boggy knelt in the mud, his knife in one hand. It's more dagger than knife really, a short, well-honed piece of steel with a bone handle. Boggy used the knife like a pick, chopping away at the ditch walls. Then he would pluck out pieces of this and that, examine them, toss some pieces away, and put others in one of the leather pouches he always carried with him.

"Yo, Louis B. Leakey," I said. "Time to go."

Boggy finished extracting something from the ditch wall—looked like a dark rock of some kind—and stuck it in the pouch.

He climbed out of the ditch. His shoes and pants were covered in mud. There were splotches of mud on his shirt and splotches of mud on his face and in his hair. The overall effect was Neanderthalic.

Charlie said, "Afraid I'm gonna have to ask you to clean that crap off before you climb into that new plane of mine."

Boggy looked himself over, as if he was only in that moment realizing exactly what a mess he was.

He kicked off his shoes, dropped his pants, took off his shirt. All he had on was a cowskin knife holster that hung between his shoulder blades from a piece of rawhide worn around his neck. He put his knife in the holster and walked bare-assed through a break in the mangroves, squatting by the water to scrub his clothes.

We stood there watching him.

Charlie said, "Think you'll ever figure him out?"

"Stopped trying years ago," I said.

15

"*hasin' Molly?* Oh yah, mon. I remember her for sure."

We were sitting in Cutie's Place, talking to Cutie.

While the double hurricanes had spelled the end for Walker's Cay, at least for the time being, they had created a windfall, so to speak, for Quentin Taylor "Cutie" Pattison.

Legions of hard-core anglers, scuba divers, and sailors still made regular treks to the tiny islands of the northern Abacos. They needed a place to eat, drink, bunk down, or tie up their boats. With the marina and resort closed on Walker's, that left Cutie's as the only option.

We had flown low over the channel separating Walker's from Miner Cay and set down in the water just beyond Cutie's brand-new docks. Seven minutes from takeoff to landing.

Most of the slips at Cutie's were filled—sportfishing boats primarily, with a few trawlers and sailboats mixed in. A cluster of new rental cottages sat just back from the dock. And the bar/restaurant had a new addition.

It had been a few years since I'd seen Cutie, and he'd become a walking billboard for his prosperity. He carried an extra fifty pounds on an already considerable frame, along with plenty of bling—a gold pendant, flashy wristwatch, and a couple of sparkly rings, one with a big "Q" in diamonds.

As Miner Cay's most prominent citizen, Cutie was the de facto mayor/godfather of the island and its three hundred or so residents. Nothing happened on Miner Cay without Cutie knowing about it.

"Hard to forget that boat," Cutie was telling us. "Women having at it like that. Never seen such a catfight."

"A fight?" I said. "Between who?"

"Between all three of the women on that boat, mon. Going at each other's throats. Couldn't tell who was scratching at who. All three of them with blond hair, long and leggity."

"Leggity?"

"Tall, good-looking women. Couldn't tell 'em apart, hardly. 'Specially when they was all in a ball fighting like that."

We had ordered food. One of Cutie's daughters brought us plates of fried snapper, peas 'n' rice, and some mixed vegetables that had come from a can. Fresh provisions can be scarce on Miner Cay.

I said, "They were fighting on the boat?"

"Started on the boat. Heard 'em yelling and screaming all the way up here. Then it continued onto the dock, getting louder and louder, them cussing each other. Then they came in here to the restaurant, sat down at this very table, and before they even had a chance to order they were going to it. One of them went after another one and then they were all three into it. Knocked the table right over," Cutie said. "The men, there was three of them as I remember, they got 'em split up and quieted down. But it was something to watch, I tell you."

I said, "You ever figure out why they were fighting?"

Cutie shook his head.

"No, and I knew better than to stick my nose in it and ask," he said. "But I've seen it happen before. People on a crossing like that, spend a few days at sea and they find out they just don't get along. Something's gonna pop."

"How long were they here?"

"One night was all. They wanted to stay longer but I asked them to move along," Cutie said. "One of 'em though, she didn't want any more of it. She got her things off the boat, rented one of my cottages. When that boat sailed off in the morning, she wasn't on it."

"Which one was that?"

Cutie shook his head.

"Don't recall her name. Like I said, they was all the same to me. But I could call over to the office, look it up. I ran her credit card."

"Yeah, if you don't mind . . ."

Cutie pulled out his cell phone and made a call. He spoke to someone on the other end and told them what he wanted.

While we were waiting, Cutie's daughter brought us banana pudding. Charlie said he didn't want his, so I took half of it and Boggy took the rest. It was good banana pudding. The pudding might have come from a box but that didn't really matter. Whoever made it had let the bananas get nice and ripe first and that made all the difference. Make banana pudding before the bananas start going brown and mushy and you might as well not even make it.

There were a few other people in Cutie's Place. A table full of guys wearing Tarponwear in various hues, fishermen over from Florida. A table of men and women, all of them wearing identical white polo shirts that bore an image of the big trawler they were traveling on and the words "Seventh Annual Bahamas Spring Fling." A few locals were taking turns at the pool table that sat at the far end of the room.

Everyone was drinking Kaliks or gin 'n' tonics or something cool and soothing. Something cool and soothing sounded nice. But if I started drinking now, then I wouldn't want to do anything else and there was lots that needed doing.

Cutie said something into the phone, then clicked it off and put it away.

"Woman's name was Karen Breakell," Cutie said. "Stayed here four nights."

"Musta liked it here," I said.

"Wasn't so much like it as she didn't have a choice. No regular air service out of here and she didn't want to charter a boat or a plane. She was waiting on the mail boat, comes around every week. Planned to take it to Nassau, then go from there to wherever," Cutie said. "But she wound up getting herself another ride."

"Another ride?"

"Yeah, another big sailboat coming from up north somewhere to charter out of Marsh Harbour. Crew was transporting it down, a big trimaran," Cutie said. "But one of them, the cook, pulled up bad sick and they had to medevac him over to Miami. So this Karen woman, she told them she could cook, and she signed on with them."

"You remember the name of that boat?"

Cutie thought about it.

"Yeah," he said. "It's called the *Trifecta.*"

"We got a problem."

"What, the bank wouldn't give you the money?"

"No, they gave me the money. That's not . . ."

"How much did you get?"

"Two thousand, just like you said."

"And the IDs worked?"

"They worked just fine. The teller even called me Miss Ryser and asked if I was enjoying my stay. It couldn't have gone smoother."

"So what's the problem?"

"Here. Take a look at this. I found it posted on a bulletin board outside a grocery store."

"That's the sailboat."

"Yeah, no shit it's the sailboat. Or one just exactly like it. Even says the name right there. Chasin' Molly. And there's a number to call if anyone has information . . ."

"Fuck."

"What are we going to do?"

"Fuck, fuck, fuck."

"I say we get rid of her and haul ass. Right now. While there's still time. Because if someone's snooping around already and looking for her then . . ."

"Just shut the fuck up and let me think. We kept all their cell phones, right?"

"Yes, all the cell phones. They're in that big duffel bag along with some of *their clothes and other crap. I thought we should have gotten rid of it, but you said keep it . . ."*

"Just shut the fuck up and bring me the duffel bag."

"You don't have to talk to me like that."

"Just bring it, dammit. I need to make a phone call."

"You calling the number on the poster?"

"Just bring me the goddam duffel bag, alright?"

16

I was feeling slightly better about finding Jen Ryser after we left Cutie's Place. But only slightly.

I knew for certain she had reached the Bahamas. But more than a week had passed since her arrival. Plenty of time to cruise down to the Exumas and visit her father. I didn't want to call Mickey until I had more information to report than "Your daughter is in the Bahamas but I don't know where exactly." Knowing that wouldn't do Mickey a bit of good. He needed something solid to grab.

As for Abel Delgado, it was heartening to know that a thoroughly amateur sleuth like myself was on the same trail as a highly trained professional. Maybe our paths would cross. Maybe we could swap some secrets of the trade. And maybe I could ask him face-to-face why he'd been dodging Mickey Ryser.

And then there was the whole thing about the fight at Cutie's Place. I wasn't all that concerned about the three young women getting into a scrape. Like Cutie said, put people on a boat under stressful conditions and the worst will come out. Especially when booze and who knows what else is added to the equation.

But most folks would sleep it off and make amends. Or at least try to. Especially if they were aboard a gorgeous new boat and on the first leg of a vacation that had probably been planned for months. They wouldn't shitcan the whole shebang, abandon their friends, and jump ship on a tiny island knowing they would get stranded there for days.

Karen Breakell.

The list of people I needed to find kept getting longer.

We piled into the seaplane, Charlie pointed us for Marsh Harbour, and thirty minutes later we were touching down at the airport just outside of town.

The plane needed some minor maintenance, loose bolts on the struts or something, something I'm relieved Charlie didn't tell us about when we were up in the air. He said he'd take care of it and catch up with us later.

Boggy and I rented a car at the airport, drove into town. Compared to Grand Cay, Marsh Harbour was Manhattan. Strip malls, Kentucky Fried Chicken, and traffic backed up at the town's two stoplights.

I got us rooms at the Mariner's Inn, near the center of things. Then we set out, going from marina to marina, asking if anyone had seen the *Chasin' Molly* or the *Trifecta*.

The first place we stopped, the dockmaster said, "You working with that other guy?"

"What other guy?"

"Guy who stuck that up."

The dockmaster pointed to a flyer on a bulletin board. It showed a Beneteau 54, a stock shot, taken off the Internet probably. Written below it—"REWARD: For information leading to the location of *Chasin' Molly*. Urgent! Call . . ."

The number on the flyer was the same one Gloria Delgado had given me. I called it and this time I got the same recorded voice that I'd heard on the machine at Delgado's office. I left my name and number and told Delgado he needed to call me right away.

We visited two more marinas. Both sported flyers on their bulletin boards about *Chasin' Molly*. At least Delgado appeared to be doing a little something to earn his pay.

We got lucky at the fourth place we stopped—Blue Sky Marina. It turned out to be where the *Trifecta* was based.

"Out on a charter," said the man behind the counter at the marina office. "Not due back until tomorrow."

"You know the crew?"

"Just got here the other day, but yeah, I met them."

"You know a Karen Breakell? She'd be in her twenties."

"Only one woman crew on *Trifecta*. Guess that would be her."

"You know where *Trifecta* is?" I said. "Sure would like to find it."

"You mind me asking why?"

"Old friend of the family," I said. "Just thought I'd surprise Karen, maybe buy her a drink or something."

"Works for me," the man said. "Hold on."

A VHF radio sat on the counter, tuned to Channel 16. The man picked up the handset.

"Blue Sky Marina calling the *Trifecta*," he said. "*Trifecta*, come in."

He gave it a few seconds and called again. Static and then a man's voice: "Read you, Blue Sky. This is the *Trifecta*."

"Yeah, Captain. What's your location?"

"Just leaving Guana for Green Turtle. Look to be there in two-three hours."

"Copy that," said the man behind the counter. He held out the handset to me. "You want to tell that friend of yours anything?"

"No," I said. "I think I'll surprise her."

17

Green Turtle Cay sits three miles offshore of Great Abaco. The only way to get there if you don't have a boat, or a seaplane, is to take the ferry, which runs on the hour or thereabouts.

I covered the twenty-five miles on the S.C. Bootle Highway to the ferry dock in less than forty minutes. A minor miracle since we had to stop twice for goats, once for chickens, and once for a truck that had dropped its exhaust system in the middle of the road after hitting a monster pothole.

We pulled into the ferry dock parking lot just as the deckhands on the *Sarah Mitchell* were casting off lines. The captain kept it at idle until we'd hopped aboard.

Two long bench seats ran down each side of the ferry's cabin. They were filled with passengers, a mix of vacationers and locals. The space between the benches was taken up by various goods bought in Marsh Harbour—crates of groceries, cases of beer and soda, boxes containing everything from dishwashers to TV sets—along with assorted suitcases and duffel bags.

The only place left to stand was near the stern. Aside from the occasional whiff of diesel fumes, the wind felt fresh on my skin. The sun was at our backs. The day was progressing nicely enough, although I had not a clue where it was heading. Still, there was motion and it seemed to be forward motion and I was just a big shrimp, going with the tide, crunching my way along, ass-first and mindless of any hungry beasties that might come along and make a meal of me.

A pod of dolphins broke surface in our wake and drafted the boat for several minutes before jetting away. I took it as a good luck sign. Not that I put much stock in signs. Or luck. The good kind or the bad kind. But when dolphins present themselves—those quirky almost-human smiles, their happy leaping, that sense of a creature so attuned to its place and so utterly pleased to be there—it is hard not to feel just a little bit hopeful.

The ferry hit a wave and jostled us around. Boggy and I held fast to the transom to keep our footing. Despite the washing he'd given his clothes, Boggy still looked a mess.

"Mind me asking you something?"

"You just did," he said.

"Mind me asking what you were doing in that ditch at the Walker's airport?"

"I found some things there."

"What things?"

"Taino things."

"The Taino used to live on Walker's Cay?"

"The Taino, they were everywhere, Zachary. On all these islands. Some called themselves Lucaya. Some Arawak. But they were all the same people—Taino."

He opened one of the leather pouches that hung from the drawstring of his pants. He pulled out a smooth black object, a stone of some kind it looked like, just a couple of inches long, maybe three inches wide.

He handed it to me.

"A zemi," Boggy said.

"Zemi. That's one of your Taino gods or something, right?"

"Yes, my people, they carve the likenesses of zemis in sacred wood."

I weighed the object in the palm of my hand, rubbed it between my fingers. The shape was irregular, but there seemed to be five distinct, rounded corners.

"Hard wood," I said. "Hard as rock."

"From the ceiba. Some they call it the silk cotton tree. It is the tree where spirits live."

"So what particular god am I holding here?"

"The years they have worn it smooth, but look and you can see the shape—the head, the four legs, the round shell. This, it is Opiyelguo-birán, the turtle zemi, guardian of the gates of death."

"Mmm, cheery," I said. "But how do you know it's not just an old piece of wood that if you squint real hard it might look vaguely like Opi- . . . some damn turtle."

"Because when I found the zemi, it spoke to me, Zachary. I could feel its power."

"That *maja acu* stuff, you been nipping at it again, haven't you?"

Boggy ignored me. He took the zemi from me and put it back in the pouch.

"You got more zemis in there?"

"Yes, several."

"Let's see."

"Not now," Boggy said. "It is not the time or place."

"But you found them in that ditch? Just lucked across them, out in the middle of nowhere, easy as that. Like going to the zemi Super Store?"

"You have to understand, Zachary, there were once thousands and thousands of Taino in these islands. Every Taino—man, woman, child—always carried a pouch like mine with different zemis in it. For power and for protection. When Tainos died, their zemis were buried with them, to look after them in the afterlife."

"So the runway at Walker's Cay, that was once a Taino burial ground?"

"I think so, yes. At the center of the island, near a high point of land. That is where Taino live, and that is where they bury their dead," Boggy said. "I am very happy that I found these zemis."

Boggy lives in a small place he built at the nursery. It's a glorified chickee hut really—a palmetto-thatched roof with a broad overhang above a platform of hard pine, not even screens to keep out the bugs. It sits near the center of the property, on the highest ground.

"I've seen some of those zemis at your place, haven't I? You've got them stuck everywhere."

"Yes, but those zemis are ones that I made." He tapped the leather pouch. "These zemis, they are much more powerful."

"Why's that? Thought you were supposed to be some high-charged shaman, a guy who has a direct line to the gods. The zemis you make, they oughta be jam-up with power."

"I am only one, Zachary."

"What's that supposed to mean?"

"In the long-ago, when there were many Taino on these islands, the belief it was strong, the belief it was everywhere. The old zemis they were filled with that belief, they were filled with power."

"What were they, like faith magnets or something?"

Boggy's eyes lit up. He smiled. Such a rare occurrence that I had to blink to make sure.

"That is a very good way to describe it, Zachary. Yes, that is exactly what they are. Faith magnets. I like that."

"Well, glad I could make your day."

Boggy looked at me. I always try to hold his gaze, but every time it's me who is the first one to look away.

"I know you don't believe, Zachary."

"I've got my beliefs."

"In what do you believe?"

"It's not like I can put a name on it or anything."

"If you cannot put a name on it, then why believe in it?"

"I believe in myself."

"A small belief."

"I believe in Barbara and I believe in Shula, OK? I believe in the thing that joins all people together and not the thing that pulls them apart. I believe in wisdom defeating ignorance, love conquering hate, good winning out over evil, some beauty being just skin deep and some ugly going all the way to the bone. I believe in skies of blue, clouds of white, bright blessed days, and dark sacred nights."

"Mr. Louis Armstrong."

"Yeah, I believe in him, too."

Boggy put a hand on my shoulder.

"That's a start," he said.

18

The *Sarah Mitchell* pulled up to the ferry dock in New Plymouth, Green Turtle's only town and as charming a place as you could hope to find in the Bahamas. Yet another Loyalist community, with its roots in the 1780s, it still had the narrow streets and tabby walls and pastel buildings that hearkened to that era, although few of the structures dated back much more than a hundred years. Numerous fires and hurricanes had seen to that.

We had at least another hour before the *Trifecta* arrived, so Boggy and I walked around.

We passed half a dozen churches, an elementary school where kids were playing dodgeball on the playground, a couple of cemeteries, five places that rented golf carts to tourists, the Alton Lowe Museum, four restaurants, three grocery stores, two hardware stores, a bank that was open only on Tuesday and Friday afternoons, and the Plymouth Rock liquor store, which was notable for the fact that it also served chicken souse for breakfast and sold real estate, your basic full-service establishment.

We walked out on Government Dock and took in the view. A group of young boys were jumping off the end of the dock, turning flips on the way down. A group of young girls were pretending not to watch, giggling among themselves.

Boats were tied off at mooring buoys just inside the harbor. Nice boats. Cruisers and charters like the *Trifecta*. When it finally arrived this was where it would be.

We walked around some more and wound up where everyone who visits New Plymouth eventually winds up—Miss Emily's Blue Bee Bar. The sign outside proudly proclaimed it the "Original Home of the Goombay Smash."

Emily Cooper passed away years ago and, being a good Christian woman, swore she never tasted the concoction that launched a zillion hangovers. The secret recipe resided with her daughter Violet. She was behind the bar.

"Hello, dahlin'," Violet said. "Haven't seen you here in too long now. Where you been keeping yourself?"

She gave me a hug. She gave Boggy one, too. We did some catching up.

Violet poured us each a plastic cup of the house specialty. Even with all the fruit juice and the froufrou, the rum, which there were three kinds of, went directly to that part of the prefrontal cortex that elevates higher thinking.

We found a table and sat down.

I got out my cell phone. I'd forgotten to charge it the night before. It was running low on juice and I was keeping it turned off unless I really needed it. Plus, roaming fees in the Bahamas are brutal.

I switched on the phone and was rewarded with an assortment of beeps and blips that let me know I was way behind on the human contact front.

A message from Mickey Ryser saying I should give him a call. A message from Barbara saying I should give her a call, too. I was still sorting through all the messages when the screen lit up with an incoming call and I clicked over to that.

A man's voice . . .

"Zack Chasteen?"

"You got me."

"Abel Delgado. You called?"

"I did. We need to talk."

"So talk."

"Face-to-face, Delgado. Where are you?"

"Listen, Chasteen, I already know about you. I talked to my wife. She said you'd bothered her."

"I paid your wife a visit, Delgado. I did not bother her. And I don't believe she would tell you otherwise."

"Oh yeah?"

"Tell you the truth, if she was bothered by anyone it was you."

"What makes you think that?"

"Just a personal observation," I said. "I've observed something else, too."

"What?"

"That you've been negligent in returning the calls of your client, Mickey Ryser."

"I just got off the phone with Ryser."

"What did you tell him?"

"That's between me and him."

"Not anymore it's not. Mickey's an old friend. He paid you good money to find his daughter. What have you done to earn it? Besides stick up a few posters around Marsh Harbour?"

Nothing from the other end of the line.

"You get any response from those posters, Delgado? Because if you have any idea where Jen Ryser is, then you need tell me right now. Anything you know, I want to know it, too."

More nothing from the other end of the line.

"You still with me, Delgado?"

"Yeah, I'm with you," he said. "You bother my wife again and I'll have your ass."

"Why wait?"

"Huh?"

"I said why wait? You can have my ass as soon as you want it. But, fair warning, my ass is part of a package deal that contains all the rest of me. So you'll have your work cut out for you. Also, I might as well tell you that I am not above a head butt. And if it gets down to the short hairs, then I have been known to bite."

A long pause from Delgado, then . . .

"You talk big, Chasteen."

"I am big."

"Where are you?"

"Wherever two or more are gathered together in my name . . ."

It got nothing from him. A great line like that, wasted.

"At this moment, I'm sitting at Miss Emily's Blue Bee Bar willfully trying to restrain myself from asking Violet for a second goombay smash. You better pray to God I don't have another one because I get even bigger and meaner with rum in me."

"Huh?"

"Let me make this easy, Delgado. Where are you?"

"Marsh Harbour. You know where that is?"

"Indeed I do. Exactly where in Marsh Harbour?"

"The Mariner's Inn," he said. "At the bar."

"Imagine that."

"Imagine what?"

"Imagine I'll be meeting you there, Delgado. Say, eight o'clock tonight. I'll bring my ass. You bring yours. We'll see who leaves with what."

They brought her food and asked her questions. They wanted to know about the money.

"When are the deposits made?"

"The tenth of each month."

"Always the same amount?"

"Yes."

"Does anyone have access to the account besides you?"

"No."

They asked a few questions about her mother and the rest of her family. Was there anyone she checked in with on a regular basis? Anyone who would get worried if they didn't hear from her?

No, she told them. She had no brothers, no sisters. There was an aunt and an uncle and assorted cousins, most of them living in Raleigh, but she was seldom in touch with them, hadn't spoken to them since her mother's funeral, except to go over some matters about her estate. And her best friends, the people she cared most about, they'd all been with her on the boat.

Immediately, she regretted telling them the truth. She should have told them she was extremely close to Molly's family, that she was supposed to call them at least every other day, that they were probably beside themselves with worry now and had alerted the police. But she didn't think of it until it was too late. She wasn't accustomed to lying.

It was her father who interested them the most.

"I really don't know that much about him," she said. "I haven't seen him in

more than twenty years. I can't even remember what he looks like. We've just spoken on the phone. And only three times."

"He owns a private island with a big house. Got his own plane. The guy must be loaded."

"I really wouldn't know."

"You know anything about the setup on that island? How many people he's got working for him there? Security, that kind of thing?"

"No idea."

"How did he make all his money?"

"I've got no idea about that either."

"Are you in his will?"

"I don't know."

"You said he was dying."

"He told me on the phone that he'd been sick. I assumed the worse."

"He's gotta be getting ready to kick. Why else would he be getting in touch with you after all these years, huh? Because if he had really wanted to see you he could have done that long before now. Right?"

She didn't say anything. But she thought: Yes, if my father had really wanted to see me he would have done it long ago.

She heard them talking low among themselves, but couldn't make out any of it.

She thought: I should have been nicer to my father on the phone. I should have flown straight there to see him when he called. I shouldn't have been so noncommittal, leaving him hanging like that, wondering when I would show up. Or if I would show up. I should have at least shown a little enthusiasm. But Molly had barely ever spoken about him. I didn't even know his name until I was thirteen. And I had no desire to seek him out—Molly had squelched any notion of that. Still, he's my father. I should have . . .

She felt a hand on her leg. It was him, shaking her.

"Jen? Answer me, dammit, I'm asking you a question."

"What? Sorry, I didn't hear you."

"Who is this guy?"

"What guy?"

"This guy, Abel Delgado."

19

It was just after 5:00 P.M. when the *Trifecta* dropped anchor at Green Turtle Cay, a hundred yards out from Government Dock. A few minutes later, several people piled into its dinghy and began heading our way.

I couldn't be sure that Karen Breakell was on the dinghy. She was the cook, the only female crew member according to the dockmaster at Blue Sky Marina. Maybe she'd stayed on the boat to get dinner ready. In which case I'd have to sweet-talk someone into taking us on the dinghy out to her. I had used up all my sweet talk on Abel Delgado. I was hoping to catch a break.

The dinghy tied off on the dock. Six people in it.

Four of them were quite obviously the party who had chartered the boat—two men, two women; the men in flowery shirts, the women in Lilly Pulitzer.

A young man in a semi-official captain's outfit—khaki shorts, white shirt tucked in, deck shoes—helped them onto the dock.

That left the young woman who was the last to step out of the dinghy. Same outfit as the young man. Blond, tall, lean, and well put together. Or long and leggity, in Cutiespeak.

She brought up the rear of the group. I approached her.

"Karen Breakell?"

She stopped.

"Yes, that's me."

"I'd like to talk to you about Jen Ryser."

Her brown eyes widened, a hand went to her mouth.

"Jen? Is she OK? Did something happen?"

"We just need to locate her, that's all."

"What's wrong? Who are you?"

I introduced Boggy and myself. I told her that I was an old friend of Jen's father and that he had asked me to help track her down. The rest of her party stopped at the end of the dock, waiting for her. She told them to go on and she would catch up with them.

"We'll be at Sundowner's," the young man said, pointing toward a bar that sat along the waterfront.

Karen Breakell wore the look of someone who had spent much of her young life around boats. Her hair was honeyed and sun-streaked. Her skin wasn't the shiny, surface bronze of a quickie vacation tan, but the deep and creamy brown that speaks of long hours spent not only in the sun but soaking up its reflection off the water, the way it burnishes the nether parts—behind the ears, beneath the brow, between the fingers—despite all diligence with sunscreen. I could just make out the first spidery lines around her eyes, the ones that come from squinting against the glare of a white-bright day. Hers was a pretty and open face, one that would wear a smile well. But she wasn't smiling as she studied me. The jury was still out about me and my motives.

She wore a good watch and she checked it.

"I need to get to the grocery store before it closes. Get some things for dinner," she said. "We're only here for an hour and then we're heading back to Marsh Harbour."

"Thought you weren't due back until tomorrow."

"Change of plans. The clients decided they want to fly home first thing in the morning. So I'm going to pick up some steaks and cook them dinner while we cruise back to the marina."

"This shouldn't take long," I said.

"I really don't know what I can do to help you find Jen. It's been nearly a week since I last saw her. I thought she would have been at her father's place by now."

"So she was definitely planning to go there?"

"Oh yeah, for sure. She was excited about it. Or maybe excited isn't the right word. Because she was nervous, too. I mean, it has been so long since Jen's seen him. What, twenty years or so?"

"Something like that," I said. "You and Jen are close friends?"

"Real close. We shared a house for the past two years. On the sailing team together and everything. Jen's great. I just wish that . . ."

She shrugged, let it hang.

"What happened at Miner Cay, Karen?"

She shot me a look.

"So you heard about that?"

"We were there earlier today. You and your friends made quite an impression with the locals."

She shook her head, blew out some air.

"We'd all been drinking a little too much."

"So I heard."

"I probably shouldn't have done what I did, but I'd had it with Torrey. I just couldn't take being on the boat with that woman for another second."

"That's Torrey Kealing?"

"Yeah, her. That saying about oil and water? How they don't mix? That was us."

"But didn't you know that before you got on the boat with her? I mean, you must have had a few weeks to plan the trip, gotten a chance to feel things out beforehand, know if there might be issues with other people."

"Oh, we'd been planning the trip for more than a year. And everyone got along just fine. But Torrey wasn't part of the original group. She didn't come along until right at the end. After the whole thing with Coach Tony and Liz."

"Coach Tony?"

"Yeah, Tony Telan. The coach of our sailing team. More than just a coach, really. A friend, too. I mean, he's just a couple of years older than us. He's in graduate school. And he's like this super-experienced sailor. Did a solo transatlantic when he was just seventeen. Been up and down the Caribbean. Knows everything there is to know about boats. He was supposed to come with us. He and Liz. That's his girlfriend. She sails, too. But a couple of weeks before we were supposed to leave, their house caught on fire. They lost almost everything. Even their dog. After that, they decided they better not come with us. So that left just me and Jen and Pete and Will. We were thinking about calling the whole thing off."

I recalled the names I'd written down on my notepad in Walker's Cay.

"Pete Crumrine and Will Moody."

"Uh-huh. Jen and I have known them since we were all freshmen. Nice guys. Pete is going to law school in the fall. At Georgia. And Will is staying in Charleston, going to medical school. Pete and I went out a couple of times when we were sophomores, but we decided we worked better as friends. Jen and Will, though, they had this kinda thing . . ."

"They were seeing each other?"

"Let's say they were hanging out a lot together, you know? Spending more time, just the two of them. I was hoping it would go somewhere. Jen deserves to find someone nice. She hasn't exactly had the best luck with men."

"What do you mean?"

"I don't know, bad choices, I guess. She's one of those girls, I don't know exactly how to describe it, but she always had to be with a guy, you know what I mean? She couldn't just be Jen. We used to talk about it sometimes. Me, when I break up with a guy I sometimes go months before I'm with another guy. I don't mind it. Tell you the truth, I kind of enjoy it that way. Guys can sometimes be so . . ."

"So guyish," I said.

She laughed.

"Totally," she said. "But Jen, the moment she broke it off with one guy it was like she couldn't stop until she'd connected with someone else. I'm not saying she was like, you know, promiscuous. It wasn't anything like that. It was more like she needed to be with a guy in order to define herself. Lucky for Jen she never had any trouble finding guys. She's pretty. She's smart."

"And she's rich."

"Which can create its own problems," Karen said. "Lots of the guys Jen attracts, they're users. It's not like Jen flaunts her money. I mean, she has nice things. Very nice things. Nice clothes, nice car."

"Nice boat."

"An unbelievable boat," Karen said. "And the house we shared, she owned it. But she was never in your face about all the money, you know? Like, here's an example . . .

"Last year, the sailing team qualified for the nationals out in San Diego. It was going to cost something like eighty thousand dollars for everyone to go, what with getting the boats hauled out there, room and board and transportation for thirty-two people. The college said it could only pay half of that, the team would have to raise the rest. So we had car washes and bake sales and we begged our parents, all the usual stuff. Two weeks before nationals we were still fifteen thousand dollars short. We thought, *Well, that's that. We aren't going.* And then Coach Tony held a team meeting and announced that an anonymous benefactor had come forward and donated the rest of the money we needed."

"It was Jen?"

"She denied it when I asked her about it," Karen said. "But, yeah, it had to be her. I mean, who else? Either her or her mother."

"How did Jen take it when her mother died?"

"Hard, real hard. Jen and her mom, they were more like sisters than mother and daughter, you know? Jen called her by her name, Molly, not Mom or something like that. They were just really, really close. I mean, I love my mother, but with the two of them it was something else. They must have spoken on the phone four or five times a day. Girl talk, everything. They didn't have any secrets. Buying the boat, the cruise, the whole thing was their idea. The two of them came up with it originally and then put together the rest of the crew. Molly was supposed to come with us. But . . ." She stopped, shrugged. "I think that's why Jen jumped at the chance to visit her father. She's had this big hole in her heart since Molly died and she was hoping maybe he could fill it."

Karen Breakell looked at her watch again.

"Look, I really need to get to the store," she said.

"We'll walk with you," I said.

20

id's Grocery was just up the street. We headed for it. I walked alongside Karen Breakell. Boggy trailed behind us.

"You said you almost called off the trip?"

Karen nodded.

"Yeah, this was right after Coach Tony had to drop out. Will and Pete aren't experienced sailors. And neither Jen nor I had enough open-water experience to feel comfortable about making the crossing. We needed a seasoned captain to go with us. And it's hard to find someone on such short notice. So we were left high and dry, right before we were scheduled to leave. Jen was really torn up about that. The sailboat trip was kinda like this tribute to her mom, something the two of them had planned on doing together and she wanted to see it through. Jen's a good sailor, but . . ."

"A Beneteau 54 is a lot of boat."

"Exactly. She didn't want to risk it just on her skills alone," Karen said. "We were all bummed about having to pull the plug on the trip. We wanted to travel in April and May, before hurricane season started. So if we were going to do it, then it meant we had to leave right away."

"So what changed Jen's mind about canceling the trip?"

"Justin Hatchitt came along."

"The captain?"

"Uh-huh. It was just total coincidence that we found him. Or he found us. Whatever, it was a lucky break," Karen said. "All because we decided to go have a few beers at the Blind Tiger. It's this bar in downtown Charleston."

"So, let me get this straight. You meet a guy in a bar and you hire him to be your captain?"

Karen laughed.

"I know, it sounds pretty sketch. But if you met Justin you'd understand. He just looks like a captain. Rugged, outdoorsy. He's got this air of confidence, like he can handle anything that comes along."

"And he had experience sailing in the islands?"

"Yeah, lots of it. He said he'd spent the winter on a big sailboat down in St. Bart's and had just finished transporting it to Hilton Head for the summer season. Not that Jen checked any of it out," Karen said. "She didn't need a lot of convincing."

"What do you mean?"

Karen smiled.

"I mean, you could practically see the sparks flying between her and Justin."

"So she hired him to be the captain?"

"That's the best part," Karen said. "Justin said he'd do it for free. He said he'd been working nonstop for almost a year, had some money saved, and he said this would be his vacation. He loved the boat once he laid eyes on it. I mean, it's brand-new, what's not to love? And, I don't know, we all just seemed to hit it off with him. It felt right. A good fit."

We reached the entrance of Sid's Grocery. The hours were posted in the window. Still another forty-five minutes until it closed.

"So what went wrong, Karen?"

"Excuse me?"

"What made you get off the boat on Miner Cay?"

She shook her head. It took her a moment to answer.

"Like I said, Torrey and I just did not hit it off. At first, she seemed like a good fit, too. But it didn't take too long for that to wear off."

"You said she was the last one to join the trip?"

"Yeah, she and Pete, they'd hooked up. He hadn't known Torrey very long, just a couple of weeks. Met her at the Blind Tiger the same night we met Justin. Then things got all fast and furious between them. Pete was, like, head over heels for her. He asked if she could come along."

"And everyone agreed?"

"Well, with Coach Tony and Liz dropping out, we had room on the boat. Torrey seemed nice enough. She said she had sailing experience. She seemed OK. She was very enthusiastic. She's got this big personality, very vivacious and talkative. Plus, she had the money."

"The money?"

"Yeah. Pete and Will and me, we didn't want Jen to get stuck with all the expense, you know? After all, here she was letting us join her on this great boat of hers and we wanted to pay our way. We decided we would each throw in two thousand dollars at the beginning of the trip and use that to pay our share of the food, gas, docking expenses, whatever. Torrey threw in her two thousand and that was that."

"So when did you decide that the boat wasn't big enough for the both of you?"

"Didn't take long. We hit bad weather right out of Charleston and had to tuck in around Savannah, behind Tybee Island, until it settled. Three days of rain and heavy wind and all of us cooped up. You know how it is on a boat. Everyone needs to pitch in. I did the cooking because, you know, that's just my thing. All the others saw what needed doing and they did it. Except Torrey. She was mostly good at bossing other people around. It started wearing thin real quick. "

"What about Jen or Justin Hatchitt? Shouldn't they have set her straight?"

"You would think," Karen said. "But by then Jen and Justin were pretty much oblivious to anything but each other."

"I thought Jen and Will . . ."

"Yeah, Will thought he and Jen had something going on, too. Like I said, it wasn't anything official. Still, it made it awkward with Jen and Justin carrying on with each other right in front of Will like that. With the weather, there wasn't anything we could do but hang out down below on the boat. Jen and Justin would go off to her cabin. Pete and Torrey would go off, too. Will and I would just kinda sit there twiddling our thumbs. It was weird. I felt sorry for Will. I could tell he was hurt. But he just shrugged it off."

"So what caused things to blow up between you and Torrey?"

"It was right after we left Savannah," Karen said. "About thirty miles offshore we hit some more weather, a squall line, and things happened real fast. We had to scramble—reef the mainsail, fasten things down, close the hatches. Everyone was busy doing something. Except Torrey, as usual.

"The roller furler on the jib snagged or something and the jib was flapping around on the foredeck. I yelled at Torrey to get off her dead ass and come help me with it. But she just sat there. Jen was down below and heard me hollering. So she hurried up to give me a hand, but she slipped as she was coming out of the cockpit and she must have hit a turnbuckle or something because it ripped her blouse and there was blood all over the place. And there was this big gash on the back of her shoulder.

"Lucky for us, Will was on board. I mean, he's not a doctor yet or anything, but he knows how to do things. He got the wound cleaned up. Not as bad as it looked but it needed some stitches, like eight or ten of them. We had to make a decision: Turn back to Savannah and take Jen to the emergency room. Or keep going and take care of it ourselves. Will and Pete and me, we were all for turning back. I mean, it was a nasty cut. But Justin and Torrey, they said we'd be in more danger if we sailed back through the storm and it was better to press on to the Bahamas. It was Jen's call and she said keep going. So Will got out the first-aid kit and he had Jen drink a lot of vodka and he stitched it up. It was ugly looking but at least he took care of it."

"And you blamed it all on Torrey?"

"Yeah, I did. But it was really just a whole lot of stuff that had been building up. And it exploded when we hit Miner Cay a couple of days later. Like I said, we all started drinking too early in the day and by the time we went ashore we were at each other's throats."

"You and Jen, too?"

Karen looked away, her face pained.

"Yeah, I said some things. Jen said some things. Mostly I was giving her a hard time for hooking up with Justin and rubbing it in Will's face. Will didn't deserve that. Then Torrey jumped into it and told me to mind my own business and that really set me off. Next I knew, we were all going at it."

"And the next morning, you got off the boat in Miner Cay and told them good-bye."

"Yeah, Jen didn't want me to go. She begged me not to. But I had my back up and the whole thing on the boat was just getting a little too weird for me. Not what I signed up for," Karen said. "I felt bad for Will because, with me gone, he was really going to be the fifth wheel. I tried to talk him into coming with me, but he didn't like the idea of hanging out on Miner Cay for who knows how long waiting for the mailboat to arrive. He wanted to go straight to Marsh Harbour and figure it out from there."

"So that's where they were heading? Marsh Harbour?"

"That was the first stop, yeah. And then the plan was to just work our way down the islands until we got to Jen's dad's place. After that, we were going to play it by ear, see what happened."

"So you think they might still be up here in the Abacos?"

"Could be. They wanted to hit as many islands up this way as possible—Man O' War Cay, Elbow Cay, make the circuit. Then hit Harbour Island and Eleuthera on the way south. I keep an eye out, thinking I'll spot them, but . . ."

A woman was coming out of Sid's Grocery. Karen grabbed the door and held it open, ready to step inside.

I gave her my card.

"Well, if you cross paths with them, give me a shout."

"Will do," Karen said. "And if you find Jen first, will you tell her something for me?"

"Sure," I said. "What is it?"

"Tell her I love her. Tell her I'm sorry. Tell her I'm still her friend."

They were talking on the deck, but this time Jen couldn't make out much of it until she heard him say, "OK, I'm going now. I could be a while. Can you take care of everything?"

"I think so. Just hurry."

"If I don't come back . . ."

"Don't say that."

"If I'm not back by morning, then don't come looking for me. Just do what you have to do. Look out for yourself. The farther you can get away from here, the better."

Jen gave it a few minutes, until she was certain he was gone. Then she called out for help, heard footsteps approach, the hatch door slide open.

"What is it?"

"I need to use the head."

Jen was pulled roughly to her feet.

She said, "Untie my hands. I'm having my period. There's a cloth bag with . . ."

"Yeah, I see it. Hold on."

When she was inside, by the toilet, Jen said, "Close the door."

"Forget it."

"But, please, I . . ."

"I said forget it. I'm not closing that door. Just do what you have to do. And make it fast, you hear?"

21

When we got back to Marsh Harbour and the Mariner's Inn, there was still an hour until it was time to meet Abel Delgado in the bar.

Charlie Callahan had checked in while we were gone. He and Boggy went off in search of dinner.

I ordered room service and made some phone calls . . .

I called Mickey Ryser's house on Lady Cut Cay. Octavia answered.

"Mr. Ryser still hasn't dragged himself out of bed, not since we got here," she told me. "Won't hardly eat nothing. I have to force food down him. And that detective man, he called here earlier."

"Mickey spoke with him?"

"You could call it that. But it was more hollering than talking. At least on Mr. Ryser's end. I think that detective man, he was wanting more money."

"Well, you tell Mr. Ryser I've got some good news," I said.

The simple fact that I had verified Jen Ryser's arrival in the Bahamas was not the stuff on which to hang hopes. But I put a high gloss on it. And I left out the parts about Jen getting hurt during the crossing and the squabble on Miner Cay. Octavia absorbed it with excitement. I felt sure she would pass it along to Mickey in such a way that it gave him a boost. He sure needed one.

I called Barbara. She had just finished putting down Shula for the night.

"She misses you," Barbara said.

"How can you tell?"

"The way she was looking around at the dinner table. And when I was kissing her good night, she was definitely wondering why you weren't there beside me."

"I'm wondering that, too."

"Not making much progress?"

"Inch by tiny inch. We've gotten luckier than I thought we would get in just one day. At least we know where Jen was even if we don't know where she is or where she's going."

"Which is a lot more than you knew when you set out."

"Yeah, I guess. One part of me keeps thinking there's nothing to worry about, this is just a bunch of kids out for a good time and they'll turn up when they turn up and be wondering why folks were so worried about them."

"What's the other part of you think?"

"The other part is still gnawing on it," I said. "But let's talk about something else."

"OK, let's talk about the present."

"You mean, as opposed to the future or the past?"

"No, I mean the present you are bringing back for Shula. When Daddy goes off on a trip he's supposed to bring back a present for his little girl."

"It's not like Daddy's had time to do much shopping."

"It doesn't have to be anything fancy, Zack. Just a pretty shell or something."

"Like a conch shell maybe?"

"Perfect. You can hold it up to Shula's ear and show her how to listen to the sea. I used to love doing that when I was a child. Yes, yes, pick her out a pretty conch shell why don't you? I know she'll love it."

I called Helen Miller in Charleston.

"Clete Boyer here," I said.

"Why hello, Mr. Boyer. How you?"

That voice again. I wondered if the rest of her was as sultry as she sounded. Then I made myself stop wondering. Shame on you, Chasteen.

"Just calling to see if you'd made any progress on those things I asked you to check out."

"Uh-huh, I see," she said. "Listen, before I tell you what I found out, how about you tell me something."

"Gladly."

"Why are you feeding me a line of horse crap about your name being Clete Boyer?"

I didn't have an answer for that. So I didn't give her one.

"I'm waiting, Mr. Chasteen."

"How'd you find out my name?"

"Christalmighty, I'm a detective. You gave me your phone number. Finding out the name a phone number belongs to, that's not heavy lifting."

"Hmmm," I said.

"Once I found out your name, Mr. Zachary Taylor Chasteen, it made it easier to find out some other things, too. Like how you served almost two years in Baypoint Federal Prison for counterfeiting, smuggling, and a couple of other pesky little felonies."

"I was set up. The conviction was reversed. Got a pardon from the governor, along with a commendation for valorous service to the State of Florida."

"Yeah, I found that out, too. And I made some calls and what I learned was that, all in all, you're a fairly decent, upstanding guy."

"Glad to know that about myself," I said. "Some days I have my doubts."

She laughed.

"Plus, my daddy, he's a big football fan, too. He remembered you playing ball for the Dolphins. He said you were pretty good until you blew out a knee. Third-team All Pro, three years in a row."

"Not the sorta thing that lands you in the Football Hall of Fame."

"Still, not too shabby. That how come you named your daughter Shula?"

"You really uncovered a lot about me, didn't you?"

"I'm good at what I do," she said. "I think it's kind of sweet, you naming your daughter after your old football coach. Good thing you never played for Howard Schnellenberger, huh?"

"A Girl Named Schnellenberger. Could be a Johnny Cash song."

"More like Weird Al Yankovic," she said. "Still, Zack . . . may I call you Zack?"

"Certainly, Helen."

"Still, Zack, none of that explains why you lied to me, now does it?"

So I hemmed and I hawed and I came clean. I told her about my connection with Mickey Ryser and how I had been enlisted to find his daughter and how that led me to listening to the messages in Abel Delgado's office and calling her.

"OK, I'll buy it," she said when I was done. "Now let me tell you what I found out."

She'd found out everything I'd asked her to find out about Jen Ryser and a lot more on top of that. Graduated with a degree in art history from the College of Charleston. Solid B-student. Captain of the women's sailing team. Delta Delta Delta sorority. No criminal history beyond two speeding tickets. Prior to setting out for the Bahamas, she'd been working at a day-care center.

"But it wasn't like she really needed to work," Helen Miller said. "Not with her trust fund."

"I figured her mom must have left her something."

"Yeah, twenty thousand dollars a month of something."

"Explains how she bought that boat."

"She paid cash for it, part of a lump sum from her inheritance. And it still left a nice little cushion in her account."

"Excuse me, Ms. Miller, but bank accounts and trust funds—isn't that private information?"

"Why, yes, Mr. Chasteen. It's very private. Then again, I'm a private investigator."

"Should I ask how . . ."

"No," she said. "You shouldn't."

I told her I needed her to check the background of the other crew members. I started telling her the names, but she stopped me.

"Way ahead of you," she said. "Paid a visit to the marina where Jen kept her boat. Chatted up the dockmaster. He told me I should contact a guy named Tony Telan."

"Coach of the college sailing team. He was supposed to go on the trip. He and his girlfriend."

"Right. Only his house caught on fire," Helen said. "Anyway, I sat down with him. Nice guy. He gave me the names of three of Jen's friends who were on the boat—Karen Breakell, Will Moody, and Pete Crumrine. I checked them out. Good kids. No blips on their records."

"Did you contact their parents?"

"I started to," Helen Miller said. "Then I decided it might freak them out for no good reason, so I held off. What do you think?"

I told her I had just spoken with Karen Breakell and shared what I had learned from her.

"As for Will Moody and Pete Crumrine, I think it's worth the risk of freaking out their parents just to know if their sons have been in touch. Maybe they've called and can shed some more light on all this."

"OK, will do," Helen said. "As for the other two people on the boat . . ."

"Justin Hatchitt and Torrey Kealing."

"That's the first I've heard of their names. No one I spoke to knew anything about either one of them. But I'll check them out, too."

"Hold on. I've got their passport numbers."

I read them off to her.

"That'll help," she said. "I did go back out to the marina and talk with the dockmaster after I spoke to Tony Telan. He remembered a couple of things that he didn't remember the first time I spoke with him."

"Like what?"

"Like this guy who visited the marina a couple of times, said he was looking for work, either transporting someone's boat for them or hiring on as a captain. Dockmaster told him the only boat he knew of that was planning to go anywhere was Jen Ryser's boat but it already had a captain and a full crew."

"This was before Tony Telan dropped out, right?"

"Yeah, must have been," Helen said. "Anyway, the guy said he might as well check it out anyway, just in case anything came up. So the dockmaster gave him Telan's name and Jen's name and how to find them. I'm thinking maybe the guy might be Justin Hatchitt."

"Sounds like a fit. Except . . ."

"Except what?"

"Except Karen Breakell told me they met Justin Hatchitt at a bar one night by coincidence. It was after the fire at Telan's house. They needed a captain. And . . ."

"And lo and behold, some guy just shows up and fills the bill."

"Sound funny to you?"

"It does when I put it with something else."

"What's that?"

"That fire at Telan's house? It wasn't an accident. State fire marshal's report was just filed last week. Definitely arson. The investigators found accelerants placed in three different locations."

"And they don't suspect Telan?"

"No, they cleared him. He and his girlfriend were renting the place. They were both asleep when it happened and they barely got out of there. Lost just about everything including their dog. An old two-story wooden house on Montague Street. A firetrap to begin with, only someone nudged it along."

"Landlord maybe?"

"Landlord's a ninety-year-old woman, lives next door," Helen Miller said. "They pretty much ruled her out right off the bat."

"You think this guy Hatchitt . . . ?"

"Might have burned down the house just to get Telan out of the way? A whole lot of trouble just to be captain on a sailboat trip."

"Not when the sailboat is worth nearly a million dollars and the woman who owns it even more than that."

Helen Miller thought about it.

"I didn't have a name before. Now I do," she said. "I'll start checking out Hatchitt. Torrey Kealing, too."

I suggested a few other things she might want to check out. And when I was done, she said, "I'm not billing this to Abel Delgado, am I?"

"No," I said. "You can bill it to me."

"Along with that hundred-dollar bonus you told me to tack on Delgado's bill?"

"Yeah, that, too," I said. "How deep am I in with you so far?"

"Oh, you're in pretty deep," she said. "And for what you want, it'll get deeper."

She gave me a dollar amount.

I let out a whistle.

"Like I told you," she said. "I'm good."

22

Charlie and Boggy weren't back from dinner by the time eight o'clock rolled around. So I paid my visit to the Mariner's Inn bar without them.

It wasn't hard to pick out Abel Delgado. He was the biggest guy at the bar and he occupied one corner of it, his stool turned so he could see everyone who came in the place.

At least that might have been his original intent. But as it stood now, Delgado was in no condition to see much beyond the salted rim of his margarita glass. He wore some kind of Tommy Bahama knockoff, aquamarine with orange palm trees, that was supposed to make him look like a real island guy. His hair was tousled, his jaw slack, and it was better than even money that he'd been slamming down drinks ever since we'd spoken on the phone three hours earlier.

He sat hunched over, both elbows on the bar, talking to a young man next to him. I took the stool on his other side. He didn't pay me any attention.

The bartender, a busty Bahamian woman wearing a red silk blouse and a toothy smile, asked what I wanted. I ordered a Kalik. She delivered it. And I sat there, sipping my beer and eavesdropping on Delgado's conversation.

It was really more of a monologue, with Delgado doing the talking, his voice thick, the words slurred. The young man offered an occasional nod just to hold up his end of the proposition.

". . . and I told the old man, I said, I got expenses you know. Plus, my day rate, a case like this, it's twenty-five hundred. And I already been on it six days, which is . . . which is . . ."

"Fifteen thousand," the young man.

"Yeah, fifteen thousand. So I said to him, I said I need that, plus my expenses before you find out what I found out. And, believe me, I'm finding out some things. Give me a couple more days and . . ."

I tapped Delgado on the shoulder. He turned and squinted at me, trying hard to focus. His head rolled, as if it were on a swivel atop his neck.

"Howya doing, Abel?"

"I know you?"

"Zack Chasteen. Here as promised."

It took a moment to sink in with him.

"You're a fucking asshole," he said.

"That's no way to make friends, Delgado."

"Fuck you, you fucking asshole."

He said it loudly and it quieted the bar.

"Easy," I said.

Delgado turned on me, knocking over his glass, splattering the two of us.

"You're trying to fuck me over, you piece of shit . . ."

He lunged at me and I grabbed his shoulders, trying to hold him off. But his sheer bulk and momentum sent me backward off the stool and both of us fell to the floor. Drunk as he was, Delgado managed to land a couple of blows to the top of my head that probably hurt his knuckles more than they hurt me. I wrenched out from under him and onto my feet. I held off the urge to kick him.

I heard women screaming, saw men backing away. I caught a glimpse of Boggy and Charlie entering the bar. Under most conditions, the sight of the two of them would rivet a crowd's attention, but right now Delgado and I had center stage.

I crouched, ready, as Delgado pulled himself up. He stood there, swaying for a moment as he got his bearings.

The young man he'd been talking to was standing now. He was taller than Delgado and in a lot better shape. He grabbed Delgado's arm, trying to hold him back. The bartender reached across the bar and tried to grab him, too. But Delgado pulled away and charged me, head down, roaring with rage.

I sidestepped him and planted a foot into his backside as he went past. It sent him crashing into a nearby table, scattering its occupants, and sending plates and glasses and bottles of beer in all directions.

Delgado lay there a moment, his face in the remains of someone's fish dinner. He shook his head, then he shook himself all over, like a dog coming in from the rain.

He got up. Winded and heaving, he came at me again. I grabbed his shirt at the shoulders and slung him into the side of the bar. He hit it hard and slid to the floor. This time he lay there a little longer.

And then he got up again. Give the guy points for perseverance. He steadied himself on a bar stool. The bartender got a hand on his shirt, but he ripped away and charged me.

He aimed high this time and I went low, ramming a shoulder into his gut, lifting him up and driving him back against the bar. I felt all the wind go out of him, heard his head snap back and hit something. When I stood up, he stayed down. His head lolled against the bar rail, eyes closed. His tongue hung from the side of his mouth. He was out for the count.

I stood there getting my wind. It hadn't lasted long, but it had sucked the air out of me. I needed to work out more often, get in better shape. Story of my life.

The bartender looked at me and said, "You know him?"

"Casual acquaintance."

"Well, either you get him out of here or I call the police and they do it."

"I'll take care of it," I said.

"I'll give you a hand," said the young man who'd been sitting beside Delgado. He was a good-looking guy—tanned, built like an athlete. I put him in his late twenties. He wore a two-week beard and his curly black hair framed a face with sharp features. He got his hands under Delgado's shoulders and pulled him away from the bar.

Boggy and Charlie joined us.

"Sorry we didn't get here earlier," Charlie said. "I swung by the airport to check a couple of things on the plane."

"Wouldn't have made any difference. He was gunning for me no matter what."

I went through Delgado's pockets and found the card key for his room. The bartender was still watching me.

"You got his tab?" I asked her.

"Sure do. He was charging it to his room."

"I'll take it."

I looked it over. The room number was written in a box at the top—221. I put a hundred-dollar bill on it, handed it back to her, and told her to keep the change.

23

etting Delgado back to his room was a four-man job. Boggy and I each grabbed a leg. Charlie took one arm and the young man took the other.

We stopped once just outside the bar when Delgado started throwing up. We rolled him on his side and let him do what he had to do and then he was out again.

When we reached Room 221, I swiped Delgado's card key through the scanner/lock on the door. I'm no good with those things. I kept getting the red light.

"Here, let me," the young man said.

First try—bingo.

We carried Delgado inside and lowered him onto the bed. The room was ice-cold, the thermostat probably turned as low as it would go. Rivulets of condensation streamed down the sliding-glass door that opened to a small patio overlooking the marina. I flipped on some lights to get a better look around.

Not much to see besides what came with the room. Empty Kalik bottles in the garbage can. Clothes on the floor. Wadded-up receipts and a yellow legal pad atop the dresser.

I gave the legal pad a look. The pages were empty. I started going through the dresser drawers.

Boggy nosed around in the bathroom. Charlie checked out the patio.

The young man leaned against a wall by the TV console, hands in the pockets of his cargo shorts, watching my every move.

He said, "You sure took care of Mr. Delgado."

"I had lots of help. Me and eight margaritas versus him."

He laughed.

"Yeah, he was out of it by the time I got to the bar," he said. "What did you do to piss him off anyway?"

"Came here to finish the job he was hired to do."

The young man cocked his head, studied me closer.

"You a detective like him?"

"Nope."

I felt around under Delgado's T-shirts and socks. Found nothing.

"But you're looking for Jen, too?"

I stopped riffling through the drawer. I looked at the young man.

"You say that as if you know her."

"Yeah, I do. I was with her on the boat. That's why I was in the bar with Mr. Delgado. I saw a flyer he put up and gave him a call and he said to meet him here."

I stepped away from the dresser.

"What's your name?"

"Will," he said. "Will Moody."

He gave me a smile and stuck out his hand. I shook it. His handshake was firm and he looked me straight in the eyes.

As I'd listened to Karen Breakell tell me about those on board the *Chasin' Molly*, I'd formed a mental image of Will Moody and his friend, Pete Crumrine. College boys. Fraternity buds probably. Crumrine headed for law school. Moody for med school. I'd imagined them as clean-cut, preppy types. Izod shirts and Duck Head pants and Topsiders on their feet. If there was anything scruffy about them it was the kind of scruffy that could be washed away in a hurry should they need to make a good impression on a dean or the parents of a girlfriend or Mom and Dad at the country club for dinner.

The young man standing before me didn't fit that picture. He looked a little older than I had imagined. He wasn't exactly unkempt. His hair was clean enough. His T-shirt and shorts, though faded, appeared recently washed. He looked like lots of young guys who spend time on boats. With them, there is the tendency to let things go, to keep grooming time at a minimum. Not to the point of slovenliness, but just short of it.

Then again, you can take an investment banker in a Barney's suit, put him on a sailboat in the islands, and witness the transformation. Within a day or two he's throwing away the Gillette disposables, wearing a bandanna, and wondering how he'd look in dreadlocks.

"So where's Jen? Does she know people are looking for her up and down the Bahamas?"

Moody grinned and shook his head.

"You guys are so blowing this out of proportion. Like I was telling him . . ." He nodded at Delgado again. "There's nothing to worry about. Jen's fine. She should be arriving at her dad's place any day now."

"Where is she right now?"

"I couldn't tell you exactly. Last I saw her . . ."

"When was that?"

"Day before yesterday," he said. "They were heading for Nassau. Then they were maybe stopping at Eleuthera or somewhere before going wherever it is her dad's place is at."

"They?"

"Jen, Torrey, Pete, and Justin."

"Why aren't you with them?"

He shrugged.

"I don't know. I'd had enough, I guess. I just wanted to get off the boat and do my own thing."

"Like Karen Breakell."

"Yeah, like that. Wonder if she ever made it off that little island we stopped at."

"She did," I said. "I saw her just a couple of hours ago."

"Yeah?"

"Over on Green Turtle Cay. She landed a crew job on a charter boat. It'll be docking here in Marsh Harbour this evening."

"You know where?"

"Blue Sky Marina," I said. "Name of the boat is *Trifecta*."

"Cool," he said. "Maybe I'll look her up. I like Karen. She's got her shit straight."

There were plenty of other things I wanted to ask him, but a cell phone started ringing. It was coming from one of Delgado's pockets. I got it just before the fourth ring.

"Is this Mr. Delgado?"

A man's voice. Bahamian accent.

"I'm an associate," I said.

There was hesitation on the other end. And then the man said, "I am calling back as we agreed."

"Is this about the boat?"

"Yah, mon. He said he would have the money for me and . . ."

The call started breaking up.

"Hold on, hold on," I said.

I hurried from the room and onto the patio. I closed the sliding door behind me. Didn't want to let the cold out. Will Moody had started after me, but stopped on the other side of the glass.

"You there?"

"Yah, mon. Right here."

"Tell me about the boat."

"First I need to see that money."

We went back and forth for a while. After we agreed on how to handle it, I stepped back inside.

Boggy and Charlie occupied the room's two chairs. Will Moody had turned on the TV and was flipping through channels. Delgado was still snoring on the bed.

I told them about my conversation with the man on the phone.

Will Moody said, "You going there now?"

"Might as well. Night's still young," I said. "But I'd like to sit down with you in the morning. Maybe we can catch an early breakfast."

"Sure, that would be great," Moody said.

"Where you staying?"

"Oh, this little place just up the road. I forget the name of it."

There aren't that many choices in Marsh Harbour. I knew most of them.

"Abaco Beach Resort? The Lofty Fig? Dunning's Cottages?"

"That last one," Moody said. "But why don't I just meet you here at the restaurant, if that's alright."

"Fine by me. Say seven o'clock?"

"That *is* early," Moody said. "How about nine?"

"Eight."

He grinned.

"OK," he said. "I'll try."

I gave the room another quick once-over while Boggy pulled a blanket over Delgado. He wasn't going anywhere. I'd check in with him first thing in the morning, maybe drag him along with me to breakfast. We could kiss and make up over coffee.

Charlie turned off the lights. The four of us stepped outside, and I pulled the door shut behind us.

24

e tol' me five hunritt dollars. And dat's what I want to see."

The man said his name was Williamson and we'd met him, as instructed, at a place called Lita's Take-A-Way.

It was on the road going south out of Marsh Harbour. Typical Bahamian fish-fry joint. Weathered shack glorified with turquoise paint and white trim. Wooden shutters propped open above a walk-up window. Old woman in a hairnet taking the orders. A couple of not-quite-so-old women working behind her in the kitchen. Fried fish. Cracked conch. Fried chicken. Conch fritters. You could elevate your cholesterol count just by breathing the air.

Picnic tables sat on a concrete slab illuminated by yellow bug lights that dangled from bamboo poles. A dozen or so men played dominoes at the tables. Each and every one of them casting an eye our way.

Williamson walked out to meet us the moment Charlie swung his rental car into the parking lot. A tall, slender, loose-limbed man with a close-cropped white beard that matched his hair. Might have been forty, might have been seventy. Hard to tell. He had more than half his teeth, but the ones he had were gnarly and stained and there were sizable gaps between them. He wore a long-sleeved white shirt tucked into long brown pants. Black sandals on calloused feet.

We had gotten straight to business.

"I'll pay you two hundred now," I said. "And the rest if it pans out."

"Three hundred now," Williamson said.

"Tell me once more what you saw," I said.

He told the story again, the same way he told it the first time. He was a lobster fisherman and a few days earlier he had been out on his boat along the west side of Great Abaco. Lobster season was over and Williamson had been pulling his traps, taking them ashore a boatload at a time to clean and repair and get ready for when the season reopened in August.

"I seen da boat, big and bare-masted, come puttering along in the still of morning," he said. "Took notice of it, too, because dat kind of boat, it don't come near da Marls too often."

At mention of The Marls, I looked at Charlie and he looked at me.

The Marls is a vast estuarial reserve that gets its name from the gray muck—a combination of clay and dolomite and shell—that is the region's most notable topographical feature. Where there's enough muck to form an islet, mangroves take root, flourish, and create dense broad canopies of green. A spiderweb network of tidal channels, miles and miles of it, cuts among the islets, flooding the estuary with baitfish and the larvae of shrimp, lobster, and conch.

Imagine a ten-thousand-piece jigsaw puzzle where every piece looks like every other piece and that pretty much describes The Marls. And it's home to some of the best bonefishing on the planet.

Charlie said, "Brings back fond memories, doesn't it, Zack-o?"

"Don't know if fond is the exact word I'd use to describe those memories."

A few years back, Charlie and I had chartered a guide for a day of fishing in The Marls. We must have caught and released two dozen bonefish. A splendid excursion.

The next day, feeling cocky about our navigational skills and looking to save a few hundred dollars, we rented a little skiff and set out into The Marls on our own. We caught some fish. We did ourselves proud. But it wasn't until the sun was a few fingers above the horizon that either one of us would admit we were lost. And not just lost but complete head-up-our-butts-without-a-clue in the wilderness.

We would follow a channel that looked like it might lead to open water only to run aground. We would follow another promising channel only to hit the dead end of a mangrove cul-de-sac. We would let the boat drift, hoping it would take us somewhere, but we wound up floating in circles.

The boat didn't have a radio. It got dark. The mosquitoes came out.

These weren't the kind of mosquitoes that could be warded off by mere slapping. These were vicious little saltwater mosquitoes unaccustomed to having large mammals in their presence, and sensing the feast of their brief lives, they were by-God relentless.

After we parted with all the blood we could afford to part with, Charlie and I hit upon the only available solution to our predicament. We dug up muck from the flats and covered ourselves in it from head to toe. It didn't totally thwart the mosquitoes, but at least the little bastards had to work for their meals.

Come morning, some local fishermen found us. And after assuring themselves we weren't lunatic exiles from the Lost Tribe of Mudmen, they led us back toward relative civilization.

Charlie caught me scratching my arms and legs.

"Yeah," he said, "just thinking about The Marls does me that way, too."

Williamson told us he had kept an eye on the sailboat as it moved past. At one point, when the boat appeared to have run aground, Williamson cranked up his skiff and headed for it, thinking he might make a few bucks by throwing the captain a line and pulling the sailboat to deeper water. But the sailboat worked free on its own.

"Dat's when I saw it, her name written right across da transom," he said.

"*Chasin' Molly?*"

"Yah, dat what it say, for true."

Late that afternoon, heading home, Williamson came across the boat again.

"Only dis time she was out of da water on skids," he said. "Had the gantry out and they was hauling her in."

"Who's they?"

Williamson looked around, as if someone might have sneaked up behind him.

"Dem Dailey brothers," he said. "They stay out the other side of Crossing Place off the road to Hole in the Wall. They got a boatyard. Do that and other things."

He told me how to get there. I got out the money and handed it to him through the car window. He looked over each bill carefully, then smoothed them out, folded them over, and stuffed them away.

He said, "I'll be sitting right here, waiting 'til you come back."

25

It was a twenty-minute drive to the Dailey brothers' boatyard, the last ten minutes of it down a crater-chocked, semisubmerged stretch of limestone that only under the most generous terms could be called a road. The Hyundai that Charlie had picked up at the airport offered exactly nothing in the way of shock absorption. Each jarring bounce threatened to splay it open.

"Perfect car for these conditions," Charlie said.

"It's a piece of crap," I said.

"Yes, my friend, but it's a rental piece of crap. That's what makes it perfect."

The going wasn't made any easier without headlights. We decided to douse them just in case the Daileys weren't in the mood for visitors. Mangrove branches clawed the windshield and scraped the side panels. Fallen limbs pounded against the undercarriage.

It was almost midnight. We could have waited until morning, but I was anxious to get a peek at where *Chasin' Molly* might or might not be. If I could just put my eyes on the boat and confirm that it was here, then that would give me all I needed to contact the police and let them step in to help with the search for Jen Ryser.

The road that wasn't really a road stopped at a makeshift gate that was little more than knobby pine poles and chicken wire. A hand-painted sign said "Private." The fence that stretched out on either side was not built for high-security purposes, but the brambles and brush that had overgrown it were almost as effective as concertina wire.

Charlie managed to turn the car around and park it pointing it out, the way we'd come in.

"Not that we could haul ass out of here on that road," he said. "Still, it's a comforting thought."

We got out and walked up to the gate. No lock and chain holding it shut, just a loop of rope over a post. I unlooped it and we walked in.

It was like entering a boat cemetery. Vessels of every kind on either side of us, big ones and small ones, from trawlers to skiffs. Some were toppled on their sides, wheelhouses ripped asunder, flying bridges torn apart. Others were flipped over completely, hulls to the heavens. None would ever touch water again. They had been cannibalized for their parts, picked to the bone like carrion in the desert.

As we moved deeper into the place, we got a feel for its layout. It wasn't particularly well lit, just one flickering light outside a squat block building that appeared to be an office of sorts. Behind it, lined up with barely an arm's length between them—three wooden cottages, each with a sagging porch and in various stages of disrepair. I was expecting dogs to come lunging out from under the porches, but none appeared. A nice piece of luck there. Nothing can put a damper on an evening stroll like dogs coming for you in the dark.

Another hundred feet ahead of us a small cove opened onto the lee of Great Abaco—dull gray water under a dark sky. A long concrete dock stuck out from a concrete seawall, a couple of small boats tied up at it. Alongside the dock sat a broad concrete boat ramp. And towering above the ramp, its wheels in tracks on either side, stood the steel gantry that Williamson had told us about.

The gantry was sturdy and substantial, capable of lifting some very big boats. Its tracks wound away from the ramp and led to a massive Quonset hut hangar. In contrast to the surrounding dereliction, the hangar stood out in the night, a gleaming white, prefabricated building easily fifty yards long and three stories tall. It looked fairly new.

The boatyard was bigger than two Kmart parking lots and we had already decided that the only way to cover it all and get out of there in a hurry would be to split up. I pointed Boggy toward the rows of boats sitting atop cradles at the far end of the property. Charlie would head to the other side and work his way along the waterfront. I would check out the hangar.

"Ten minutes," I said. "Back here."

They split off and I continued straight ahead. The hangar loomed larger and larger the closer I got to it. A forklift was parked outside the hangar. A broad garage-style door made of corrugated aluminum was the only entrance I could see. I pulled up on the handle, but it was locked tight.

I walked down one side of the hangar and found no windows that would offer a glimpse inside. There were probably skylights up top. And the hangar's thin vinyl skin, stretched tight on a skeleton of metal ribs, would let in enough ambient light during daytime to illuminate the building without much need for artificial light. Boxy compressors stationed every thirty feet or so fed huge, snakelike ducts that blew cool air into the hangar. All in all, a high-tech and no doubt costly piece of work.

I walked all the way around the hangar and returned to the entrance. I was giving the handle another pull when I heard the last sound anyone wants to hear when you're snooping around someplace where you really shouldn't be: The kachuck-kachuck of a shell being chambered in a shotgun.

Whoever was holding the shotgun didn't have to tell me to freeze. The instinct was automatic. Same with lifting my hands over my head.

A high-beam lantern flipped on and lit up the scene. My silhouette against the hangar made me look gigantic, but I felt damn puny with a gun at my back.

"Turn around real slow."

I turned and squinted against the light. I saw three faces but couldn't tell much about the men who belonged to them. The bright beam made it impossible to pick up any details.

The one holding the lantern said, "Who the hell are you?"

I told them my name.

"What do you think you're doing out here?"

I told them I was looking for a boat.

"So you just come sneaking around in the middle of the night? You planning on stealing this boat or something? That what you planning to do?"

"No. I just wanted to see if it was here."

"We got lots of boats. Exactly what kind of boat are you looking for?"

"A Beneteau 54. New one. It's called *Chasin' Molly*."

I heard them mumbling among themselves. Then the one with the lantern nodded toward the block building.

"Start walking," he said.

26

They sat me in a cheap white plastic chair, tied my wrists behind me, and wrapped duct tape around me and the chair.

The chair was in the middle of a big, cluttered room. The door was at my back, open windows on either side. On the ceiling directly above me, two long fluorescent bulbs cast a bluish aura on the surroundings.

It was more warehouse than office—power tools, cans of marine paint, sawhorses, the pervasive odor of resin and fiberglass. On the floor—greasy rags, oil-soaked dirt, and random heaps of trash. Cobwebs consumed the corners of the ceiling. A breeze passed through the door and windows, provoking small torrents of dust.

One of the men—he looked to be the oldest, in his thirties—sat behind a wooden desk. He wore a tight white T-shirt with a tattoo displayed on one forearm. An anchor with roses entwined around it. An old-school tattoo, like sailors used to wear. Something done in a drunken whim in some foreign port. Or prison. Not the artful filigrees sported nowadays by everyone from hipsters and housewives to schoolgirls.

Another brother, in his twenties, sat on the edge of the desk. He was shirtless with a pistol stuck in the waist of his jeans.

The third one couldn't have been more than eighteen or nineteen. He kept the shotgun pointed at me from the far side of the room.

Looking at the Dailey brothers was like looking at those computer-generated images the cops use to show what missing persons looked like

ten years ago and what they might look like now. Variations on a heredi-
tary theme and a predictable arc of aging.

Same eyes, same basic build, same set to their jaws, all of it reflecting an
undistilled strain of meanness. Reddish brown hair. On the youngest, it
fell nearly to his shoulders. Middle brother kept it trimmed above his ears.
And the oldest one wore it cut tight in deference to an eroding hairline.

Their genetic stock and pigmentation was not predisposed toward
long hours under an unyielding tropical sun. The youngest of them, the
one with the shotgun, owned a thin face still relatively unblemished and
the beginnings of a mustache, not so much because his face needed it but
just to show he could grow one. The middle one, plumper in the cheeks,
displayed the onset of carcinomas-in-waiting—discoloring on the forehead, a festering blotch on his nose. And the older brother, the one with
first-stage jowls and a double chin, had an ugly canker on his lower lip
and crusty outbreaks along his brow. Case studies for the annals of der-
matology. Having had plenty of pieces of my own self lopped off over
the years, I'm more than casually observant about such things. The Dailey brothers should have spent some of their disposable income on sunscreen.

The one behind the desk, the oldest one, said, "You some kind of cop?"

I shook my head.

"Insurance man?"

I shook my head again.

"Then why you interested in that particular boat?"

"Belongs to the daughter of a friend of mine. She's gone missing. I
figure if I find the boat it might lead me to her."

The one behind the desk worked his mouth around. His smirk became a snarl.

"That what you figure, huh?"

I didn't say anything.

"Who told you to look here?"

"Just a hunch," I said.

"Bullshit. Who told you?"

I shook my head.

"Donnie," he said. "You might have to loosen his tongue."

The middle brother, the one with the pistol, hopped off the desk and
planted himself in front of me. He pointed the pistol at my right knee.

Then at my left knee. Then at a spot in my forehead that I didn't want to think about.

"Who?" the oldest brother asked.

"Screw you," I said.

Donnie took a step and whacked the pistol against the side of my head. I saw stars and diamonds and prisms of light, and I went somewhere else for an instant, and then all the pieces came together and I was back in the chair. Coach Lowe used to say: "*Only hurts if you rub it.*" And I couldn't. For what comfort that was worth.

"Who?"

"Must be an echo in here," I said.

Donnie smacked me again. This time the stars and diamonds took longer going away. I shook my head to get rid of them. And still it was like the whole room was underwater.

Something sour came up at the back of my throat. I coughed and gagged trying to hold it back.

"Last time," big brother said. "Or else Donnie puts a slug in your knee."

The sour stuff was not to be denied its destiny. It gushed up, I hurled and it drenched Donnie.

"Son of a bitch," Donnie said.

He stepped back, pointed the pistol at my knee . . .

A flash of silver, something flew past me. And I actually thought: *It's a goddam bird, a crazy goddam bird flying straight through the room.*

The blade of Boggy's knife sank into Donnie's arm, at the hinge of his elbow. He screamed, fell to his knees, dropped the gun.

After that, everything happened all at once: Charlie raced in from behind me, took down Donnie . . . Boggy dove across the desk, floored big brother . . . A shotgun blast, the desk splintered . . . I pushed up with my feet and toppled over in the chair . . . Another blast from the shotgun, the floor exploded beside me . . . I rolled with the chair . . . Another blast into the desk . . .

Big brother yelled, "Hold off, Sonny, goddammit! Stop!"

I lay on my side, couldn't move. It gave me a skewered view of things: Charlie with the pistol held to Donnie's head . . . Sonny, backed up in a corner, shotgun leveled at his waist . . . Boggy rising from behind the desk, an arm locked around the neck of the oldest Dailey brother, whose shoulder was splattered with red.

Donnie stared at the knife in his arm.

"I'm stuck! I'm bleeding!"

Sonny, the kid with the shotgun, took aim at Charlie. Charlie pressed the pistol harder against Donnie's head and pinned him on the floor.

"Don't do it," Charlie said.

"I'll shoot your sorry ass, believe me, I will!"

Charlie eyed the kid, eyed the shotgun. He said, "You already got off three shots and you didn't hit anyone."

"He hit *me*, goddammit," big brother said.

"OK, strike that," Charlie said. "He didn't hit anyone he aimed at. I'm liking my odds."

"Fuck you," Sonny said. He moved along the far wall, trying to get a better angle.

Charlie yanked Donnie up from the floor. He put Donnie between himself and the shotgun.

Donnie kicked and screamed.

"I'm bleeding, I'm bleeding!"

Big brother shouted, "Shut the fuck up, Donnie!"

Charlie steadied Donnie's arm and looked at the knife sticking out of it.

"In there pretty good," he said.

Then he grabbed the knife and pulled it out in one swift movement. Donnie screamed as the wound spewed blood.

"I'm bleeding to death! I'm dying."

"Yeah," Charlie said. "You might be at that."

Donnie grabbed the wound with his free hand, tried to stop the flow. Blood seeped between his fingers.

Boggy moved from behind the desk, pulling big brother with him. Charlie handed him the knife and Boggy cut away the duct tape that bound me to the chair. I stood.

Sonny still had his shotgun leveled at us. He was frantic now, swinging the gun from side to side, moving from one foot to the other, not sure what to do.

"Now the way I figure it," Charlie said, "that twelve gauge of yours—it's a shitty old Remington—it can hold seven shells. I can't tell from here if you've got it plugged or not. But let's say you've got it plugged. That means only three shells. And that means you're empty."

Sonny looked down at his gun, then at big brother.

"Ronnie," he said. "You alright? I didn't mean to shoot you."

"That's OK, Sonny. I know, I know . . ."

Sonny edged along the wall. Charlie turned to match his move, holding Donnie up in front of him. The wound didn't seem to be bleeding as much as before, but Donnie was going limp. Shock was setting in.

Charlie looked at me. He nodded to the doorway. I began backing toward it. Sonny swung on me, then back on Charlie.

"But let's say that gun of yours isn't plugged," Charlie said. "I'm betting you don't leave it sitting around your house fully loaded. I'm betting that when you and your brothers ran out here to find my friend Zack, you didn't go to all the trouble of sticking seven shells in it. You were in a hurry. You stuck three shells in it. Maybe four. Probably not five . . ."

Sonny slapped a pants pocket.

"I got plenty shells right here," he said.

"Good for you, boy. Good for you," Charlie said. "But this nine-millimeter I'm holding, it's an automatic. And it's got a full clip. By the time you reload, I'll have a bullet in both of your brothers and plenty left over for you," Charlie said. "So let's not go down that road, OK?"

Ronnie strained against Boggy's grip. He said, "Just keep your head, Sonny. We'll get out of this."

Boggy put his knife to Ronnie's neck and walked him toward the door.

"You good to hold this one, Zachary?"

"Yeah," I said. "I'm fine."

Boggy handed me the knife. I got an arm around Ronnie's neck and poked the knife into his back just to let him know it was there. He jumped. I might have poked a little too hard. So sue me.

Boggy pulled a bandanna from his pocket and walked back to where Charlie held Donnie. He pried Donnie's hand from the wound and tied off the bandanna around it. He helped Donnie stretch out on the floor and knelt beside him, applying pressure to the wound with both hands.

No one said anything. After a minute or two, Boggy spoke softly to Donnie, "The bleeding, it has almost stopped. You keep holding it. It is not as bad as it looks, but you need to see a doctor."

Charlie aimed the pistol at Sonny now, both hands on it.

"We're going to step out of here, real peaceful," Charlie said. "And we're going to take your brother with us. So don't do anything stupid."

"Where you going with him?" Sonny said.

"Don't you worry," Charlie said. "You just stay right there."

Charlie and Boggy backed away, and when we were all outside, I tightened my armlock on Ronnie and pointed him toward the hangar.

"Let's take a look inside that thing and see what we can find."

"I don't have the keys on me," Ronnie said. "I keep 'em in my desk."

I heard the sound of Sonny racking more shells into the shotgun.

"Let's leave it until the morning, Zack," Charlie said. "We can come back with the police."

Sonny appeared in the doorway, gun leveled.

"I got a full load now, you son of a bitch."

I gave Sonny another poke with the knife.

"Talk to your brother," I said.

"Be cool, Sonny," Ronnie told him. "Be cool and everything's gonna work out."

We started moving toward the gate and the car. From inside the block house, Donnie hollered: "Sonny, get back here. You gotta take me to the doctor."

"Shut the fuck up, Donnie," Sonny said.

He moved out of the doorway and trailed us at a distance. He stopped at the gate as we loaded into the car.

"Where you taking Ronnie?" Sonny yelled. "You hurt him, I'll come after you."

He kept the shotgun pointed at the Hyundai as we pulled away.

27

All the way down that bumpy limestone road, I asked Ronnie Dailey questions. Was *Chasin' Molly* in the hangar? Had he seen Jen Ryser? All I got was nothing.

I gave him another poke.

"How about I start cutting off parts of you with this knife?"

"Go ahead," he said. "Start cutting."

We got to where the limestone road met the hard top. I opened the back door and pushed him out.

"Stay sweet. Don't ever change. See ya real soon," I said.

"Fuck you," said Ronnie Dailey.

I gave Boggy his knife and he returned it to its sling. When we got a little farther down the road, I asked Charlie to hand me the pistol he'd taken from the Daileys. I waited until we were crossing a small bridge over a narrow cut in the mangroves. I rolled down the window.

"Now, Zack," Charlie said. "That's a nice gun."

"Contradiction of terms," I said.

And I flung it into the water.

I leaned up from my seat, gave Boggy and Charlie each a slap on the back.

"The two of you did some pretty good work back there," I said. "I appreciate it."

Both of them nodded.

"Only I was wondering . . ."

Charlie said, "Wondering what, Zack?"

"Wondering if you saw them come up and grab me by the hangar?"

They both nodded.

Boggy said, "I was watching from behind one of the boats."

"I was down by the dock," Charlie said. "Saw it all."

"And you saw them drag me into that room and sit me down in the chair and tie me up?"

They both nodded.

"We came up in the shadows," Charlie said. "And we were watching from just outside the door."

"And you saw that one brother whack me in the head with a pistol?"

Charlie winced.

"Bet that hurt, huh?"

"And then you saw him whack me again?"

They both nodded.

"And yet you stood out there, watching, until I was whacked silly and he was getting ready to shoot me before you chose to do anything about it? That's what I was wondering about."

"Timing," Boggy said.

"Timing? What the hell do you mean, timing?"

"We were waiting for you to puke, Zachary."

Charlie laughed.

"Waiting for me to puke? How could you possibly have known I was going to puke? I didn't even know I was going to puke until it happened."

"I knew you would do something. You always do," Boggy said. "And when you puked it was good timing and everything went according to plan."

"Plan, hell. You didn't have a plan. You were standing out there, enjoying the show, making things up as you went along."

"Now, Zack," Charlie said. "That's a little harsh, don't you think? Considering we just saved the day."

"I'm just saying . . ."

Charlie said, "I think you oughta practice."

"Practice what?"

"Puking on demand like that. Maybe it can get your ass out of a jam when we aren't around."

I leaned back in the seat.

"Still got a bad taste in my mouth."

"We can fix that," Charlie said.

There was a store up ahead. Charlie parked the car and went inside and came out carrying a twelve-pack of beer and some beef jerky and some red-hot peanuts.

When we got back to the Mariner's Inn we sat on the patio behind my room and drank and ate and didn't talk much. There was no postmortem of the altercation at the Dailey brothers' boatyard. No talk of how we took it to them and how we got away.

The beer went fast and Charlie stepped to his room and brought back a bottle of Havana Club, the seven-year-old, and we turned our attention to that. Boggy threw down a glass, called it a night, and excused himself.

Somewhere in the very early morning, after the adrenaline settled and the nerves stopped being all jingly and jangly, Charlie reminded me that we hadn't stopped at Lita's Take-A-Way to pay Williamson the rest of his money.

"Bet he's still sitting right there, waiting," Charlie said.

"Bet he is, too."

"I could drive us out there."

"Yeah, you could."

"Only, I've been over-served."

"Yeah, you have."

"You could drive."

"Yeah, I could."

"Only, you've been over-served, too."

We kept talking around it and wound up agreeing it was a far wiser thing to settle up with Williamson by the light of day.

The rumble of the boat's engine roused her from her sleep. The engine idled for a few minutes, then revved and backed off and revved again. And then the boat was moving.

She was feeling stronger now. They had fed her well enough and given her plenty of water and fruit juice. The deep weakness that had plagued her was gone. In the beginning, it had helped her sleep and make it through days of doing nothing. But now the tedium was setting in. She was restless, anxious.

Nudging her face against the mattress, she succeeded in working the blindfold down just enough so she could peek out over the top, but not so much that she couldn't get it back up in a hurry when they came to check on her.

She also managed to loosen the bindings on her hands and legs. Not to the point that she could free herself—the knots were too tight for that—but enough that she was no longer so constricted. With enough effort she could roll over in the bed.

She moved to her side and looked around the cabin. It was early morning and soft light came in through the two portholes. The door leading to the head and the main cabin was closed.

The boat ran for at least half an hour, full throttle. The water started out calm and then it got rough and bumpy and then it got calm again.

The boat slowed and idled along and then stopped as the engine was thrown into neutral and then reverse and then neutral. Jen heard the anchor line being fed out. The engine—reverse, neutral, reverse. And then the anchor caught hold and the engine went silent.

Jen strained to hear the two of them talking up above, but she couldn't make out anything. And then there was no sound at all—no voices, no movement on the deck. Just the gentle slap of water against the hull.

She called out, "Hey. Down here!"

No one answered, no one came.

She called out again. She waited. And still no one came.

This hadn't happened before. Always when she called, someone had eventually come down below to find out what she wanted.

Had they abandoned her? What if they had left for good and made their escape and now she was stuck here, alone in a floating coffin? How long could she survive without food and water? If she screamed would anyone hear?

She screamed. She waited. She screamed again. She waited some more.

Nothing.

The tiny cabin had grown hot and stuffy. She fought off the panic. She took long, deep breaths and told herself: OK, OK. Do something. Do anything. This is it. You have to get out of here. Now or never.

She wiggled herself to the edge of the bed. Another heave and she tumbled onto the floor. She landed on her stomach. She rolled onto her back, feet pointed at the door, a body length away.

Her arms were underneath her and that hurt but it helped her raise herself up just a little. She scooted her butt toward her feet and drew up her knees the best she could. Then she straightened out her legs and did it again. Like an inchworm, moving toward the door.

And finally her bare feet touched it. She moved a little closer and planted her feet flat against the door. It slid easier than she expected and when it was open enough to get her legs through she slid it open all the way and inch-wormed through the doorway and into the main cabin.

Ten minutes it took her. She was sweating and exhausted and her shoulder hurt more than ever. What little energy she had left drained out of her when she looked around the main cabin and saw the steps, six of them, leading to the main hatch. The main hatch was closed. But that didn't really matter because how was she ever going to get up the steps?

She screamed. She screamed again.

She lay there, panting, trying to calm herself. Minutes went by.

And then she felt something—a bump against the boat. Footsteps on the deck. Someone had heard her.

"Down here! I'm down here!"

The hatch popped open. A figure outlined against the bright sky.

Him.

He leaped down beside her, bypassing the steps. He grabbed her by the hair and pulled her up.

"What do you think you're doing?"

"Nothing, nothing. I was just trying . . ."

"Trying to get out of here? Trying to escape?"

"No, no. I wasn't. Really."

She began to cry. She hated herself for it. She wanted to fight him, to kick and hit. But she was broken inside. She had been terrified to see him. But, at the same time, relieved that he—that someone, anyone—was here.

"Water," she said.

He brought it to her and helped her drink it. When she was done, he said, "Now, I want you to do exactly like I tell you. You got that?"

"Yes, yes. I understand."

"And you better not try anything funny. Or, I swear to God, that'll be it."

"I promise. I'll do whatever you say."

"Good." He reached into a pocket, pulled out a cell phone. "Because we're going to give your father a call."

28

The hangover wasn't as bad as I deserved. By quarter 'til eight I was out of bed and fairly presentable, with the help of three Alleve and five minutes of sitting on the shower floor with hot water massaging the back of my head.

I rounded up Boggy and Charlie, and we went to the hotel restaurant for breakfast. We got coffee and eggs and sausage and toast, and by the time nine o'clock rolled around, Will Moody still hadn't joined us.

We drove the mile or so to Dunning's Cottages and asked a woman in the office if she could ring Will Moody's room and tell him we were there. She looked at the guest book.

"No Will Moody here," she said.

"Has he already checked out?"

"Never was here."

"Tall guy, beginnings of a beard, dark hair, in his twenties."

She shook her head.

"No," she said. "Not here."

We got back in the car.

Charlie said, "So what do you think?"

"I'm still chewing on it," I said. "But while I'm chewing, how about we find the police station."

The officer working the front desk at the Marsh Harbour police station listened as I told him we had information about a possible boat theft. He didn't speak. He didn't nod. He didn't write anything down.

"You have a seat," he said. "Superintendent will be with you."

We sat in metal chairs. We watched the ceiling fan turn. We listened to the officer talking on the police radio.

A woman came in and told the officer she wanted to file a report about her neighbor. Something about his dog killing one of her roosters.

Another woman came in and said she wanted to see her husband who had been arrested the night before. The officer had her sign a logbook. Then he unlocked a door and showed her down a hall.

Thirty minutes passed. It was closing in on ten o'clock.

I approached the officer at the desk.

"Think the superintendent could see us now?"

"He'll be along. Have a seat."

"Is the superintendent even here?"

The officer looked at me.

"He'll be along," the officer.

Another thirty minutes went by. Charlie and Boggy went outside to get some air. They came back in. I walked up to the front desk again.

There's nothing people in the islands dislike more than pushy Americans who can't tear themselves away from the clock and get cozy with the "Mon, soon come" mentality. I respect that. I really do. And I appreciate a good case of the slows as much as anyone.

But this was pushing it.

"Excuse me," I said, "but do you have any idea when the superintendent can see us? Because I've got plenty of other things I could be doing."

"Suit yourself," the officer said.

"Suit myself what?"

"Go do these other things. The superintendent he usually does not come in until after lunch."

"Why didn't you tell me that to begin with?"

"The superintendent's comings and goings are not your business. He is a busy man."

"Would it help if I filled out a report or something?"

"Not necessary," the officer. "You come back and we make a report then."

"You want me to leave my name and my contact information so you can call me when the superintendent is in his office?"

"Not necessary. You come back after lunch."

"Thanks so much for your time."

"My pleasure," the officer said. "Enjoy your stay in Marsh Harbour."

I owed Williamson two hundred dollars for his tip about spotting *Chasin' Molly*, but I still wanted to see the boat for myself before I paid him. And there was no way I was returning to the Dailey brothers' boat-yard unless the police were with me this time.

So we went back to the Mariner's Inn to kill time until the superin-tendent saw fit to show up at his office.

We dropped by Abel Delgado's room and knocked on the door. I was hoping the events of the previous evening might have humbled him, at least to the point that we could have a civil, sober conversation and I could convince him that his work for Mickey Ryser was done. I was thinking maybe I'd drop a little cash on him, just to help soothe any wounds and get him on his way back to Miami. He didn't really deserve any more money, but the posters he'd put up had ultimately led us to Dailey's boat-yard and that was worth something.

But Delgado didn't answer the door. I went to the office and had the receptionist call his room, but he didn't answer that either. I left a mes-sage asking Delgado to get in touch.

We went to my room and sat around watching ESPN Sport Center. Fewer things are more pathetic than grown men sitting around watching taped highlights of games they don't really care about. But it was either that or three channels of gospel music, the Home Shopping Network, or Nickelodeon. We were on the third loop of the Ducks besting the Coy-otes one–zip in thrilling NHL action when my cell phone rang.

"Zack-o!" Mickey Ryser greeted me. "She just called. I spoke with her. She's on her way here."

"Jen called?"

"Just got off the phone with her," Mickey said. "She's flying into George Town this afternoon. I'm sending someone to pick her up."

"Good news," I said.

"Damn straight it is."

"She mention anything about *Chasin' Molly*?"

"Just to say that everything's alright. Nothing to worry about. Music to my ears," Mickey said. "So you know what that means, Zack-o."

"What?"

"You need to get off that sorry ass of yours and get down here with my boat."

29

There were good reasons for me to stick around Marsh Harbour.

I had unfinished business with the Daileys. I wanted to settle all accounts with Abel Delgado. And I wanted to make sure he was on his way home.

But there were more prevailing reasons to get to Lady Cut Cay with Mickey Ryser's boat.

The fact that Jen Ryser had finally surfaced made finding *Chasin' Molly* somewhat of a moot proposition. At least until she could shed further light on the subject.

Mickey had sounded good on the phone. Full of vigor, anxious to see his daughter. A new lease on life, such as it was.

The sooner I got his boat to him the better. And then I could go home. An easy decision.

I put some money in an envelope along with a note to Delgado that read, "This will get you back to Miami. Thanks for your help."

I knocked on Delgado's door again, but still no answer. So I left the envelope with the receptionist at the Mariner's Inn and asked her to make sure Delgado got it.

Then we checked out. We turned in our rental cars at the airport. And we hopped aboard Charlie's plane for Nassau.

———

On the thirty-minute flight south, I kept thinking about what Will Moody had said the night before. Maybe I had blown everything out of proportion.

So what if Jen Ryser and her friends weren't sticking to any particular schedule? So what if they hadn't communicated regularly with those who might want to hear from them? They were adults. They were capable of making their way in the world without someone like me coming along to check on them. And even if they weren't capable of it, they were entitled to screw up all on their own.

Maybe I had imagined something bad where no bad existed. Maybe, as much as I was reluctant to admit it, I'd been wearing old-fogey goggles. Maybe I'd been viewing the innocent meanderings of six young people on a boat with the prudish disingenuousness of someone who was just a little envious—of their youth and everything that went with it. Untethered lives. Casual hookups with the opposite sex. Living in the moment.

Ah, for the days, Chasteen.

There is the tendency of one generation to run wild, break rules, enjoy itself, and then condemn those who come along next to give those indulgences a new spin. Especially when the youngsters seem to be having too damn much fun.

"Don't criticize what you can't understand/Your sons and your daughters are beyond your command/Your old road is rapidly agin' . . ."

Dylan sang the words before I was born, but they still resonated when I was growing up. I embraced them then, honored them as a personal anthem. It seemed hypocritical to discard and dishonor them now.

I tried to envision Shula, cutting her path in the world. She would settle into her own generational tribe, with its own music, mores, and politics; its own hairstyles, handshakes, and slang. All of it a natural product of time, place, and circumstance.

Try as we might and even if we wanted to, Barbara and I would be unable to shape our daughter in our likenesses. All we could do was guide her and love her endlessly. Teach her the difference between right and wrong. To be comfortable in her skin. To think for herself. And then let her fly.

Twenty or so years down the road, she would set out on an adventure of her own. At least, I hoped she would.

And I'd be cool with it.

I wouldn't pass judgment. I wouldn't cling. I wouldn't meddle. I wouldn't worry.

The hell I wouldn't.

30

Charlie delivered us straight to Dilly's Marina, east of Paradise Island and not far from downtown Nassau. He put the seaplane down just outside the channel and motored us to the dock. The plan called for Boggy and me to take Mickey's boat to Lady Cut Cay. Charlie would fly us back to Miami.

"When do you think you'll get to Mickey's place?" Charlie asked.

"I'm guessing if we make it out of here by dark, then we should arrive well before noon tomorrow. You flying straight there?"

"Seeing as how I've got some lead time, I might take a little detour."

"Detour?"

"Yeah, there's this gal I know over on Andros. And I was thinking maybe . . ."

"Don't get tangled up too long."

"Kinda depends on if her husband's around."

"And if he is?"

"Then I'll only be tangled up a little while."

As promised, the marina had Mickey's boat ready to go. More accurately, Mickey's boat was a motor yacht. And nothing could have adequately prepared me for the sight of it.

Radiance it was called and the name fit. Sixty-eight feet of gleaming craftsmanship. Double-planked mahogany hull painted bright white with a varnished teak trim. Teak handrails with stanchions of bronze and stainless steel. The pilothouse perched prettily atop the main deck with a V-grooved overhead of white oak and a four-seater bench behind the wheel. The aft deck held another expansive sitting area—a fine place for cocktails—its settees and chairs protected from the elements by canvas covers in a shade of beige that complemented the paint on the trim.

It was a Trumpy, a lineage of yachts founded by John Trumpy, Sr., a German immigrant and naval architect who arrived in America in the early 1900s and designed yachts for all the big-deal tycoons of that era. The DuPonts, the Guggenheims, the Dodges, and the Chryslers, they all owned Trumpys, along with Howard Hughes. In 1925, Trumpy designed a 104-foot yacht called the *The Sequoia* for a Philadelphia businessman. Later bought by the federal government to intercept Prohibition smugglers, it eventually became the official presidential yacht and served every U.S. head of state from Herbert Hoover to Gerald Ford. Then Jimmy Carter came along and ordered it sold at auction in 1977 in a symbolic cost-cutting gesture. He would have been better off getting rid of the vice presidency instead.

Only some 450 Trumpys were ever built. *Radiance*, circa 1971, was one of the last, launched shortly before Trumpy's son, John Trumpy, Jr., closed the family's iconic Annapolis shipyard. From the days of Cleopatra's barge, yachts have always been floating egos, only nowadays they displace a whole lot more water than in years past. Mega-yachts they're called. The largest ones, owned by assorted Middle Eastern sheikhs and sundry sultans of software, stretch more than five hundred feet, wretched excesses in fiberglass with all the soul of silicon semiconductors.

Radiance packed more heart into her sixty-eight feet than any mega-yacht six times its length. From the moment I stepped aboard her I was smitten.

The main salon was Jay Gatsby meets Rudyard Kipling with vintage rattan chairs and wicker settees and a coffee table that was once a Balinese temple door. A massive oil painting of a salt marsh—an Elizabeth Barr original—disappeared into a bulkhead at the press of a button to reveal a twenty-eight-inch plasma television. The galley ran almost the full beam of the boat with a Sub-Zero refrigerator and freezer tucked under teak countertops and a full-size four-burner stove. A master stateroom with a queen-size bed and two guest staterooms, all with en suite heads. Crew quarters in the bow. The pilothouse was elegant in its own fashion without being too damn fussy. You could ride out a big blow in it and rely on all the latest electronics, from the Standard Horizon depth sounder to the Simrad Radar/Chartplotter/GPS.

The marina's boatyard manager spent a couple of hours giving Boggy and me an exhaustive tour of *Radiance* and sharing her various quirks— how she ran best at a notch or two back from full throttle and how she favored port slightly in following seas. While we were waiting for the dockhands to finish gassing her up—two diesel tanks, each holding 440 gallons, glad it was on Mickey's tab—I made some phone calls from the pilothouse.

Barbara didn't pick up, but I left her a gushy message and finished it off with kisses for Shula.

Helen Miller answered on the second ring. I told her she could pull the plug on her end of things since Jen Ryser had finally surfaced.

"You want to hear what I found out anyway?"

"You going to charge me for it?"

"Damn right I am."

"Then lay it on me."

Helen Miller had followed up on my suggestion to check further into the backgrounds of Will Moody and Pete Crumrine. Both came from well-to-do-families. Moody's father was partner in an Atlanta pediatric practice. Crumrine's mom ran an advertising company in Nashville and his dad was a dentist there. Neither family had heard from their sons. And both were concerned about it.

"Cute-looking guys, too. I found them on Facebook. Got a couple of photos. Blond surfer dudes. If I was only a few years younger . . ."

"You said blond? You sure?"

"Yeah, I printed out their photos for my file. Got 'em sitting right here in front of me. Pete Crumrine is curly blond, almost a mini 'fro. Will Moody, he's got this kind of Tom Petty look. Hair's almost white, long and straight. He's real skinny."

Not the Will Moody I met.

"Zack, are you there?"

"Yeah, sorry. Right here."

"So anyway, I'll call the parents back and let them know you crossed paths with Will Moody and that he said everything was fine. They'll be relieved to hear it," Miller said. "As for Justin Hatchitt and Torrey Kealing . . . are you sure you wrote down the right passport numbers?"

"I'm sure. Why?"

"I called in a favor with someone I know at the passport office in Charleston. Nothing clicks."

"What do you mean nothing clicks?"

"I mean the numbers you gave me don't correspond to any sequence of numbers in the system."

"So you're telling me the passports are fake?"

"Appears that way."

"But how do you fake a U.S. passport these days? I thought that was next to impossible, since 9/11 anyway."

"Same thing I asked my contact at the passport office. She said there can be a giant difference between the way a passport looks and the way it acts."

"The way it acts?"

"Uh-huh. Meaning, it's not all that hard for someone with even basic forgery skills to make a fake passport that looks like the real deal. It might work for some identification purposes, like cashing a check or using a credit card at a retail shop or something, but it will come up short when it gets plugged into the system."

"That's when it has to act like a passport, with the computers and everything?"

"Right," Miller said. "And the system is fairly foolproof. The new passports, since 2004 anyway, all use biometrics. They're encrypted and encoded with all kinds of identifiers. There's still a significant gap, working the new ones into the system as the old ones expire, but even with the old ones there's a long data trail, crosscheck upon crosscheck, and immigration agents are highly adept at spotting any fake passports used by people trying to get into the U.S. The airlines, too, they're plugged into the system. If this Justin Hatchitt and Torrey Kealing had fake passports and they used them to try and buy a plane ticket out of the country it would have set off all kinds of bells and whistles."

"But since they left by boat . . ."

"Since they left the country by private boat, they didn't have to go through any TSA boarding procedures. They had to show their passports when they entered the Bahamas, but the Bahamas, like most Caribbean countries, doesn't have a customs and immigration computer system that links directly to U.S. Homeland Security."

I flashed on Mr. Bethel at Walker's Cay, his entries going into a ledger book, not the computer. A forged passport, it would be easy enough to get it by him.

"Of course," Miller said, "it would catch up with them when they tried to reenter the U.S."

"*If* they tried to reenter the U.S."

"Exactly. This Justin Hatchitt and Torrey Kealing, they could be running away from who knows what, with no intention of ever coming home."

31

It was just shy of sunset and we were pulling away from East End Point, the Atlantis Resort's towering oddness at our back, when my cell phone rang. It was Lynfield Pederson.

"Where the hell are you?"

I told him I was about one mile off New Providence Island, heading south.

"What are you doing there?"

I told him Jen Ryser had finally shown up and that I was taking her father's yacht to Lady Cut Cay.

"You need to turn around, Zack. Get back to Nassau. I'll fly over from Harbour Island and meet you. Then I'll escort you to Marsh Harbour. It will be better that way."

"Escort me? What are you talking about?"

"Jesus Christ, Zack. You got any idea what's going down?"

"Apparently not."

"Got a dead guy at the Mariner's Inn. Name of Delgado. Know him?"

"Delgado's dead?"

"Police up that way, they think you might have had something to do with it."

"Delgado and me, we had a little run-in at the hotel bar last night, but that's all there was to it."

"Yeah, the police know about that. Got the story from the bartender and about a dozen other witnesses. They all say you beat him up pretty good."

"Wasn't much of a fight. I spent most of it just stepping out of his way."

"They say you knocked him out."

"It was the alcohol more than anything I did. Delgado was in the bag when I got there. He'd been drinking all day."

"But you and him, you got into some kind of argument and you had it out, right?"

"Wasn't much arguing to it. He said a few words. I said a few words. And he came at me. After it was over I helped carry Delgado back to his room and put him in his bed. He was sleeping like a baby when I left."

"That's the thing, Zack. Some of those witnesses, they saw you carrying Delgado into his room. I spoke to the superintendent up there . . ."

"I tried to speak to him, too."

"Oh yeah? What about?"

"Tell me about Delgado first."

"Superintendent and me, we aren't real close. He's kind of a prick . . ."

"Hmmm," I said.

"But he knows you and me got a history. He was superintendent in Freeport a few years back when you got mixed up in that thing with Victor Ortiz and those Panamanian counterfeiters."

"That thing put me in prison for almost two years."

"Yeah, and the superintendent didn't like it how you got yourself cleared of all the charges. Blew back on him. Made him look bad. Else he thinks he could be the commissioner by now, sitting in a fancy Nassau office calling all the shots, instead of getting busted down to Marsh Harbour," Pederson said. "So he was real anxious to reach out and let me know he's looking at a murder here."

"Murder?"

"He thinks someone smothered Delgado. Still waiting on the coroner's report, but the superintendent saw what he saw. Bruising around the mouth and nose. Tongue all bit up and swollen. Bloodshot eyes . . ."

"He was drunk, Lynfield. Of course he had bloodshot eyes. I woke up this morning, my eyes were bloodshot."

"Yeah, but I'm talking eyes shot full of blood, man. Veins popped, bulging out. Not a pretty sight. Plus, the housekeeper she had to use her key to get in Delgado's room—it was about one o'clock this afternoon—and there he was on the bed. Pillow still over his face."

I stepped away from the wheel and let Boggy take over. I tried to make sense out of everything Pederson had just told me.

"This morning, before I checked out of the Mariner's Inn, I left a message at the front desk for Delgado. I left an envelope for him, too."

"Police know all about the message and the envelope. Envelope had five hundred dollars in it. Police have it now."

"OK, that should prove I didn't kill Delgado. Else why would I leave that for him?" No sooner were the words out of my mouth than it hit me. "No way. No damn way. They think I left that envelope just to make it look like I didn't kill Delgado?"

"Be a clever thing to do."

"But . . ."

"Turn the boat around, Zack. Don't get off it. Stay put. Wait for me at the marina. I can be there in under an hour."

"I didn't kill Delgado."

"There's more, Zack," Pederson said. "You want to hear it?"

"It get any better?"

"Not really, but you need to know it," Pederson said. "There's this boatyard out the other side of Crossing Place."

"Dailey brothers."

"That's them. Seems someone set fire to this dry dock facility of theirs last night. Burned it clear to the ground, including the twenty-seven boats they had inside. It's still burning, matter of fact. That whole end of the island, people got smoke stinging their eyes and stinking things up, like roasting fiberglass weenies at a cookout or something."

I didn't say anything.

"The Dailey brothers they wrote out statements. Each one of them separately. And they all three of them told it the same. Said you and two other guys—I'm guessing that would be Boggy and Charlie Callahan—said they caught you sneaking around in the boatyard a little before midnight. Said the three of you attacked them, stuck one of the brothers with a knife, carried off another brother and tossed him out of a car on the main highway."

"Didn't toss him out. Charlie stopped the car. I opened the door and let him out."

"So you aren't denying you were out there?"

"We were out there. But we didn't set fire to anything. The Dailey brothers say we did?"

"What the Dailey brothers said was all of them were at the hospital getting the one of them stitched up when one of their wives woke up and saw the hangar in flames."

"I didn't do it."

"There's more," Pederson said. "You know a young woman by the name of Karen Breakell? In her twenties, works on a charter boat out of Blue Sky Marina?"

I told him I knew her.

"She was leaving the marina late last night. Alone. Told a friend on the boat she was going into town and see if she could catch last call somewhere. She was walking across the marina parking lot when someone knocked her in the head. Knocked hell out of her. Might have done worse to her, but the security guard—he's this old fellow, can't hardly move—he hears her screaming and he hollers to see what's the matter. Time he gets to where she's at, she's lying in blood. They got her in the hospital."

"She going to be OK?"

"Hasn't come around yet. Doctors say it could go either way. Soon as she's stable, if she's stable, they'll try to medevac her to Miami," Pederson said. "Dockmaster at Blue Sky Marina told police that a guy matching your description came around there yesterday asking about Karen Breakell. Told him he was an old friend of the family. Had an Indian-looking fellow with him. Then one of the crew on her boat, young guy, the first mate, he verified that someone like you and this same Indian-looking fellow were there on the Green Turtle dock when Karen Breakell came ashore to get groceries. He said she acted real upset after she'd spoken with you."

"I didn't do it. I didn't do any of it."

"You keep saying it . . ."

"I keep saying it because it's true. Dammit, Lynfield, you know me. It sound like something I would do?"

He took longer to answer than I would have liked.

"The fire maybe," he said. "I've known you to light a fire."

"Aw, come on, man. Setting a fire like that to get at someone, that's chickenshit. Smothering a man in his sleep. Attacking a woman in the dark. That isn't me either. You know that."

"Yeah, I know it," Pederson said. "But the superintendent up in Marsh Harbour, he doesn't know it. All he sees is these three separate things, a triangle like, and you're at all the points in the triangle and it's easy for him to connect the lines in between and you're walking them, too. Someone sure was busy last night, Zack. And everything's pointing in your direction."

Pederson asked me why I had gone looking for Karen Breakell. I explained that she had jumped ship at Miner Cay and I was hoping maybe she could give me some insight on where to find Jen Ryser.

He asked me what I'd been doing out at the Dailey brothers' boatyard. I told him I'd received a tip that I'd find *Chasin' Molly* there. And I told him I'd gone to the police station and tried to report it, only the desk officer insisted I speak directly to the superintendent and the superintendent never showed.

"Of course," I said, "they probably think it's a clever bit of subterfuge on my part to show up at the police station to report a missing boat when I'd already burned down the place where that boat was supposed to be."

The cell phone signal was growing weaker the farther we pulled away from New Providence Island. I lost Pederson. He called me back.

"Those Daileys are a long line of no good," he said. "Wouldn't surprise me if they were up to something. Still, Zack, that doesn't get you out of this. I have to ask you to turn yourself in."

"And then what?"

"And then, like I said, I'll escort you up to Marsh Harbour and you can tell the police there what you told me."

"And then they'll put me in jail."

Pederson didn't say anything.

"That's what they'll do, Lynfield. I know it. You know it, too. What are we looking at here? Murder, trespass, assault, kidnapping, arson, another assault, maybe attempted murder. Am I leaving anything out?"

"You're in a fix, Zack. I'm not going to lie to you. But I'll do everything I can. You'll have the right to an attorney . . ."

"Right to an attorney? Hell, sounds like you're already reading me the Miranda Act. Only, oh yeah, you don't have the Miranda Act here in the Bahamas, do you? Police suspect someone of doing something and they can throw them right in jail, innocent people, and it can be months, years maybe, before they get out. I've been in jail, Lynfield. I'm not going there again."

"You're putting me in a tough spot, Zack."

"The police in Marsh Harbour, do they know I'm on a boat out of Nassau?"

"Don't think so," Pederson said. "I didn't know it myself until I got you on the phone. All they've verified so far is that you left Marsh Harbour this morning on Charlie Callahan's seaplane."

"So buy me some time."

"Not like the buying-time store is open, Zack. And even it were open, it's not like I got much spending power. They're going to be looking for you all up and down these islands. Not much I can do to get in the way of that."

"I just need a day or two. Tell them you couldn't find me. It's not a total lie. Because you haven't found me. Not really. We're just talking on the phone."

"Aw hell, Zack, I don't know . . ."

The call broke off again. I waited for Pederson to call me back. While I was waiting, I tried to picture the triangle he had been talking about, tried to envision all the people at all the points. One face kept appearing.

When the phone rang, I answered it.

"Will Moody," I said.

"What are you talking about?"

"A friend of Jen Ryser's. Will Moody. He was sitting at the bar with Delgado when I got there last night. He helped me carry Delgado to his room. I handed him Delgado's card key to open the door. I don't remember him returning it to me. He could easily have gone back in there and . . ."

"You're saying this guy killed Delgado, Zack? What's the motive?"

"I don't know. But Moody was also asking me about Karen Breakell. Where could he find her? How much he'd like to see her. I told him what boat she was on and when it would be getting back to Marsh Harbour. I set her up. I can't believe it. I set her up and he went there and beat hell out of her."

"Again, Zack, I gotta ask: What was his motive? If Moody and Karen Breakell were friends, college classmates and everything, why would he . . ."

"But see, here's the thing," I said. "Will Moody might not be Will Moody. The Will Moody I met doesn't match the description of the Will Moody on Facebook. The Will Moody I met was big, with dark curly hair and a beard. The real Will Moody, the one whose photo Helen Miller saw, he's . . ."

"Hold on, hold on. What do you mean Will Moody might not be Will Moody? Who's Helen Miller? What's this Facebook shit? Zack, I'm sorry, but you aren't making a bit of sense."

The phone went dead. This time it didn't ring again.

32

I didn't sleep that night. Boggy and I stood two-hour watches at the helm, but instead of bunking down, I walked the deck of *Radiance*.

Part of me was keeping an eye out for the Royal Bahamian Police patrol boat that I was certain would intercept us at any moment. I didn't think Lynfield Pederson would give me up. No, he would stall his colleagues as long as he possibly could. But the police were casting a wide net. They could easily dredge up something that would lead them my way.

The *Nassau Guardian* would probably have a story about Delgado's murder, if not in the next day's edition, then surely the day after. It would mention that the police were searching for a suspect, namely me. The paper would run my mug shot. Someone at Dilly's Marina would see it. And that would be that.

The other part of me was trying to get a handle on The Person Who Was Not Really Will Moody and why he would kill Abel Delgado.

Money? No, because Delgado didn't have any.

The fake Moody, whoever he was, had told me he had seen the posters Delgado put up around Marsh Harbour. That's what led him to the Mariner's Inn. He wanted to give Delgado information about Jen Ryser's whereabouts and tell the detective the same thing he told me: Call off the search. There was nothing to worry about. Jen Ryser was safe and sound and on her way to visit her father. Which turned out to be true. So why tell Delgado that and then turn around and kill him?

And if someone who lied about his identity told me there was nothing to worry about, should I be worried? Absolutely.

And why would this same guy go after Karen Breakell, assuming it was him who attacked her?

That didn't add up either.

The equation fell apart completely when I tried factoring in the fire at the Dailey brothers' boatyard.

I tried attacking it from another direction. Maybe none of the three events were related. Maybe one person killed Abel Delgado, another attacked Karen Breakell, and yet another burned down the Daileys' hangar.

That fell apart, too. Marsh Harbour is not without its share of violence, but all three of those things happening on one night represented a random crime spree of unprecedented proportion in those parts.

That left only one other direction to go: Whoever was behind this had done it with every intention of laying the blame on me. They had done a smart job of it. And I had pitched right in and given them all the help they needed, leaving behind a messy trail and providing witnesses every step of the way.

But why?

Who the hell were Justin Hatchitt and Torrey Kealing?

And how did they fit in with everything?

33

First light found us at the top of the Exuma chain and moving past Norman's Cay, yet another Bahamian island with a colorful (translation: notorious) past.

Back in the late 1970s, Carlos Lehder decided to set up shop on Norman's, using it as a distribution center for his cocaine cartel. Lehder didn't buy the entire island, but he claimed it as his own, bringing in a small army of gun-toting Colombians and attack dogs, and making it clear he didn't like visitors or neighbors. Before long most of the locals packed up and moved away.

What's truly interesting to note is that Lehder ran his operation out of Norman's—in plain sight, with a new airstrip, lots of construction, and plenty of comings and goings—for almost five years. Which speaks volumes about the Royal Bahamian Police.

If I wanted to empty my Bermudan bank account, I could probably buy my way out of the Bahamas with a guarantee that the cops wouldn't pursue charges against me.

But just the thought of that pissed me off.

And so the morning unfolded, cay after cay after cay—Warderick Wells, Over Yonder, Big Farmer's, and Musha—until we zeroed in on Lady Cut Cay.

Compared to its closest neighbors, the nearest one maybe two miles away, Lady Cut Cay had decent elevation. A rocky bluff rose on the windward side, tabled out at the middle of the island, and sloped down to a cove and a sandy beach on its lee. Apart from a landing strip at the south tip, thick vegetation covered most of the terrain. At the island's summit, brush had been cleared in a wide swath around a three-story, slant-roofed house. It added to the house's prominence and gave it a stark, commanding presence.

We hadn't called ahead, mainly because I wasn't getting a cell-phone signal. I didn't want to use the radio on *Radiance* because the call would go out on public frequency and there was no telling who might be listening.

But I'd left the radio on so I could monitor it. I heard a squawk of static and then a voice, Mickey's voice.

"Lady Cut Cay calling the good ship *Radiance. Radiance*, are you there?"

Boggy was at the wheel.

"Answer him?"

I shook my head.

"We'll be there soon enough."

The radio squawked again.

"Lady Cut Cay calling *Radiance*. Come in, *Radiance*."

A few moments of silence, then: "Yo, Chasteen, how about you answer me? You got your ears on or not?"

So much for anonymity on the airwaves.

"Spotted you heading for us, Zack-o," Mickey said. "We'll come down and meet you on the dock."

34

The depth finder showed only seven feet of water leading up to the dock. *Radiance* drew six feet. She could probably make it, but rather than embarrassing ourselves by running aground, Boggy and I anchored her fifty yards out and took the dinghy in.

A made-in-the-Bahamas sportfisherman, an Albury Brothers 27, with twin Suzuki outboards, was tied off at the dock. Behind it, Mickey Ryser stood ready to greet us.

Mickey leaned on a cane, but otherwise appeared remarkably improved from when I had seen him just four days earlier. Barefoot, his skinny legs sticking out of baggy khaki shorts. Another splendidly tacky shirt—pink hula girls and purple palm trees. A broad-brimmed straw hat shaded his face but not so much that it hid a wide grin.

"Zack-o, Boggy . . . I want you to meet my daughter."

The young woman beside Mickey was almost as tall as him. Blond hair pulled back from a face that held high cheekbones and full lips. But it was the eyes that got you. They were big and brown with a hint of green, hazel I guess you'd call it. They were like shattered glass, refracting light so you couldn't quite find their center. She wore a short white T-shirt over low-slung red Capri pants and the gap between them showed off a flat, brown tummy with a small gold hoop in her navel.

Mickey patted her back and eased her our way.

"Jen," he said, "these are two of the fellows who have been running around, looking for you."

She offered me her hand, then Boggy, and flashed a shy smile that didn't go with her face.

"Sorry for the inconvenience," she said. "I had no idea my father would go to all that trouble."

"Just anxious for my little girl to get here," Mickey said.

He pulled her to him and put an arm around her shoulder. She snuggled against him and patted his chest.

"So how you like that little boat of mine, Zack-o?"

"Some boat," I said.

"You need to get yourself one."

"Outta my league," I said. "Beside, I've got three other boats already."

"Not like this one."

"No, it's a classic, Mickey. They don't make them like this anymore. But the upkeep," I said, "I bet it's a bitch."

"Ah, it's not bad. A little paint here, some teak oil there. Nothing to it."

"You're lying," I said.

Mickey laughed.

I said, "Any word from Charlie Callahan? I was halfway expecting he might beat us here. And halfway not."

"He radioed a couple of hours ago. Said he'd be here early afternoon."

"Must have gotten tangled up," Boggy said.

A big golf cart, a three-seater, rolled onto the dock. An older man, Bahamian, in his sixties, got out and grabbed our bags. Mickey introduced us to him—Curtis, his name was—and told him to put our bags in the second-floor guest rooms.

"What's Miss Rose got going for lunch, Curtis?"

"Got some stew snapper on the stove," Curtis said.

"Some guava duff for dessert maybe?"

"Thought I saw some of that, too."

"I hope so," Mickey said. "Zack, you have not had dessert until you've eaten Miss Rose's guava duff."

We watched as Curtis left in the golf cart.

"Curtis and Miss Rose, that's his wife, they kinda came with the island. Worked for the people who owned it before me," Mickey said. "Curtis takes care of the boats and fixes anything needs fixing. Miss Rose, she handles the cooking and the cleaning. Their grandson, Edwin, lives here, too, and helps them out. Curtis has him raking the beach today. He's as good with a boat as his grandfather. It was both of them who ran the Albury and picked up Jen when she flew into George Town yesterday. You'll bump into Edwin sooner or later."

We loaded into Mickey's golf cart. Boggy and I settled into the backseat. Mickey took the passenger's side.

"You drive, honey," he told Jen. "I'll play tour guide and tell you which way to go."

We followed a rutted road that circled Lady Cut Cay as Mickey showed off this and that—a desalinization plant, big generators, an incinerator system for getting rid of trash. Even had a good-sized greenhouse, more a shade house really, for growing plants to help landscape the place. Living on your own private tropical island is not a proposition for those without sizable resources.

We made a swing by the beach. Its open-air pavilion held a big dining table and some comfy-looking lounge chairs. A catamaran sat under the coconut palms. We passed a small brackish pond surrounded by mangroves before reaching the grass airstrip. The road continued on the other side of the airstrip to the rocky bluff I'd spotted from *Radiance*.

At the top of the bluff we got out to soak in the view. Cat Island lay a hundred miles to our east, but it was easy enough to imagine that we were looking out on the wide-open Atlantic. Compared to the flat, glassy water on the lee side of the island, the windward side presented big, frothy breakers that crashed on the rocks below. The wind blew hard and Mickey had to speak loudly to be heard above it.

"Makes you glad to be alive, doesn't it, Zack-o?"

He slapped me on the back and kept a hand on my shoulder.

"I can see why you like it here." I draped an arm around him.

"Just glad you could enjoy it with me. Means a lot, man."

I couldn't think of anything else to say, so I gave his shoulder a squeeze and we stood like that for a moment, taking it all in. As we pulled apart, I caught Jen watching us from the other side of the golf cart, alongside Boggy. Her look was dark, as if she didn't know quite what to make of me, but brightened instantly as her eyes met mine.

"Ready to roll?" she chirped, hopping behind the wheel again.

I was anxious to ask her questions—Where was her boat? Where were her friends? Where had she been all this time?—but I figured it best to feel my way and ease into it. Mickey was so clearly enjoying himself that I didn't want to do anything that might spoil the moment.

The house was even more spectacular up close than it had been at a distance. The design was modern, the Sarasota School of Architecture transplanted to the tropics, with wide overhangs, ceiling-to-floor windows and doors, balconies and private niches everywhere you looked. A broad wooden deck off the living room that opened east to the rocky windward side of the island.

Mickey's nurse, Octavia, hurried out of the house as we pulled up. She stood at the end of a walkway, fists planted at her waist, a scowl on her face.

"Where you been, Mr. Mickey? Thirty minutes late for your medicine."

"Calm down, woman," Mickey said. "Thirty minutes isn't going to kill me."

"Yeah, but I just might. You get inside this house right now," Octavia said, hustling him away.

Jen smiled as we followed them along the walkway, under a sea grape arbor, to the front door.

"The two of them act like an old married couple," she said. "But he sure listens to her."

"Your father looks a lot better than when I saw him a few days ago," I said.

"That's the same thing Octavia said." She shrugged. "I wouldn't know. I really don't have anything to compare it to."

"How was it to see him after all these years?"

She spoke to me over a shoulder.

"Strange," she said. "For both of us, I guess."

We stepped inside and before I could ask her anything else, she pointed us toward a set of spiral stairs.

"Your rooms are up there," she said. "I'll find out from Miss Rose when lunch will be ready and ask her to call you then."

35

Jen Ryser didn't join us for lunch.

"I'm afraid she's all done in," Mickey said. "I told her to get some rest and be ready to go later this afternoon. I'm planning for all of us to get out on *Radiance*, maybe turn it into a sunset-dinner cruise."

We sat at a free-form cypress table on a patio off the kitchen. Our view was of the tranquil bay and the cays that stretched south to George Town, on Great Exuma.

Miss Rose, a slender woman in a flowered dress, an apron tied off at her waist, served the stew snapper over rice, sliced tomatoes on the side. She brought out a bottle of pepper sauce.

"Goes nice if you can take it," she said. "Curtis grows the peppers."

I doused the snapper with pepper sauce and my mouth was still on fire when the guava duff came around. Its sweetness helped calm down the burn. So much so that I asked for seconds, which delighted Miss Rose to no end. She positively beamed when Boggy asked for thirds and followed her into the kitchen, probably to lick the pan.

"You boys are welcome to stay here as long as you like. Charlie, too," Mickey said. "I've got plenty of room. And I'd enjoy the company."

"Thanks, but I don't want to get in the way of your reunion, Mickey. We'll be heading out first thing in the morning."

He didn't press the point. I didn't blame him.

"So what do you think, Zack?"

"About what? The house?"

"Screw the house. It's just a house. I'm talking about Jen. She's something, isn't she?"

"Oh, she's something," I said.

"Every time I look at her, I see someone different. Sometimes it's Molly—the way Jen holds herself, her eyes. Sometimes I see me. She's got a lot of me in her, too, don't you think, Zack?"

"A beautiful young lady."

"Fashion-model beautiful, if you ask me. But she's not all ditsy like that. She's smart, too. Smart as a damn whip. Got a good head on those pretty shoulders. I laid it all out for her."

"Laid out all what?"

"Laid it all out about me and how I don't have that long and how all this is going to be hers. I had my lawyer do up the papers. Some of it goes to some charities. A little something for Curtis and Miss Rose, a few others. But mostly it goes to her. We cried some, the both of us. And then we had some laughs, too. Me telling her about all the things I remember from when she was a little girl. She used to call me Doo-Dah. I don't know why, she just did. We both got a kick out of that. And there was this little red wagon I used to pull her around in and I would sing to her and she would giggle. You know what she told me, Zack?"

"What's that?"

"She never got rid of that little red wagon. A couple of times, Molly wanted to pitch it out, but Jen never would let her. She still has it to this day. She told me she always had it to remind her of me. Isn't that something?"

"Yeah, it is. It really is."

Mickey shook his head. He was tearing up. He grabbed a napkin and dabbed at his eyes.

"Sorry," he said.

"No need to be."

"I screwed up, Zack."

"How's that?"

"Letting it go so long like this, between me and her. I should have reached out before now."

"I'm sure you had your reasons, Mickey."

"Yeah, I thought I did, too. But looking back on it now, those reasons really didn't amount to anything. It was all just pride and hurt feelings and getting so wrapped up in myself that I couldn't look beyond and see the big picture. It was selfish, Zack. It was goddam selfish, that's all it was. And now look at me. I'm swimming like hell trying to make up for lost time, but knowing I'm bound to drown. It's a hell of a thing."

I didn't say anything. Mickey looked at me.

"Wish I'd had a chance to meet that daughter of yours when I was at your place," he said.

"She's a humdinger," I said.

"I bet she is. You don't ever let go of her, you hear?"

"I don't intend to."

"No matter what happens between you and Barbara . . ."

"Nothing's happening between us."

"I'm just saying, no matter what, you can't let anything come between you and your daughter. You gotta promise me that."

"Promise," I said.

He stuck his hand across the table and I held on to it.

I still hadn't told him about the call from Lynfield Pederson. Right then might not have been the most appropriate time, Mickey being all torn up like he was. But I didn't know what purpose could be served by not letting him know he was harboring a fugitive from justice. It wasn't fair.

Before I could start in on the story, Octavia stepped out on the porch. She tapped her watch.

"Time for your shot," she said.

"Thank you, Dr. Mengele," Mickey said. He got up from the table. "Sorry, Zack, but these damn shots knock me out. I'll catch up with you in a couple of hours."

36

A nap would have been nice, especially after the sleepless night before. I stretched out on the bed in my room. I stared at the ceiling. It was a nice ceiling, some kind of tongue-and-groove wood thing. Cedar maybe. I stared at it for fifteen minutes. Then I got up. Sleep can be way overrated.

I went downstairs and wound up in the kitchen. Boggy was still there. He sat at a table with Miss Rose.

Curtis stood at the sink, washing dishes. A young man stood beside him, drying the dishes that got washed. Edwin, the grandson, I assumed. He was tall and broad-shouldered and he was training his hair to grow into dreads. They had a long way to go. It made his head look like a picture of the sun drawn by a five-year-old.

An automatic dishwasher was built into the counter. Lots of good, sensible people prefer not to use them. Even the so-called silent diswashers make too much noise. The noise is a conversation killer. And kitchens are all about conversation. Which stopped when I entered this one.

Miss Rose got up from the table. She began putting dishes away in cupboards. Curtis and Edwin pretended I wasn't there.

Boggy looked at me.

"Go for a walk, Zachary?"

"Sure," I said. "I need to make room for another one of Miss Rose's fine meals."

Miss Rose smiled but didn't say anything.

We stepped out the kitchen door and set off down the rutted road, taking the fork that led to the dock. It was midday hot and what breeze there was disappeared as we descended. It was as if the foliage sucked up the breeze and spit it out as heat.

"So," I said, "did you finish off that guava duff?"

"You think that is why I went into the kitchen, Zachary?"

"There some other reason?"

"Fact-finding mission."

"Taino Super-Sleuth Tip Number One: You want to find out stuff, you talk to the hired help."

"Ah so, Guamikeni."

"Give it up, Boggy Chan."

"The three of them, they are much devoted to Mickey Ryser. He is a good man and they love him."

"And this information is valuable to us how?"

"They do not like the girl."

"She's been here what, a day? And already they don't like her?"

"You read *Blink* by Malcolm Gladwell?"

"You mean you did?"

Boggy gave me a long look.

"First impressions matter," he said. "Instinct is everything."

"And they instinctively didn't like her, right from the start?"

"That," Boggy said. "And there are things she has done."

"What things?"

"Small things, maybe. But together they make a picture of a person. She is very attached to her cell phone."

"Lots of people are. A character flaw, maybe, but not a giant one these days. Sadly."

"She got very angry when she could not make calls. Apparently there is no coverage on this island."

"Knew I liked this place."

"Mickey Ryser told her she could use the radio, call anyone she wanted, even patch the radio to the cell phone of whoever she wanted to call."

"Expensive. Plus, not very private."

"Mickey Ryser he said he would do this for her, but she got mad and said no and went to her room."

"Which begs the question: Who is it she needs to call so badly?"

"Also, Miss Rose came upon her last night in Mickey Ryser's den. It was late, after midnight, and Miss Rose couldn't sleep."

"Must be going around."

"Miss Rose stood in the shadows, away from the door, and watched as the young woman went through Mickey Ryser's desk and all its drawers. Miss Rose, she is very upset by this."

"Understandably. Did she take anything?"

Boggy shook his head.

"No, Miss Rose, she does not think so. She had to hurry away before the young woman saw her."

"Anything else?"

Boggy nodded.

"It is about Mickey Ryser. When he returned here a few days ago, he brought much money with him. Two suitcases of it. Curtis he carried the suitcases for Mickey Ryser and helped him put the money in a safe."

"The safe, it's in his den?"

"I did not ask and they did not tell me."

"And they are worried that the girl is trying to find it?"

Boggy shook his head.

"No, it is not that so much. They say it is a very good safe and only Mickey Ryser can open it. Mostly I think they are sad about the money."

"Sad? Why?"

"Because it means Mickey Ryser knows he is going to die and he is getting together all his money so the government cannot find it after he is gone."

"A man after my own heart."

"And they are sad, too, because after Mickey Ryser is gone they do not know what will happen to them."

We walked for a while and didn't talk. It got even hotter as we moved out of the shade and into the clearing near the foot of the dock.

I said, "That all you got?"

"There is one more thing, Zachary."

"I'm listening."

"It is very bad news for you."

"I can handle it."

Boggy put a hand on my shoulder and gave me a somber look.

"That guava duff? I finished it off. And I licked the pan."

37

We were sitting at the end of the dock when we heard the sound of Charlie Callahan's seaplane. It swooped in low and circled the island. Charlie wiggled the wings, an aerowave, and put the plane down well offshore.

He motored in, stopped a few yards from where we had anchored *Radiance*, and threw out anchors of his own.

Boggy and I took the dinghy out to get him. He stood on one of the pontoons and started barking at me the moment we got there.

"Exactly what kind of shitstorm have you started, Chasteen?"

"You tell me."

"Got your face on the front page of the *Guardian*."

"They use a good photo?"

"Old one. In a Dolphins jersey. You had helmet hair."

"Damn," I said. "They need to update the files. I'm way better looking now."

"Cut the crap, man. What's going on?"

"Wanted for murder, on the run. Same old, same old."

"Wanted for a bunch of other things, too, according to that story."

"You were there. You know what happened."

"Yeah, I *was* there. Which explains why things are hot for me, too. This little friend of mine on Andros . . ."

"How was your entanglement, Charlie?"

"Fine, thanks. Nice of you to ask. Wish it could have lasted longer,"

Charlie said. "Only this little friend of mine, her phone rings this morning, wakes us both up. It's a girlfriend of hers, works dispatch for the Andros police. She knows about the two of us. She says there's an all-Bahamas bulletin out, looking for a Maule-MT-7-420. A red one. Owned by none other than me. She asked my friend if she had seen me."

"Your friend lie?"

"Yeah, she lied, but she didn't like it. Let's just say I didn't get the send-off I deserved. Might explain why I'm a little cranky."

We pulled up to the dock and tied off the dinghy. Charlie looked around.

"Hell of a place," he said. "Leave it to Mickey, huh?"

"How did you get away from Andros without the police noticing?"

"I'm one slick son of a bitch, that's how. My friend lives down at Cargill Creek, but I tucked in up the coast a bit, near Small Hope Bay. Had her drive up and get me. Mostly I was worried about her husband knowing I was on the island. Turns out he was gone to Nassau for the week. So I was feeling good about things. Real good. And then all this happened."

"You didn't have any trouble flying out of there?"

"Yeah, I had trouble. A world of trouble," Charlie said. "I got her to drive me up to where I'd tucked away the plane. Only I'd get ready to take off and here would come someone. Fishermen mostly, but I didn't want anyone to see me if there was any way I could help it. And it was broad daylight, you know? Once it was a police boat came by. Another time it was a search plane flying low."

"Think they were looking for you?"

"Had to think that. They were sure as hell looking for something," Charlie said. "I have to tell you, Zack, I was sitting there thinking: *Screw it, just give yourself up. You didn't do anything. You're innocent. You'll get out of this. Eventually.*"

"It was the eventually part that bothered me."

"Yeah, me, too," Charlie said. "So I saw these thunderheads building in the east. They kept building and building and I kept sitting there waiting on them. A couple-three hours. Sweating my ass off in the cockpit of my plane, thinking all the time someone's gonna find me. Storm finally got there and, I'm telling you, it cut all-to-hell loose. Lightning and thunder and must have been forty-knot winds. But it by God cleared out the boats from the water. And I flew right into the teeth of it. Couldn't see shit. Nothing I hate worse than taking off into a squall."

"Thanks for coming," I said. "Appreciate it."

"Yeah, so now what? I'm here and"—he pointed out to the plane—"that's as good as a billboard advertising me. You got any ideas?"

We wound up enlisting the help of Curtis and Edwin. They took us up to the greenhouse and found a big roll of shade cloth—black plastic with a fine mesh. We cut a half-dozen lengths about a hundred feet each. We didn't tell Curtis and Edwin why we needed to camouflage the plane and they didn't ask.

Charlie pulled the seaplane as close as he could get it to the beach. The pontoons dug into the sand, but he said it wouldn't be any problem getting it out as long as there were just a few inches of water.

We draped the shade cloth over the plane and tied it down. When we got done we stood back and looked at it. It looked peculiar. But it didn't look like a seaplane. And it didn't look red.

It took some of the edge off Charlie. He spent a few moments admiring the surroundings, his gaze drifting up to the house.

"Hell of a house." He looked at me. "Please tell me it's got a bar."

38

By midafternoon, Mickey Ryser was rallying the troops for an outing on *Radiance*.

"You sure you strong enough for that?" Octavia said.

"Just the sight of that boat makes me feel better," Mickey said. "That and having my daughter here with me."

"I don't like boats," Octavia said. "I get sick on 'em."

"Then don't go," Mickey said. "Any medicine I need, I can take it with me. You stay here. Take it easy. Relax."

Octavia didn't argue with him.

But Jen did. She said she was too exhausted to go out in the boat. I heard Mickey pleading with her from her bedroom, their voices carrying down to the second-floor living room where I sat with Boggy and Charlie.

"It'll only be for a couple of hours, honey. Just a quick little shake-down cruise."

"You go. I don't feel like it."

"But I want you on the boat. It means a lot."

"Some other time. I'm tired."

"You can rest on the boat. There's a big couch in the salon. AC and everything."

"Where are you going anyway?"

"Thought we'd run down to George Town, then turn around and run back."

Something about that must have helped change her mind.

"OK," she said. "I'll go."

Aside from the fact that the police were on the prowl for us, it was a fine day for cruising on a million-dollar classic yacht.

Charlie said the story in the *Guardian* hadn't mentioned anything about Boggy and me being seen last aboard *Radiance*. Maybe the people at Dilly's Marina hadn't made the connection. Or maybe they had made the connection and chosen not to contact the police, figuring that Mickey Ryser's sizable business with them bought some degree of silence. I could only hope.

I still hadn't told Mickey about the trouble that was chasing us. And once I saw how his spirits and physical condition seemed so markedly improved just by being aboard *Radiance* with his daughter and his friends, I decided against telling him altogether.

Why spoil the occasion? Why dump a bucket of misery on the guy? Let him enjoy what time he had left. I'd get out of this mess, smooth things over. I could tell him about it then. Better that way.

We ran south for an hour, Mickey at the helm, beaming like a boy with a brand-new bike. Curtis and Edwin had joined us. They had removed the canvas covers from the chairs on the aft deck and were sitting there with Boggy and Charlie, the covers stowed neatly beneath the gunwales.

I was in the pilothouse with Mickey and Jen. The three of us held down the captain's bench, Jen in the middle, a big straw bag by her feet. Her long white linen top was sheer enough to show the bright blue bikini beneath it. She wore a floppy yellow hat and big sunglasses.

Mickey had some tunes going, a vintage ska mix, but we could talk above it. I turned and looked at Jen.

"So where's this boat of yours? Sounds like quite a rig."

It took her a moment to answer.

"Sold it," she said.

Mickey looked as surprised to hear it as I was.

"You did what?"

"I sold it." She shrugged and gave Mickey's arm a squeeze. "I got to thinking about it and I decided that it was really selfish of me to go sailing all over the place when I should be here when you needed me. I can always get another boat. But there's not another you."

Mickey kissed her forehead and wrapped an arm around her. She rested her head on his shoulder.

"Where did you sell it?" I asked her.

"Marsh Harbour."

"Where in Marsh Harbour?"

She sat up and looked at me. It was not a friendly look.

"A marina."

"What marina?"

It got me a glance from Mickey.

"What difference does it make, Zack-o? It's her boat. She can do what she wants with it. I just hope she sold it for a good price."

Jen smiled.

"I did. I got a real good price for it . . . Doo-Dah."

She laughed. Mickey laughed, too.

"You mean, the marina bought it outright? Because most of the time, a marina will just act as the agent and get a commission after the boat sells. It can take a while. Especially the boat market being what it is these days."

Jen blew out air, annoyed.

"I sold the boat to the marina. They gave me money for it. I put the money in the bank. Anything else you want to know?"

"Yes, actually. What about your friends?"

"What about them?"

"Well, I know Karen Breakell found a job on a charter boat. And Will Moody, I saw him the other night. But what about the others? Justin and Torrey and the other one . . . Pete. Pete Crumrine."

She studied my face.

"You really did your homework, didn't you?"

"What about them, Jen?"

"They're cool with it," she said. "They totally understood. I mean, who wouldn't understand something like this?"

"Are they still in Marsh Harbour?"

"I don't know. Maybe."

"Or did they go home?"

"I told you, I don't know. I got on the plane and flew down here and they could be anywhere now for all I know."

Another look from Mickey, this time a little perturbed.

"Enough already with the third degree, OK, Zack? She's safe. She's here. That's all I care about."

He gave Jen another hug, but she squirmed out of it and stood up from the bench. She grabbed her straw bag.

"I'm going below," she said.

39

As we neared George Town and the broad, flat waters of Elizabeth Harbour, I went below to use the head. There's not much town in George Town, just a one-way main drag that circles past a business district with a couple dozen low buildings, then splits off to opposite ends of Great Exuma.

A narrow finger of land stretches from the road into the harbor. In another week or so it would be filled with thousands of people, a happy throng from throughout the Bahamas who come each year to watch the National Family Island Regatta and to party for four days nonstop. Except for a few vendors erecting booths the place was empty.

I had my cell phone with me. As I stepped into the main salon it gave a little beep, letting me know I had service. I immediately turned it off. Cops in the States track suspects on their cell phones. I didn't know if Bahamian cops had the technology, but I didn't want to chance it.

As I neared the head, the salon's aft door slid open. Jen stepped inside. She was studying the cell phone in her hand. And she was also on course for the head. She looked up, not particularly happy to see me, and not bothering to hide it.

I gave a gallant sweep of a hand.

"Please," I said.

"Thank you," she said.

The door slid shut behind her.

I was fairly certain she intended to use the cell phone from inside there. And I was tempted to stand outside and eavesdrop.

So tempted, I did just that.

I didn't lean against the door with my ear up to it. But I did strain to hear anything I could. I didn't hear much. No sound of Jen talking. No sound that might typically be associated with a woman using the head. Mostly what I heard was the boat's engine droning along.

And then my ears adjusted, I filtered out the engine, and I heard it. Barely audible but I heard it. A faint tap-tapping.

Jen sending a text message.

Five minutes passed. I made some distance between myself and the door. Another five minutes. I found a chair, sat down.

She finally emerged.

"All yours," she said.

We didn't stop at George Town. Mickey turned *Radiance* around and we headed north, back the way we came.

There were a couple of hours of daylight left. And just shy of Lady Cut Cay, near a shoal where the water glimmered with three shades of blue, Mickey backed the engines to an idle and told Curtis to let out the hook.

"Nice little patch reef here if anyone wants to jump in and take a look around," he said.

I grabbed a mask and fins from a locker. So did Boggy and Charlie.

"It'd be good to find some conch," I said. "Have Miss Rose turn it into conch salad for dinner."

Curtis shook his head.

"No conch down there," he said.

"What do you mean there's no conch?"

"All fished out. Conch are scarce in these parts," Curtis said. "You want to find conch you need to go south to Acklins or Crooked Island, around there."

We jumped in and finned around. I split off from Boggy and Charlie, having a ball in the water, chasing schools of blue tang and snapper, trying to reach out and touch them, watching them swirl away.

I was rounding an outcropping of brain coral when I looked down and saw the conch. A big one, the size of a dinner plate, its rusty-gold shell standing out like a neon sign against the sandy sea bottom. I dove down and grabbed it.

Back on the boat, I showed off my prize. Curtis just shook his head, like he couldn't believe what he saw.

Boggy said, "*Cohobo*."

"What's that?"

"Is Taino word for conch," Boggy said. "And it bodes well that you found it, Zachary."

"Bodes well for dinner," I said. "And I can take the shell to Shula."

Boggy took the conch from me, looked at it closely.

"The conch," he said, "it is good for many things."

He promptly set about cleaning it and managed to remove the meat without marring the shell. The inside of the shell was a study in gradations of pink, light on the edge of the lip, then flaming as the shell spiraled inward upon itself. It was a big, mature conch, its crown long and pointed.

I scrubbed it off and stuck it out of the sun, under some sheets of canvas beneath the gunwales. A perfect gift for Shula. I would hold it to her ear and show her how to listen to the ocean. I would tell her stories. I missed her something fierce.

Mickey made his way down from the pilothouse and stood by the transom, looking out on the water.

"How was it, Zack?"

"Water felt great. Nice little reef."

"One of my favorite spots," Mickey said. "Saw a hawksbill turtle last time I was here. That was a while ago."

"You oughta jump in and give it a look. Might see that turtle again."

Mickey smiled.

"You're right," he said. "I oughta."

Mickey started strapping on his fins. Jen leaned against the gunwale, watching him. He looked at her.

"Why don't you join me?"

"Sure, why not," she said.

She pulled off her white linen top. She looked good in the bright blue bikini. I noticed it. So did Boggy and Charlie. But a buddy's daughter, you just don't stare.

Mickey stepped to the swim platform. He eased into the water as Jen put on her gear.

Mickey yelled, "Come on in!"

Jen stood on the edge of the platform, her back to us.

Only now I did stare. Because I was looking at her flawless skin, the back of her shoulders, tanned and smooth and without blemish.

And then she jumped in.

40

I knew Mickey and Jen wouldn't stay in the water for long. Despite all his spunk and mettle, he would tire quickly. I had only a few minutes at the most.

Jen's cell phone was probably in the straw bag she had carried aboard, the straw bag she snatched up and hauled off with her after our little set-to in the pilothouse.

The bag wasn't anywhere on the deck. I stepped inside the main salon. Wasn't there either. I went up to the pilothouse. No luck.

I made my way down to the main stateroom. And there sat the bag on the bed. I sifted through it, found the cell phone.

I am no expert when it comes to cell phones. I never owned one until after Shula was born and then only after considerable prodding from Barbara.

The cell phone I held wasn't anything like my cell phone. The power was off. It took me a good minute to figure out how to turn it on. The screen lit up and I didn't recognize any of the icons.

Barbara text messaged all the time, constantly it seemed. I had never tried it. And I had no idea where to find the messaging function on this phone.

I punched my way through various icons. Got an e-mail directory. It was empty. Got an address book. It was filled with names but sorting through it seemed a waste of time.

Finally punched an icon that opened the text messages. The most recent thread automatically popped up on the screen.

No names on the messages, just phone numbers. I began reading them in reverse order:

- *G2g.*
- *When?*
- *Tomorrow. They'll be gone. Have plane.*
- *When?*
- *No!!!*
- *Come tonight?*
- *No!!! They hear.*
- *Shit. I'll call you.*
- *Out in his boat. Big problem. Visitors.*
- *Wtf? Where ARE you?*

I didn't hear her walk up behind me.

"Excuse me?"

I turned around. She was still wet from her swim, a towel around her neck. She grabbed the cell phone from me.

"Just what do you think you're doing?"

"I could ask you the same thing."

"Huh?"

"You aren't Jen Ryser."

She drew herself up.

"What are you talking about?"

"I don't know who you are, but you aren't Mickey Ryser's daughter."

"Are you insane?"

"Possibly. But I don't think Jen Ryser would just sell her boat like that. She named it after her mother. She just wouldn't let it go. It meant too much to her."

She didn't say anything.

"Something else. Jen Ryser has a scar on her back. You don't."

"What scar?

"From when she got cut on the crossing to Walker's Cay. Will Moody stitched it up on the boat. Karen Breakell told me about it. Karen Breakell, who's in the hospital, in a coma. You know anything about that?"

She started to say something, then stopped.

"Start talking, Torrey," I said.

"What did you call me?"

"Torrey. Torrey Kealing. That's who you are, isn't it? Because you damn sure aren't Jen Ryser."

"You're fucking crazy. I'm not going to listen to this."

She stormed off. I didn't stop her. We were on a boat. Where could she go?

By the time I made it topside, the engines had cranked up and *Radiance* was pointing toward Lady Cut Cay. Curtis manned the helm, Edwin beside him.

I joined Boggy and Charlie on the aft deck, told them what was going down. We could see into the main salon. Mickey on the rattan couch. The young woman pacing the floor in front of him, on a rant, arms flailing.

She showed Mickey the cell phone. She pointed out at me. And then she started crying. She collapsed onto the couch, face in her hands. Mickey patted her back and drew her close.

Charlie said, "So if she's not Jen Ryser, who is she?"

"I'm guessing the third woman on the sailboat. Torrey Kealing."

"Any idea who she was messaging?"

"Been trying to figure that out."

"One of the guys on the sailboat?"

"Could be one of them."

"That Will Moody guy . . ."

"Yeah," I said. "Something's going on with him. Just can't pin it down. A little too neat for him to show up like he did. Something doesn't fit. But it could be someone else, someone we don't know about."

In the main salon, the young woman still had her face buried against Mickey's chest. Mickey looked out at me—a world of pain in his eyes.

"So, that girl in there," Charlie said. "She was pretending to be Jen Ryser so she could get money from Mickey?"

"No other way to figure it. And not just a little pocket money. The whole package. She knows Mickey only has a little time. So she shows up, says she's his long-lost daughter, and hopes Daddy will leave her something. Mickey had his will rewritten a few weeks ago, after he first spoke to Jen on the phone. I don't know all the details, but he's leaving her a bundle."

"Pretty ballsy scam," Charlie said.

"Could have worked, almost did. Mickey hasn't seen Jen in more than twenty years. He doesn't know what she looks like. This one, this Torrey Kealing, she shows up saying she's Jen when he's expecting Jen to show up, why not believe her?"

Inside the main salon, Mickey got up from the couch. He took a moment to steady himself on a chair before making his way to the galley. He pulled a bottle of water from the refrigerator, brought it back to the couch, and gave it to the young woman.

Boggy said, "What now, Zachary? We go to the police?"

"We'll let Mickey finish things in there. See how he wants to handle it."

It was shaping up to be a killer sunset. Still an hour away, but already the sky was warming up for the big show—streaks of gold against a blue backdrop darkening into purple.

Charlie said, "This doesn't necessarily get the heat off you, does it, Zack?"

"No, but it's a beginning. Time to let the police in on it. They can unravel everything."

"You believe that?"

"Have to believe it."

We watched the sky some more. Curtis backed off the throttle as we closed in on the dock at Lady Cut Cay.

Charlie said, "Kinda leaves everything where it started, doesn't it?"

"Yeah," I said. "So where the hell's the real Jen Ryser?"

The boat was anchored somewhere. It had been anchored for the better part of a day.

A long distance to get there, through most of the day before and into the night. Across a lot of open water. Big swells, pounding seas, one hellacious squall. The boat heaving up and slamming down.

It had bounced her off the bed and when he came down to check on her he was furious.

"I told you not to move."

"I fell. The waves. I couldn't get back up."

"I can't keep coming down here just to check on you."

He made her take a pill. He put it in her mouth and gave her water and held her mouth shut until she swallowed.

And after that she slept. She wasn't sure how long. But when she awoke the motion had stopped. The noise, too. They were anchored.

He came down to check on her every hour or so. He had little to say. He was brusque and impatient and whenever she needed to use the head he stood right outside and kept telling her to hurry up.

Then he would go back up top. He never left the boat. She could hear him up there, sometimes pacing the deck.

Waiting. For whatever would happen next.

41

Curtis brought *Radiance* all the way in. He jockeyed the engines and pulled alongside the dock with nary a bump. Edwin hopped off the boat and looped its bow and stern lines around pilings.

"You get off and then I'll anchor her out," Edwin called down from the pilothouse.

We stepped off the boat and waited on the dock. It was several minutes before Mickey emerged from the salon. The young woman stayed in there, watching us from the couch.

Mickey looked weak and drained. He used his cane to make it across the deck. I offered a hand as he stepped onto the dock. He pushed it away.

"I can make it on my own," he said.

"You OK?"

He squared off in front of me.

"I'm fine," he said. "But you need to leave. You need to leave right now."

"Mickey, what . . ."

He put up a hand to silence me.

"I don't want to hear it. I don't know what the hell you think you're doing. I don't want to hear a thing. I just want you gone."

In the salon, the young woman got up from the couch. She moved close to the window and stared out at us. She folded her arms across her chest.

"Look, I don't know what she told you," I said. "But she . . ."

"She told me all I needed to hear, dammit. You've been after her since we got on the boat. Asking her all those damn questions."

"She's not your daughter, Mickey."

He looked away. Then he fixed me with an angry glare.

"What proof do you have of that?"

"Her story about selling the sailboat, for one thing. It doesn't make a bit of sense."

"Just because it doesn't make sense to you doesn't mean it's not true."

"Jesus, Mickey. Just think about it. Ask her to produce a bill of sale, a bank deposit, anything. No one just up and decides to sell a boat like a Beneteau 54 and finds a buyer right off the bat. It doesn't happen."

Mickey's jaw clenched.

He said, "You got anything besides that?"

"I found one of your daughter's friends, Karen Breakell. She told me Jen had an accident on the crossing. Got a bad cut on her shoulder. They had to sew it up on the boat. That woman in there . . ."

Mickey dismissed it with a flick of his hand.

"Jen told me all about that. She told me this Karen girl was drunk the whole time and didn't know what was going on. She told me she couldn't wait to get her off the boat. Jen said it was another girl who got cut."

"Torrey Kealing?"

"I don't know. What difference does it make? But I'll tell you one thing: I don't appreciate you invading her privacy the way you did. Getting her cell phone, looking at her messages. What the hell, Zack?"

"She was messaging someone from the boat."

"OK, she was messaging someone. There a law against that?"

"She was messaging someone and telling them not to come yet. Not to come here to this island. Not until tomorrow. She tell you who that was? Or why they are coming here?"

"Matter of fact, she did tell me about that, Zack." He looked at me. "It was her boyfriend."

"Boyfriend?"

He let out some air.

"She didn't want to tell me about him before now. She said she wanted to meet me face-to-face first, see how it went between the two of us and go from there. But she's got this boyfriend . . ." Mickey shook his head. "I think he was a big reason she got rid of the sailboat, wanted something a little smaller for just the two of them. What she did, she said she went to this marina in Marsh Harbour and struck a deal with them where they would keep the sailboat and she would take this other boat, a powerboat. Some kind of cruiser, I don't know. Worth a whole lot less than her sailboat. Once the marina sells her boat, they'll settle up on the difference. And that explains that. You satisfied?"

"This boyfriend, she tell you his name?"

"Will Something. I didn't get the last name. All I know, she was messaging him and that's what you found. Sticking your nose where you had no business sticking it. She's upset. You owe her an apology."

I looked at Boggy and Charlie. They were as done-in by everything as I was. I looked at Mickey.

I said, "Abel Delgado's dead."

Mickey flinched at the news.

"What are you saying?"

"I'm saying someone killed Delgado night before last in Marsh Harbour. In his hotel room."

"Who?"

I shook my head.

"Don't know."

"Goddam. That's awful," Mickey said. "But what does that have to do with us? You're not saying . . ."

He turned and looked at the young woman standing on the other side of the salon window. Her face was unreadable. He looked back at me.

"You're not suggesting Jen had anything to do with that, are you?"

"She's not Jen, Mickey. I don't care what she's telling you and how much you want to believe it. I'm sorry. She's not your daughter."

Mickey's eyes twitched. He shook with anger. He reached into his pocket and pulled out a passport. He handed it to me.

"You look at that and you tell me what you see."

I opened the passport. The photo was of the young woman in the salon. The passport said her name was Jennifer Anne Ryser. I handed the passport back to Mickey.

"I don't know what to tell you," I said.

"You can tell me you made a mistake."

"The passport could be fake."

"Can't fake a U.S. passport anymore, Zack. Not since 9/11."

"It can look like a passport, but it might not act like a passport."

"What the hell is that supposed to mean?"

"She's playing you, Mickey. Let's you and I go back in there right now and talk this through with her. I've got plenty more questions I could ask."

Mickey shook his head.

"You've asked her all the questions you're going to ask." He tapped a finger on my chest. "You need to leave. You need to leave right now."

42

We retrieved our bags from the house and headed down to the sea-plane. The tide was up and the plane floated in plenty of water. We took off the shade-cloth camouflage, rolled it up, and stuck it under the chickee hut on the beach. Then we waded back to the plane and settled into our seats.

Charlie started the engine, let it warm up.

It was dark now. *Radiance* was still at the dock. It was too far away for me to tell for sure, but the salon lights were on and I could only guess that Mickey and the young woman were still sitting on the couch, talking.

Charlie said, "You sure about this, Zack?"

"Yeah, I'm sure. Unless you've got a better idea."

"I'm low on fuel," Charlie said. "Ate up a bunch of it fighting that squall off Andros. I can't make it all the way to Harbour Island on what I've got."

We had decided that the best course of action would be to connect with Lynfield Pederson and lay out everything for him. That way, maybe he could run interference while things got sorted out and I wouldn't get thrown in jail. Trouble was, if we called Pederson on the plane's radio it would alert other police to our whereabouts and, well, it could compli-cate matters. So that meant flying to Harbour Island to see Pederson in person.

"Where's the closest place to get fuel?"

"Airport in George Town."

"Any chance of flying into there without the police knowing about it?"

"Chance is slim to none. And Slim, he's done left town. Got a police station right next to the terminal," Charlie said. "Could try Barraterre, about a dozen miles north of George Town."

"It got an airport?"

"No, but I used to keep some honey pots there."

"Honey pots?"

"Fuel drums," Charlie said. "Back in the day, I had fuel stashes all up and down the islands. Tuck in, fill up, and get the hell out. Still know folks in Barraterre. Might rustle up someone who could help out."

"It's worth you giving it a shot," I said.

"Especially when it's the only shot I got."

Charlie motored the plane slowly offshore, putting *Radiance* farther behind us. We were approaching the south tip of Lady Cut Cay, bouncing gently along the water.

Charlie looked at me.

"You ready, Zack?"

"Let's do this thing," I said.

I opened the door on my side. The air coming in was warm and sticky. Boggy handed me a waterproof bag. It held a pair of binoculars, a big beach towel, some bug juice, and a bottle of water.

"See you soon, Zachary," Boggy said.

I stuck out one leg onto the plane's pontoon. Then I pulled the rest of myself out, balancing there with a hand on a strut.

"OK, what I'm going to do is flip off all the lights," Charlie said, talking louder now to be heard above the engine. "That's when you jump. I'm only gonna leave the lights off a couple of seconds. Because there's a pretty good chance Mickey is watching us and if the lights are off any longer than that he'll notice it and think something is up. So jump and get your ass as far away from the plane as you can. And then I'm outta here. You got it?"

"Piece o' cake."

"On three," Charlie said.

He counted it down and when the lights flicked off I leaped from the pontoon and into the water. Not an Olympic-caliber entry—the Bulgarian judge would have given it a 6—but it put plenty of distance between me and the plane.

By the time I surfaced, the plane's lights were back on and it was speeding away.

The water was shallow, only up to my chest. I stood there, watching the plane take off. As it gained altitude, it made a lazy loop back toward Lady Cut Cay and passed right over *Radiance*, Charlie just making sure that Mickey spotted him leaving the island.

I slung the bag over a shoulder and waded toward shore.

43

The binoculars weren't the night-vision kind, so they didn't help at all. Not that it mattered. There wasn't much to see.

I found a spot of high ground between the landing strip and the dock. The underbrush was thick but I stomped it down enough so that it didn't keep scraping against me.

I could look out between some wax myrtles and see *Radiance*. If I turned the other way and bent back the branches of a bramble bush, I could see up to the house.

All in all, a decent little hidey-hole. Not that I wanted to set up permanent housekeeping. But it would do me well enough until Charlie and Boggy made contact with Lynfield Pederson and could get back here. In the meantime, it would let me keep an eye on things in case there were any visitors, such as so-called boyfriends in powerboats.

About an hour after I came ashore, I spotted a figure walking down the dock toward *Radiance*. Octavia. Checking on Mickey, making sure he took his meds, maybe giving him a shot.

Shortly after Octavia left, the lights went off in the boat's main salon and I saw Mickey and the young woman walking along the dock. They got into a golf cart and drove away.

A few minutes later, *Radiance* moved from the dock and came to rest at anchor about fifty yards out. I saw its dinghy putt-putting back to the dock and then Edwin and Curtis got into their golf cart and drove away.

The lights went off in the house not long afterward, and that was pretty much it for the evening's excitement.

I stripped down to my briefs, hung my shirt and shorts over a tree limb. The clothes wouldn't dry overnight, not with all the humidity, but at least it would air them out, get rid of some Zack funk.

The little biting beasties weren't bad, not with the breeze, but I lathered up with bug juice anyway in the name of pre-assault deterrent. I spread out the beach towel, wadded up the waterproof bag for a pillow, and stretched out on my back.

I was hoping to look up and find a majestic firmament unfolding on my behalf. No better place for stargazing than the Out Islands. But clouds had blown in from the west, and instead of an expansive view of the heavens, the sky was a soggy gray blanket, looming low and oppressive.

Funny how the mind works at times like this. Seldom did I recall much from my high school Latin class, but I did now. The Latin word for island is *insula*. From which we also get "insular" and "isolated."

So here I was, on this island, where things had started out rosy enough then quickly gone to hell. And now I was feeling pretty insular and isolated.

An A-plus in vocabulary, Zack. Poor, poor pitiful you.

I rolled over onto my side and was rewarded with a glimpse of the rising moon trying to shine forth from behind a heavy haze. It was kind of like a burlesque queen performing a fan dance. The fact that the moon wasn't fully exposed made it larger than life and all the more alluring.

I stared at it for a while. I had no pretense of actually falling asleep. The ground was hard and I was wound tight. No way would I doze off.

Pretty moon, though.

Not quite a full moon.

The full moon still a few days off.

And by then I'd be home.

Home.

I like my dreams with a soundtrack. And for this particular dream, I had me some Marley:

Don't worry/'bout a ting/'Cause every little ting/Gonna be alright

I was in bed with Barbara, bouncing Shula on my stomach. Lots of giggling going on. The windows in the bedroom were thrown open. A baby cardinal landed on the sill and started chirping its fool head off.

Rise up this mornin'/Smiled with the risin' sun/Three little birds/Perch by my door step

Dreams. Sheesh.

Part collective unconscious, part the outside leaking in.

Then two more cardinals appeared. And they made this trio. Daddy sang bass, momma sang tenor. All that goofy crap.

Singin' sweet songs/Of melodies pure and true/Sayin', this is my message to you-ou-ou

It was the "you-ou-ouing" that finally roused me out of dreamland.

I jolted up. The sun was out.

And there stood Edwin, on the other side of the wax myrtles, in a clearing by a golf-cart path, an iPod plugged into his ears, singing his fool head off.

He was getting into it, too. Eyes closed. Hitting the high notes. Facing the east and waving his hands. Like he was conducting a sunrise reggae symphony.

I moved, trying to get deeper into the underbrush, so he wouldn't see me. It was the moving that caught his eye.

He jumped. I jumped.

He said something like, "Ou, ou, ou . . ."

I said, "Edwin, easy now."

He kept backing off, looking like he might run. Couldn't blame him. Me showing up outta nowhere, on this little island where no one ever showed up unless everyone knew about it.

I stood up.

"Edwin, be cool."

He recognized me. Still scared as hell. But he recognized me.

He pulled out the earbuds.

"What you doing here?"

"Just keeping an eye on things."

Edwin thought about it.

"Something wrong?"

So I sat him down and told him everything he needed to know. When I was done we sat around and he thought about it some more.

Then he looked at me.

"You hungry?"

44

Edwin brought me johnnycakes wrapped in aluminum foil, still warm from the kitchen. There was a pork chop in there, too.

I sat in my hidey-hole, Edwin watching me gobble down food.

"You put the fright in me," he said.

"Sorry. Wasn't expecting anyone to come out this way."

"I come out here most every morning," Edwin said. "It's my singing spot."

"Your singing spot?"

"Yeah, it's a good spot. Look out that way you see the bay. Other way, you see the ocean. I come here, punch up a playlist on my iPod, put in my buds, and I sing." He tapped his shirt, where the iPod was. "Got 2,763 songs right here in my pocket."

"Whole lot of singing."

"Got everything by Buju and Tosh. Got all the Marleys—Bob and all his sons, got Ziggy and Damian and Stephen and Julian."

"Got Ky-Mani?"

"Yeah, I got him, but he goes a little too hip-hop. I like it roots, you know?"

"What about Rohan? You got him, too?"

"Rohan don't sing. You think he would. Married Lauryn Hill, had some kids. But mostly, Rohan he's all about the clothes. Runs that Tuff Gong line. Doing pretty good at that."

"I met him once."

"Oh yeah? How's that?"

"He used to play football. University of Miami. Then up in Canada for Ottawa."

"Don't follow much football."

"Yeah, well . . ."

Edwin looked at me.

"How you think I sound? You can tell the truth."

"You sound like something out of a dream," I said.

Edwin grinned.

"Yeah, I save up some money, I'm going to Miami and cut a CD. I already got my singing name, the one that'll be on the CD. You want to hear it?"

"Sure, what is it?"

"Ex-Man Eddie. The Ex part that's for Exuma. And Eddie that's me. Edwin White. Ex-Man Eddie. You like that?"

"It's a good singing name," I said.

"Sounds kinda hip-hop, but that's what'll fool 'em. They expecting something raw, maybe dancehall, or reggaeton even, and I give them some smooth old sounds. You know who I like best, who I model myself after?"

"Who's that?"

"Alpha Blondy. You know Alpha Blondy?"

"He's African, right? African reggae."

Edwin looked surprised.

"You know some stuff. Old guy like you. Took you for some Parrothead, but you know it."

"My wife," I said. "She knows it better than me. I just get it by osmosis."

"Alpha Blondy. Comes from Ivory Coast. Sings in French, sings in English. Sings in Arabic and even Hebrew. He got da real Jah love, mon. Singing for all the world."

I finished gnawing all the meat from the pork chop and wrapped up the bone inside the aluminum foil. Edwin took it from me.

"I told Daddy Curtis and Momma Rose you were out here."

"And?"

"And they said if that girl's up to something then it's a good thing you didn't leave."

"You think she's up to something?"

Edwin shrugged.

"Hard to say. You first see her you think she's all sweetness because she's got that smile and she looks fine and she says the right things. Then you study her and you watch her eyes and you see something else. Something cold inside." He shuddered. "She was up late again last night, going through Mr. Mickey's office, wandering the house. Momma Rose caught her at it, only this time she said something. Told her she shouldn't oughta be going around doing that. The girl, she lashed out at Momma Rose. Told her if she didn't watch herself wouldn't none of us have a job."

"Your grandmother should say something to Mickey about it. He needs to know."

Edwin shook his head.

"Says it's not her place. She sees the way Mr. Mickey looks at that young woman, seeing his own flesh and his own blood. No good would come of anything she might say."

Edwin said he had work to do, but he would come back around lunch-time and bring me something else to eat.

I told him I was hoping I wouldn't be sitting there much longer.

With luck, Boggy and Charlie had made it up to Harbour Island the night before. Only a matter of time, they'd be back, bringing Lynfield Pederson with them. And together we'd blow the cover off whatever it was Torrey Kealing was trying to pull.

45

The sun moved high and burned away the clouds. Shade became an elusive thing. The breeze punched the time clock and knocked off early. Heat settled in like the overnight guest who wouldn't go away, drank all your liquor, and expected three meals a day.

And so I passed the morning and no one came.

I kept watching the sky for a red seaplane, coming in low from the north. But all I saw were frigate birds circling on thermals and big silvery jets flying high and heading for the mainland.

The only boats moved well to the west, traveling the main channel south to George Town or north to wherever. All kinds of boats. Big boats, small boats. Some moving fast and some moving slow. The wake from the big ones would sometimes make it all the way to the island, reduced by distance and rippling against the beach below—tiny, perfect waves against the white, unblemished sand.

Edwin returned at lunchtime with a paper plate covered in foil—baked chicken, peas 'n' rice, some sheetcake for dessert. I took a few bites, then stuck it aside, wrapped it up in the towel so ants wouldn't get at it. The day too hot for eating food. Even by my broad standards.

Edwin had brought along some ice water in a jug so I satisfied myself with that. I drank it too fast and felt my temples pound.

"What's going on at the house?"

"Just this and that. Mostly nothing," Edwin said. "Mr. Mickey he's in his office doing work. The girl, she only just now got up. Momma Rose tried to feed her something, but the girl she said she wasn't hungry. Said she's going to go sit on the beach. I'm supposed to go down and rake it clean and put her out a chair."

"Anyone call on the radio?"

Edwin shook his head.

"Just the usual chatter. Boats talking to other boats. People passing time."

Edwin left and I moved to a spot a few feet away, where there was more shade under a gumbo limbo and I had a clearer view of the beach.

Where were Boggy and Charlie? They should have returned long before now. Either bringing Lynfield Pederson with them, or him coming along on his own, maybe bringing some of his people with him if he thought it necessary.

How would Pederson do it? Sit Torrey Kealing down and have a talk with her. Just the two of them, Pederson coming off like this big, black Bahamian cop with sleepy eyes and a slow way, letting Kealing work herself deeper and deeper into a hole thinking she could talk her way past him.

I would sit down with Mickey, try to mend fences. He wouldn't like it, how I'd gone behind his back. But he'd come around, he'd understand. Especially when Kealing's story started falling apart. Mickey would take it hard. It would tear him up and set him back. All of it made worse knowing that his daughter was still out there somewhere.

Had Torrey Kealing, this pretty impostor on the play, bossing the hired help like she already owned the place, had she killed Jen, she and whoever was working it with her? Killed Delgado, too? Torched the Dailey brothers' boatyard? Put Karen Breakell in a coma? Scorching and burning their way down the islands.

It would all come out.

But where was everyone? What was taking so long?

I looked down toward the beach, saw Edwin with a rake, making small piles of the wrack that had come ashore, gathering the piles in a wheelbarrow and carting it away. He came back with a beach umbrella, blue canvas with a white flower print, and planted it in the sand. Came back again dragging two lounge chairs, put them on either side of the umbrella. One for Kealing and one for Mickey, he felt like coming down and joining her maybe.

Half an hour passed. I took off my shirt, drenched it with ice water from the jug, and draped it around my neck. It worked for about five minutes. Then I was sweating again.

Torrey Kealing appeared on the beach. Same blue bikini as the day before, same big straw bag. She put the bag down on a chair and pulled out her cell phone. She looked at its screen. Then she tossed it into the bag.

She walked to the edge of the water and touched a toe to it, testing. She walked out about shin deep and waded along the shoreline. She kept looking out at the main channel as she waded, all the way to the dock, then turning around and wading back the other way and stretching out in the lounge chair.

She was fidgety. Getting out her cell phone and looking at it again. As if a signal would just magically appear. She dug holes in the sand with her feet. Then she got up and waded into the water, going deeper this time, swimming a few strokes, then just sitting low in the water so all I could see was her head.

She got out and shook her hair and gathered it into a long ponytail and wrung it dry. She walked to the other end of the beach, away from the dock, to where the beach ended and the mangroves began, about a quarter mile, directly below the spot in the shade where I sat watching her.

She stood there, looking out at the main channel. Then she shaded her eyes as if she saw something, waded out a little farther.

I picked up the binoculars and trained them on the channel. I saw a boat veering from the marker, heading our way.

When he came down to the cabin he took off her blindfold. He put her backpack on the bed beside her.

"Need to get you into some clean clothes."

He reached into the backpack, pulled out panties, shorts, and a maroon College of Charleston T-shirt. He pulled her from the bed. He untied her hands and feet.

"Get undressed."

"Do you mind if I go into the head?"

"Do it here. Not like I haven't seen it before."

She was slipping into the clean clothes when the voice came from outside: "Hallooo. Halllooo. Anyone there?"

A look of panic in his eyes. He pushed her back onto the bed.

"Don't move. Don't do anything. You understand?"

She nodded.

He rushed out of the cabin and climbed the ladder to the deck.

And she immediately ran to the head. She stood on the toilet and strained to look out the vent.

She saw: A wooden fishing boat idling a few yards out, the young man in it holding up a lobster.

The young man called out, "Fresh, mon! Just pulled them this morning . . ."

She started to scream, but the boat rocked and she slipped from the toilet onto the floor. By the time she crawled back up, he was already waving the fisherman away.

"No, thanks. I'm good . . ."

"Make you a deal, mon. Ten dollars each."

"No, I don't want any lobster. Go on now . . ."

"Fresh, mon. Fresh as can be."

"Bullshit. It's not lobster season. Get out of here . . ."

The fisherman scowled and tossed the lobster in an ice chest. He revved his engine and began to pull away.

She got down from the toilet. She reached behind it and found the Leatherman she had hidden there. She fumbled with it, opening first the scissors and then the pliers before finally finding the knife.

It wasn't a big knife, the blade only three inches long. But it would have to do. Now or never.

She heard his footsteps cross the deck, him coming down the ladder. She flattened herself against the wall of the head, watched as he passed by its door and stopped, seeing she was no longer by the bed.

And she sprung out, aiming the knife for a point in his throat she thought might be the jugular.

In that same instant, he spun around, the knife catching him in the collarbone, cutting skin but doing no great harm. He rammed an elbow into her temple, knocking her down. He fell upon her, twisting her arm, grabbing the Leatherman, and throwing it to the other side of the cabin.

He backhanded her across the face, once and then again. He seized her under the chin, raised her head so the two of them were eye to eye, blood dripping from the wound on his chest onto her T-shirt.

"I . . . will . . . kill you," he said. "Don't think that I won't."

He bound her feet and her hands, tighter than ever before, and left her lying on the floor.

He went up top. She heard him crank the engine and pull the anchor.

That had been more than an hour ago. Since then, the boat had run a steady course.

Now, the engine throttled down a notch and she felt the boat turn.

46

The boat looked to be a forty-footer or thereabouts, blue hull with a flying bridge. It was about a mile offshore. I could see a figure at the main helm, but the binoculars wouldn't let me make out much in the way of detail.

I lowered the binoculars and looked down at the beach. Torrey Kealing had left the water and was hurrying back toward the lounge chair.

I put the binoculars on the boat again. It approached slowly and when it was about a half mile away it turned sharply and pointed toward the pass at the south end of Lady Cut Cay.

Torrey Kealing was under the umbrella now. She gathered her straw bag from the chair and stood there, watching the boat.

The boat picked up speed as it entered the pass and as it rounded the end of the island it was no longer visible from where Kealing stood on the beach. She watched its wake for a moment, then turned and walked toward the dock.

From my vantage point I could track the boat as it circled the island. It moved closer as it motored along the east side.

I adjusted the lens on the binoculars but the glare off the windows of the main bridge wouldn't let me see who was at the helm.

I followed the boat as it made its way past the rocky bluff and into the pass on the north side of the island.

Torrey Kealing was at the end of the dock now and she was looking to her left and to her right. She spotted the boat as it cleared the pass and set course for the dock.

She waved at the boat.

Behind her, Curtis and Edwin appeared at the foot of the dock. They held back, waiting to see what the boat was going to do, ready to help if they were needed.

The boat slowed down, gliding now toward the end of the dock. Kealing saying something to the person at the helm.

Curtis and Edwin headed out on the dock, but Kealing waved them back.

And then the boat was at the end of the dock, pulling up alongside it, barely stopping as Kealing tossed her bag aboard it and then hopped over its gunwale and onto the deck.

Only then did I get a good look at the figure at the helm. Shirtless, dark curly hair, tall and well muscled, a thin beard—the same guy I'd met in the bar at Mariner's Inn. The guy who claimed to be Will Moody. The guy who, I was pretty sure now, must be Justin Hatchitt.

He nudged the boat away from the dock and pointed it out, engine running slow.

"We need to get out of here," she said. "Now."

"What are you talking about? I thought he fell for the daughter thing."

"Oh, he fell for it. He fell for it big time. But there were these guys here yesterday . . ."

"What guys?"

"One of them was the guy in the bar, the night you did that detective."

"Chasteen?"

"And two of his friends. Chasteen knows something is going on. He was asking all kinds of questions. He kept telling Ryser I wasn't his daughter. But Ryser wouldn't listen to him. He told Chasteen and his friends to leave."

"So what's the problem?"

"It's not going to work like we planned. I'm not going to be able to stay here, pretending to be his daughter, waiting until he dies. It's not going to work. Chasteen has probably already gone to the cops . . ."

"I don't think so."

"What do you mean?"

"I caught some news this morning, something about how the police are still looking for him. They don't know where he is."

"I don't care. I don't like it. It's fucked up. It's not going to work. We need to get out of here. We need to . . ."

"Hold on, hold on."

"What do you mean hold on? Hurry up and get us out of here, Justin."

He nodded down below.

"We've still got her."

"Yeah, so what? Get rid of her, ditch her. I don't care. Let's just go."

"We didn't do all this to wind up with nothing."

"We got a few thousand. We get into George Town maybe we can find a bank, get more from her account and fly south, lay low. But we have to go. We have to . . ."

"What about Ryser?"

"What about him?"

"Guy like that, sitting here on this island, waiting to die. You don't think he has some money?"

47

Torrey Kealing getting on the boat, I hadn't expected that. The boat maybe fifty yards off the end of the dock now, not far from *Radiance*, pointing out to the channel, throttled down, still going slow.

I could see Kealing and Justin Hatchitt through the binoculars. On the main bridge, arguing it looked like.

I scanned out to the channel. No other boats heading this way. And no sign of Charlie Callahan's seaplane.

I looked at the boat. It had moved past *Radiance*, into open water, still on its slow course toward the channel. Torrey Kealing stepping away from the main bridge now, going below.

I lowered the binoculars. I grabbed the jug of water and took a long drink from it. My shirt hung from a tree limb. I shook it out and put it on. I rolled up the towel and stuck it in the waterproof bag.

Thinking: *OK, they're leaving. Game over. Let the police catch up with them. Not my job anymore. Get up to the house, tell Mickey what's going on. Then get on the radio and call Lynfield Pederson. Check in with Charlie and Boggy. Find out where they are.*

But when I looked at the boat again, it had turned around and was motoring toward the dock. Hatchitt worked the helm. I couldn't see Torrey Kealing. She was still down below.

Curtis and Edward headed toward the end of the dock as the boat pulled alongside. Hatchitt stepped away from the helm and had the boat tied off before they could get there.

And now Hatchitt was hopping onto the dock, holding something at his side. A boat hook, to fend off from the pilings? But why would he need that if the boat was already . . .

A shotgun.

Curtis and Edwin froze as they saw it, then both turned and ran the other way.

Hatchitt fired and Curtis went down, grabbing his leg. Edwin stopped, hands above his head.

Hatchitt kept the shotgun trained on them as two figures appeared on the boat. Torrey Kealing, shoving another young woman forward onto the dock, the second one wearing a maroon T-shirt, arms bound behind her.

Curtis sat up now, holding his leg, in real pain. Edwin pulled off his shirt and tied it around the wound. He helped Curtis to his feet and Hatchitt kept the shotgun on the two of them as he followed them off the dock, the two women bringing up the rear.

And I could see now that Torrey Kealing held a pistol at the back of the other woman's head.

Jen Ryser. It had to be Jen Ryser.

Her long blond hair tumbled around her shoulders. She shook it back to keep it out of her face. Barefoot, unsteady. Stooping over just a little with the pressure of the pistol at her head.

The three-seater golf cart sat at the foot of the dock. Hatchitt pointed Curtis and Edwin into the middle seat. He stood on the rear platform, one hand on the roof of the golf cart, the other keeping the shotgun on Curtis and Edwin.

Kealing sat Jen Ryser down on the passenger side, then slid behind the wheel. The golf cart lurched away, up the rutted road toward the house, disappearing behind the trees.

From where I stood, the house was almost a mile away. Down the hill, the dirt path winding through the swampy lowlands and around the brackish pond, before hitting the long grade that led up to the house.

Impossible to beat them there. But I started running anyway.

48

When I reached the edge of the clearing that circled the house, the golf cart was parked at the back door. No sign of anyone. They were all inside.

I hung back behind thatch palms and tall brush, scoping out the property, trying to figure out the best way to approach the house without being seen.

What to do, Chasteen, what to do?

Try sneaking into the house, getting the drop on them somehow?

A big somehow. More like a no way. They had guns. And I'm not the stealthiest guy on the planet. Things could get ugly quick.

Still, I needed to get an idea of what they were up to in there before I could figure out a plan of attack.

The clearing was wide—about forty yards on every side of the house. A forty-yard dash. My best time ever just shy of five seconds. More than twenty years ago at the NFL trials, right before the Dolphins drafted me. I flattered myself to think I could make it in seven or eight seconds now. Plenty of time for someone to look out a window and see me.

Where in the house were they?

They had entered through the back door. Figure they found Miss Rose in the kitchen. Maybe Octavia was in there, too. They had hustled them along at gunpoint with the others, looking for Mickey Ryser.

Edwin telling me earlier: *Mr. Mickey, he's in his office doing work.*

Had he still been there when they arrived? And having found him there were they all now in the office?

As good a guess as any. Go with it. No time to sift through all the options.

Mickey's office sat on the first floor of the house, the side with a view of the dock and the beach. I moved through the trees and brush until I reached the opposite side of the house, the ocean and rocky bluff at my back. From there, I could see across the broad deck and into the living room. No sign of movement in there. All the doors and windows closed, the AC compressors droning.

I studied the best way to cross the clearing—a straight shot to the deck. The deck sat on low four-by-four posts, maybe two feet of elevation. Enough for me to squeeze under the deck and crawl through to the other side. I'd see how things looked on the other side when I got there.

I took off across the clearing, crouching as low as I could while still hitting stride. Five yards out from the house and I dove, landing in the sand by the deck, next to a bougainvillea bush. I lay there for a long moment, hearing nothing but the AC compressors.

I flattened out, slithered my way under the deck, peeked out to the other side of the house. Mickey's office had a big ceiling-to-floor window that offered a magnificent view to the west. The sun was high and there was a glare off the window, but not so much that I couldn't see inside.

Mickey on the far side of the room, sitting behind his desk, both hands on the desktop, facing the window. Justin Hatchitt on the other side of the desk, shotgun cradled in an arm now. He was doing all the talking. Jen Ryser sat on the floor at his feet, arms still tied behind her.

Torrey Kealing sat on a corner of the desk, back to Mickey, her pistol pointing across the room. I couldn't see the others, but I remembered the layout of Mickey's office. A couch, two chairs around a coffee table. That's where the four of them—Curtis, Edwin, Octavia, and Miss Rose—were sitting.

I strained to hear what they were saying inside, but the compressors drowned out everything.

Justin Hatchitt telling Mickey, "It's all up to you now, mister."

Mickey saying, "How much do you want?"

"Whatever you got. The quicker we get it, the quicker we're out of here."

"And nobody gets hurt? My daughter stays here with me?"

"Yet to be determined. For all I know you don't have jack-shit. In which case . . ."

"I've got money," Mickey said.

"Let's see it."

"First you untie my daughter. Do it now."

"You aren't calling the shots here, pal."

"You give me something. I give you something. It's how things work."

"How about I give you . . ." Hatchitt uncradled the shotgun, pointed it square at Mickey's chest, aiming from his hip.

"You shoot me you won't get the money."

"If it's in this house, I'll find it. Or one of these others will find it for me."

"It's in a safe. I'm the only one knows how to open it."

"Show it to me."

"Untie my daughter."

A burst of static from the radio that sat on the table behind Mickey's desk.

"Bama Tiger calling Instigator. Instigator come in . . ."

Hatchitt said, "Who the fuck's that?"

"Just boats talking to other boats," Mickey said. "Nothing to do with us."

But Hatchitt came around behind the desk, kicked the table, and knocked the radio onto the floor. He stomped down on it, cracking open the case, then stomping on it some more.

"That'll take care of that," he said. "Now show me the money."

Mickey stepped out from behind his desk. He went to a corner of the room and peeled back the sisal rug. He knelt and began punching in the combination on the metal safe built into the floor.

49

I'd seen all I needed to see. Busting into the house and going straight at them wouldn't end in anything but disaster. But I couldn't just stay under the deck watching everything go down, letting them get away.

What if . . .

Just the seed of an idea. Not a solution, but a stopgap maybe. Something to stir the pot, throw them off balance. And maybe give me an opening.

I scooted back under the deck and hightailed it across the clearing, the exact way I came. I ran through the tall brush, circling back and finding the rutted road well below the house.

I ran down the road, all the way to the dock. I stopped halfway out, where the dinghy for *Radiance* was tied off at a piling. I untied it, gave it a big push, and the little skiff glided away from the dock.

The Albury 27 was in its slip on the other side of the dock. I untied it, held the bowline as I walked it out to the end of the dock, and gave it a good push, too.

That left the big blue-hulled boat, the one Hatchitt arrived in. I let loose its lines and pushed away from the dock, hopping aboard.

I went to the helm. The key wasn't in the ignition. That was OK. I wasn't going anywhere in the boat. I just wanted to put it well out of reach.

And the radio. I needed to get on it.

It sat in a console to one side of the helm. I didn't need the keys to turn it on. It was hardwired to the electrical system. I flipped a switch, saw it light up. I heard static, some voices talking. I grabbed the handset.

"Mayday! Mayday! Mayday! This is Lady Cut Cay. Emergency. Send help. Mayday! Mayday! Mayday!"

I was pretty sure that a Mayday signal was typically reserved for boats and ships and planes. Screw it. This was an island in peril.

And with the radio now out of commission in the house, I could make the call without alerting the others to what I was up to.

But there was no response. I called again.

"Mayday! Mayday! Mayday!"

No response.

The boat was only about ten feet out from the dock. It had stopped drifting. The wind was out of the west and light, but the boat had a lot of broadside and it was being pushed back to the dock.

I tried one more time with the radio. Again, no response.

The boat was bumping against the dock now. I stepped away from the helm and gave the boat another shove out. Then I slipped off my shoes and shirt and went forward onto the bow. I grabbed the bowline and dove into the water with it.

I tied the line around my waist and swam out, pulling the boat behind me. It started off slow, but I got it turned, pointing straight into the wind, getting a little momentum. I did the breaststroke and then the crawl, mixing it up.

I pulled the boat out past where *Radiance* was anchored. I didn't want the wind to blow the boat back to the dock. I began swimming toward its transom, thinking I would pull myself aboard and toss out the anchor, hold it there while I swam back to the dock.

Then two things happened:

I heard the radio crackle and a voice say, "Lady Cut Cay. This is George Town police dispatch. Please switch to Channel 11. Lady Cut Cay, do you read?"

And I looked ashore to see the golf cart coming down the road and stopping at the foot of the dock. Three people in it—Justin Hatchitt, Torrey Kealing, and Jen Ryser.

Part of me wanted to climb aboard the boat and grab the radio.

The other part knew the only thing I had going on my side was that they didn't know I was out there.

If they wanted to leave the island, they had to come get the boat. And I'd be ready when they did.

50

I hung off the far side of the boat, holding on to the bowline, peeking around the bow toward the dock.

The three of them walked to the end of the dock. Hatchitt with the shotgun in one hand, a duffel bag in the other. The woman carried a second duffel bag and held a pistol at Jen Ryser's back. Jen's hands were still tied, but she seemed steadier on her feet.

It must have spooked them a little to see the three boats adrift. The dinghy had floated far to the south and was circling in an eddy well off the beach. The Albury had floated in the other direction. It was about the same distance from the dock as the blue-hulled boat, but there was no reason for them to go after the Albury. They didn't have the key to it.

They had to come here. To me.

They stood there, thinking it over, talking about it. Then Hatchitt put the shotgun and the duffel down on the dock. He slipped off his shoes and dove in.

He was a good swimmer with a powerful stroke. No wasted motion, efficiency of breath. He was making good time. Another minute or so and he'd be here.

I had to figure out a way to do this. He would board the boat over the transom. Should I grab him while he was still in the water at the stern of the boat? Should I wait until he had his hands on the transom rail and was occupied with pulling himself up? Or should I wait until he got on

the boat, then slip aboard behind him while he was focusing on cranking the engine?

He was closing in. Another thirty seconds maybe . . .

I didn't like the idea of grappling with him in the water. He'd be
winded from the swim, but I was pretty winded, too. From running
across the island, crawling under the deck, running down to the dock,
swimming out to the boat. I still had some kick left in me, but I liked the
idea better of confronting him on the boat.

I pulled back from the bow and began working my way toward the
transom.

Could I make it up behind him without him hearing me? The top of
the transom was at least four feet above the water. Without a swim ladder
down, you had to put a foot on one of the outdrives and boost yourself up.
If he managed to get to the helm and crank the engine before I got on
board . . . or while I had a foot on the outdrive. Not a pretty picture.

I could hear his final strokes now as he approached the boat, heard
him slap a hand on the hull. I looked around the side and there he was,
catching his breath for a moment, then putting a foot on the outdrive,
starting to pull himself up . . .

An instant decision: I couldn't let him get on the boat.

I thrust up from the water, got both hands on one of his feet. I pulled,
thinking he would fall backward into the water. But he managed to get
a grip on the edge of the transom and held tight.

I wrapped myself around his leg, pulling down with all my weight. He
was on his stomach. He couldn't see me. But his free foot found me—a
heel to my throat. He kicked again and again—my mouth, my nose. I
tasted blood. Another kick and I loosened my hold. He squirted out and
onto the deck.

I was fast out of the water and onto the outdrive. I raised myself up
onto the transom. And there he was—throwing open a long lazaret near
the helm, pulling out a shotgun, wheeling around on me.

Momentum was carrying me onto the deck, but I kicked to my left off
the transom in the instant the gun fired.

I felt the sting in my right thigh as I hit the water. I dove and kept going down. Above me I heard the concussive boom of another shot in my
direction.

Trying to get my bearings. Which way to go? The water was clear and he could easily spot me. I hadn't heard the sound of the engines turning over yet. Had to put distance between us.

Radiance was somewhere to my left. If I could make it there . . .

I turned, lungs already tightening. My thigh burned. I put a hand to it, felt the hole in my shorts, a fleshy lump of me. Saw pink streaming from the wound as blood melded with salt water.

Needed air, needed air bad. I told myself: *Five more strokes.* I crunched them out and surfaced . . .

Another boom and pellets pinging the water all around me. A quick gulp and on my way back down I spotted *Radiance* still another thirty yards ahead.

I made it halfway and came up for air again. Another shot, this time wide to my right, the pellets farther apart.

I could make out the hull of *Radiance* beneath the surface. It was swinging on its anchor line, nose to the wind, transom angled away from the blue-hulled boat.

I came up, gasping for air. The first time I tried to pull myself aboard, I slipped back into the water. Second try I got my belly onto the transom, then flopped over onto the deck.

51

checked out the wound in my thigh. Still bleeding, but not nearly as bad as I had feared. Some raw flesh, another trophy for the Chasteen scar collection. But nothing arterial. I'd been lucky.

And now I could hear the engines cranking on the blue-hulled boat. I crouched along the gunwales and saw it turning toward *Radiance*, its bowsprit high in the air as Hatchitt bore down on the throttle.

I headed for an aft ladder and climbed up to the pilothouse. I ran to the helm, flipped on the radio, and grabbed its handset.

"Mayday! Mayday! Mayday! This is Lady Cut Cay! Come in . . ."

The police dispatcher. What channel had he told me to switch to?

But before I could do anything, I heard a voice: "Zack, come in. Zack, is that you?"

Lynfield Pederson.

"Yes, it's me. Where *are* you?"

"Little Farmer's Cay, heading your way. What's . . . ?"

His words lost as a gunshot shattered a pilothouse window, just behind me. Hatchitt had pulled alongside *Radiance* and was running his boat from the flying bridge. It was open and gave him a perfect position for firing at me.

Another shot tore through another window and I hit the floor. I crawled across it, taking the interior ladder down to the main salon. I stayed low, moving into the galley, its cabinets and cupboards offering some protection for any shots that Hatchitt might make through the salon windows.

I could see his boat, circling *Radiance*, as he tried to figure out where I was. For all the cover the galley offered, I didn't like being pinned down in it. When Hatchitt boarded *Radiance* and came looking for me, as surely he would, I'd be forced to go deeper into the boat, down to the cabins. A dead end, a trap. He would have me.

Pederson said he was at Little Farmer's Cay. Several islands north in the chain. At least twenty minutes away. Too much time.

I pulled open drawers looking for something, anything, I could use as a weapon. But Mickey had taken all nonessential items off *Radiance* before it went into the Nassau boatyard for repairs. It hadn't been re-stocked yet.

I looked outside. The blue-hulled boat was off *Radiance*'s bow, Hatchitt leaning over a rail on the flying bridge trying to figure out where I was.

I couldn't let him corner me in here. I needed to get on the deck, find a spot to conceal myself. That way, when Hatchitt boarded *Radiance* and headed inside to look for me, I might be able to slip aboard his boat and get away.

Oh yeah, Zack. Simple as that. What a masterful piece of strategy. Still, it wasn't like I had a lot of options.

Once aboard his boat what would I do? Head back to the dock. Only . . . Torrey Kealing had a pistol and it was trained on Jen Ryser. How to get past that?

I raised up behind the galley counter so I could get a look toward shore. Torrey Kealing had moved away from Jen, toward the end of the dock, straddling the duffel bags. The shotgun left behind by Hatchitt was at her feet. She was shouting something to Hatchitt, but I couldn't make it out.

The engines on the blue-hulled boat lowered to an idle. I figured Hatchitt would bring the boat alongside *Radiance* and board from the aft. I needed to do something.

I crawled through the galley door onto the aft deck's sitting area. I opened a storage locker near the bulkhead. Wasn't nearly large enough to fit me inside.

The rattan couch sat on high legs. I could squeeze under it, but I'd be easy to spot.

I looked along the gunwales. The canvas chair covers were still stowed near the transom from our outing the day before. I could get under-neath them. As good a hiding place as I was going to find at this point.

I felt *Radiance* rock as the other boat bumped against it. Had to hurry.

I lifted the canvas covers and stretched out beneath them, flattening myself against the gunwale. My hip was resting on something hard. I reached down to find the conch shell I had scrubbed clean and stuck it there to give to Shula. After the flare-up with Mickey, I had forgotten to take it off the boat.

Boggy telling me, *"It bodes well that you found it, Zachary."*

I didn't know what it boded. All I knew was that my hand fit neatly into the shell, sliding inside the lip and gripping the spine. It was like wearing a big pair of brass knuckles, brass knuckles with a rigid, pointy end, like the onion dome of some Russian church.

I got settled under the canvas covers. Brass grommets were spaced along edges and I positioned one of them so I could see onto the deck.

Shallow breaths through my nose. I tried not to move. The sun beat down with its full afternoon rage. It was stifling under the canvas. The heat a liquid thing, nauseating and all-consuming. I fought back the urge to squirm, to lift up a corner of the canvas and let in some air.

I couldn't see beyond a small portion of the aft deck, but I heard Hatchitt as he tethered his boat alongside *Radiance*.

He called out, "Show yourself, Chasteen. You come out, I won't shoot. All you have to do is promise to let us get out of here."

I heard him step onto the deck. His feet came into view as he moved slowly into the sitting area. A good sign that he hadn't spotted me already.

I gripped the conch shell, willing the rest of me to be still. I held my breath.

He took a couple of steps and stopped by the galley door, looking through the window.

All he had to do was go inside. Go inside and then head down to the cabins looking for me and that would give me all the time I needed to jump on his boat and get out of there.

He reached for the galley door, then stopped just short of opening it. He turned. He stood there a moment. And then he strode toward the transom, heading straight for me. I saw the shotgun rising . . .

I sprung up, flinging the canvas over him. A blast from the gun, tearing a hole through the canvas, missing me.

I charged him, driving him back against the gunwale, the force of the impact releasing his grip on the shotgun and sending it overboard. We tumbled to the deck and he flailed beneath me, trying to get out from under the canvas.

I slammed the conch shell against the side of his head. It stunned him. I hit him again, just a glancing blow. Still, his body went slack.

I pulled myself off him, headed for the other boat. Just as I was boarding it I heard a roar from behind and turned to see him coming at me, the canvas still draping his torso as he leaped and knocked me into the cockpit of the other boat.

I landed hard on my back, knocking the breath out of me. I lost my grip on the shell as he landed on top of me. And now he covered me in the canvas, bunching it across my mouth and nose, butting my head with his head.

I fought for air and flopped beneath him trying to get purchase with my feet. I bucked up, toppling him to one side, and then I was upon him, the canvas still between us, covering his head now.

He tried to roll out from under me, managed to free both arms from beneath the canvas. He grabbed my neck, digging his fingers deeper and deeper.

The conch shell lay just beyond him. I pinned his shoulders with my knees and his fingers clawed into my neck, his thumbs finding my windpipe and squeezing it with ungodly force as I leaned out to grab the shell, touching its lip, dragging it closer, and then finally getting a grip on it.

The canvas folded over his face as I clasped the shell and brought it to me. The world was going wobbly. I couldn't breathe. I raised the shell and brought it down with both hands, its pointed end striking his head. He groaned and let out air.

I struck him again and he dropped his hands from my neck.

Many times I've thought back on that moment. Yes, I could have stopped right there.

But the rush of air into my lungs—adrenaline and anger and some atavistic urging from my very core. A final blow, brought down with everything I had and the sickening sound of a skull rent apart.

Blood seeped across the canvas cover—his death shroud.

52

Yeah, there was remorse, the kind of remorse that will hang with me forever, the kind of remorse where I will wake up at two o'clock in the morning and it will be staring me in the face, asking, *Why, Zack, why?* Justin Hatchitt was not the first man I had ever killed. There were two that preceded him. I could justify them all. That didn't mean I could live with it.

But right then was not the time to settle up accounts in my soul. I untethered the boat from *Radiance*, pushed off, and turned for shore. Torrey Kealing stood at the end of the dock, still straddling the two duffel bags. She had both hands on the pistol and it was pointed out at me.

Behind her, Jen Ryser had begun to back away. That was good. Keep going, Jen. Keep going.

I came in slowly, the engines chug-chugging just above idle. When I was about thirty yards out, Torrey yelled, "Where's Justin?"

"Put down the gun."

"Where's Justin? Let me see him."

"He's dead," I said. "Put down the gun."

I heard a pop, saw her arms jump. I flinched long after any bullet would have hit me. The shot didn't even hit the boat.

I ducked down as she emptied the pistol. The first several shots went wide but she zeroed in with the last two, one dinging into the flying bridge, another ripping into the hull.

I kept bringing the boat in, driving blind.

No more pops.

When I raised up, the dock was only ten yards away. Torrey grabbed the shotgun, leveled it at me.

And from behind her Jen charged, head down, bulling into Torrey's back, the shotgun firing high as both of them tumbled off the end of the dock.

I cut the engines and let the boat glide. I ran to the side.

Torrey surfaced and swam away from the boat. I let her go.

I looked around for Jen, right and left. Finally she bobbed to the surface. With her arms bound behind her, she was struggling to get her head above water. She coughed and sputtered, on the edge of panic.

I leaned out and pulled her in. I carried her to a bench in the cockpit and set her down. I found a knife in the console and cut her hands free.

She stared at the bloody canvas on the cockpit floor.

"Is he really . . . ?"

I nodded.

"Who are you?"

"A friend of your father's. I knew your mother, too. I met you when you were just a little girl, a long time ago."

"Last week was a long time ago," she said.

"It's over, Jen. You beat them."

She started to say something, stopped. She tried again and this time she broke down. I put an arm around her and held her close as she sobbed.

Torrey Kealing stopped swimming. She treaded water, catching her breath, looking back at us. There was nowhere to go and she knew it. A young woman lost and the world closing in.

I could go get her. Or not. I was pretty wrung out.

A voice over the radio: "Lady Cut Cay, Lady Cut Cay. Come in, do you read?"

I looked out toward the channel. Saw a big boat throwing off wake and heading our way. I grabbed the handset.

"I read you, Lynfield. Talk to me."

"Shit, Chasteen, how about *you* talk to me?"

"Got one dead on the boat. Another one in the water. Alive. Need you to fish her out on your way in."

"What the hell's going on, Chasteen?"

"Too much to tell," I said.

53

It took the better part of a day to smooth out everything that needed smoothing out.

Pederson called in a doctor from George Town. She took care of the wound in Curtis's leg, plucked some twelve-gauge shot out of my thigh, and examined Jen Ryser. She dispensed some painkillers and antibiotics, told us we'd be fine, and headed back to George Town.

While all that was going on, Pederson was on the radio with the police in George Town, getting Charlie and Boggy out of jail.

Charlie gave me the whole story when he and Boggy returned to Lady Cut Cay later that afternoon. After dropping me off in the seaplane the night before, they had made the short hop to Barraterre looking for fuel.

"That place has gone to hell since the last time I visited," Charlie said. "Got a real law-abiding element living there now. Upstanding citizens and all that. It's sad."

Someone spotted the seaplane as it approached the fishing village and identified it as the same one the police were looking for. They summoned the local authorities and within minutes of landing Boggy and Charlie were hauled off.

After refusing to tell police where to find me, they had been denied the opportunity to call Lynfield Pederson.

"Police here sure are territorial," Charlie said. "Those George Town boys got their backs up about Lynfield coming down and messing around on their turf."

Boggy and Charlie spent the night in jail and it was almost noon the next day before they were able to convince the George Town police that something was going down on Lady Cut Cay. By then, Lynfield Peder-son was already on his way there from Harbour Island, having covered for me as long as he possibly could.

"We tried like hell to get someone there sooner, Zack," Charlie said. "But we had already pissed them off and they weren't about to act real fast on our behalf."

"Kinda makes me feel bad for cussing you the way I did," I said. "But just kinda."

Pederson spent several hours interviewing Torrey Kealing before send-ing her off on a police boat to George Town. In Kealing's telling of it, you could already see her cobbling together a defense she might use in court. She was a victim, an innocent young woman seduced by Justin Hatchitt, fearful for her life if she didn't go along with him.

They had worked a couple of boat thefts together, subcontracting for an outfit that set up yachts for them to steal in Florida and the Carolinas. That was their connection with the Dailey brothers. They earned a few thousand bucks per boat for their end of it.

"Hatchitt had himself some bigger ideas," Pederson told me when the two of us sat down afterward.

Hatchitt found *Chasin' Molly* on his own and began laying the ground-work to steal it—hanging around the marina, spreading the word that he was looking for work on a boat. After learning that Jen Ryser had lots of money, and plenty more likely to head her way after Mickey died, a more ambitious plan evolved.

"He set the fire that burned down that house, the one belonging to the fellow who was supposed to go on the trip," Pederson said.

"Coach Tony and his girlfriend."

"Yeah, then Hatchitt made it a point to show up at the bar in Charles-ton on the same evening when Jen Ryser and her friends were trying to decide whether to scuttle their trip. Torrey was there, too, staging her own little seduction—of Pete Crumrine. She and Hatchitt, they didn't want the others to know they were a couple, since Hatchitt intended to put the moves on Jen Ryser," Pederson said. "Fellow must have felt real confident in his courting skills."

I remembered something Karen Breakell had told me about Jen: *"It was more like she needed to be with a guy to define herself."*

Far be it from me to delve into the psychology behind it. An absent father. The need to please. Basic self-esteem issues. We've all got our own little ticks. And natural-born predators like Justin Hatchitt are quick to take advantage where any advantage exists.

According to Torrey Kealing, Hatchitt had "brainwashed" her into thinking the two of them could assume brand-new identities and live the good life with their newly found riches. Since Mickey hadn't seen his daughter in more than twenty years and had no idea what she looked like, it would be easy enough for Torrey to become Jen Ryser. Hatchitt knew a thing or two about altering passports. And the fact that Torrey and Jen shared some basic physical characteristics—tall, blond, athletic— was a bonus. Hatchitt would assume the identity of Will Moody, at least for the short term, until he needed to become someone else.

"There were a couple of bags on that boat of theirs that had all sorts of stuff in them," Pederson said. "Cannibalized passports that they'd stolen, different photos, lamination sheets, a portable laminator."

It was essential that *Chasin' Molly* make it to the Bahamas and everyone on the boat go through customs and immigration before Hatchitt and Kealing put the murderous end of their plan into action.

"That way, when someone from back home got worried and came looking for them, it became a Bahamian problem. Another layer of bureaucracy to slow down the hunt. Plus, the two of them didn't seem to have a high regard for the ability of the Royal Bahamian Police and its investigative prowess," Pederson said. "Imagine that."

They hadn't counted on Karen Breakell bailing out when they reached Miner Cay. The plan was to drug her and toss her overboard on the passage to Marsh Harbour, just like they did with Will Moody and Pete Crumrine.

Neither had they counted on Abel Delgado showing up so quickly, sticking up posters, trying to sniff out where they might be.

"The way the Kealing woman tells it, Hatchitt didn't go into Marsh Harbour that night with the idea of killing Delgado. But he got a little jumpy when you showed up. Then when you answered Delgado's cell phone and took the call from that fellow . . ."

"Mr. Williamson," I said. "The one who said he had seen *Chasin' Molly* being hauled ashore by the Daileys."

"Yeah, that's when Hatchitt decided he had to act fast to cover up the trail."

"Kill Delgado, burn down the Daileys' boatyard . . ."

"And almost kill Karen Breakell."

"That one's my fault," I said. "I led Hatchitt straight to her."

"Don't be hard on yourself, Zack. Makes you feel any better, the Breakell woman came out of her coma. She's going to be alright."

"And to think you suspected me . . ."

Pederson shot me a narrow look.

"Come on, admit it," I said. "You had your doubts."

"I never once thought you attacked that woman."

"But killing Delgado? Burning down the boatyard?"

Pederson looked away.

"Hatchitt had you wrapped up pretty good for it, Zack. Give me that at least."

"Yeah," I said. "I'll give you that."

There still was nothing directly linking Justin Hatchitt to Delgado's murderer. But Pederson was expecting that to come, as soon as they had the results of forensic evidence taken from the pillow used to smother Delgado.

As for the Dailey brothers, they were already in police custody in Marsh Harbour.

"Still waiting to charge them with something officially but that's only a matter of time," Pederson said. "A couple of insurance investigators are already there, sifting through what the fire left behind. They've been able to identify at least four vessels that were reported stolen by their owners. Probably more to come."

"Any evidence that *Chasin' Molly* was in there?"

"Not yet. But Torrey Kealing verified that she and Hatchitt left it with the Daileys. Said they traded for that other boat, the one they showed up here in."

"Not a great trade," I said.

"No, but they were anxious to separate themselves from the sailboat. What they were thinking, if the whole thing worked with Torrey Kealing becoming Jen Ryser and all that, they were going to file an insurance claim for *Chasin' Molly* being stolen and collect on it that way."

"Some cojones," I said.

"Big brass ones," said Pederson.

The police superintendent in Marsh Harbour was still trying to horn in on things. He wanted to haul all of us up there for questioning. But Pederson interceded, saying he had conducted all the necessary interviews.

"I told him that to duplicate the efforts would be a tremendous waste of government resources in this time of dwindling revenues when we must all of us be very sensitive to any superfluous drain on public funds."

"You actually said all that?"

"Yeah, only I wrote it down and gave it to the *Nassau Guardian* first, as part of my official statement. I don't think you're going to hear anything else from that superintendent," Pederson said. "There was another reason I didn't want him butting in on the investigation."

"What's that?"

"Those two duffel bags of cash that Mickey Ryser handed over to Kealing and Hatchitt? I have a sneaky suspicion our friend in Marsh Harbour would have called the money in as evidence and Mickey would never see it again."

"You going to mention the money in your report?"

"Been thinking about that. Been thinking it might complicate things, create a whole lot more paperwork that I don't want to deal with," Pederson said. "Bring more than ten thousand dollars in U.S. currency into the Bahamas and you're supposed to declare it and fill out forms. I can't imagine Mickey did any of that."

"And you're just going to turn a blind eye to it?"

"Don't see how it's going to hurt anybody. Give the man a little peace, let him enjoy what time he's got left."

"Good of you."

Pederson shrugged.

"But I did count that money. Just so I'd know."

"And?"

"Five hundred thousand," Pederson said. "In each bag."

54

We left Lady Cut Cay early the next morning. But not before sitting down to a going-away breakfast from Miss Rose—big bowls of chicken souse with more of her johnnycakes.

Curtis was on the mend and already giving Edwin a long list of chores for the day. I was hoping Mickey would feel like joining us, but Octavia said he wasn't up to it.

"Yesterday took it out of him," she said. "He'll bounce back, though. That man's got him some steel."

Jen Ryser was remarkably improved by sleep, a shower, and Miss Rose's cooking. We didn't discuss her ordeal over breakfast. We talked instead about what she'd studied in college—art history—and what career she intended to pursue—not a clue.

"I started off being interested in museums and curating and art restoration," she said. "But then I realized it would mean being cooped up in stuffy old places and I'd miss being on the water. So I guess I'm still trying to figure out everything."

She was pleasant and composed and, unlike too many people her age, not so self-absorbed that conversation with her became a one-sided event. She asked good questions. She listened. I liked her a lot.

She was sitting by Mickey's bed, the two of them talking, when I dropped in to say good-bye.

"I don't even know how to begin to thank you," she said.

"Aw shucks, ma'am, weren't nothing. Just doing my job."

She looked at me.

"What is your job, anyway?"

"I grow palm trees."

"But he's really a Zack of all trades," Mickey said. "The palm trees, they're just a front."

Jen smiled. She got up from her chair.

"I'll leave you two to chat," she said.

We watched her go.

Mickey said, "She said she'd be staying here as long as I want her to."

"How are things going between you?"

"Slow," Mickey said. "There's lots of holes to fill in."

"You'll get there."

"Yeah," Mickey said. "We will."

I sat down beside the bed. Neither one of us spoke for a while.

Then Mickey said, "I was an asshole the other day. I really had it wrong."

"If I'd been in your place, I'd a probably had it wrong, too."

"Guess we see what we want to see. And sometimes it blinds us to what's really there," Mickey said. "Sorry I acted the way I did."

"No apology necessary," I said. "It all worked out."

"Only because you're a stubborn son of a bitch who went sneaking behind my back."

"I'll put that on my résumé."

He looked at me.

"I don't know how to begin to thank you either."

"Aw shucks, mister, it weren't . . ."

"Shut the hell up," Mickey said.

We sat quietly for a while.

"I don't care what you say, I owe you, Zack. I owe you big time."

"You don't owe me a thing, Mickey. You paid in advance. Long ago."

He stuck out his hand. I took it. I held on to it and it was a long time before I let it go.

55

On the evening of the full moon, we gathered outside Boggy's place on top of the hill at the nursery. Just the four of us. It was past Shula's bedtime and her eyes were droopy. She perked up after Boggy set fire to a pile of driftwood he had collected from the beach. Flames danced toward the sky.

Boggy danced, too. It was something to behold.

His skin was covered with oil that made him shine in the light of the fire. I asked him what kind of oil it was and he said, "Manatee fat." I'm pretty sure he was joking.

He wore his official Taino shaman outfit, which was little more than a leather jock strap. It showed a whole lot more of him than I really needed to see. Barbara, however, seemed riveted by the spectacle.

"For someone so short," she said, "he's really quite . . ."

"This is a sacred ritual," I said. "You're not supposed to gawk."

"I'm just saying . . ."

"He's a shaman. That's like a priest. Don't look down there," I said. "Or you'll go to Taino hell."

Boggy did his dance around the fire a few times. He lifted a gourd filled with one of his wretched concoctions. He said a few Taino words. He drank whatever was in the gourd. Then he danced some more.

Shula clapped her hands. She was loving the show. And she seemed to understand that it was all for her.

The gourd juice must have started taking effect because Boggy began to sing. Not a particularly catchy ditty, short on melody, but he sang loud and with feeling and that counted for something.

Two pouches sat on a rock near the fire—one made out of leather and the other blue satin with a gold drawstring. Boggy opened the blue satin pouch and pulled out a conch shell. It was a massive conch shell, by far the largest one I had ever seen.

I tried not to think of the conch shell I had used to kill Justin Hatchitt. But it was impossible to keep it out of my mind. It would always be there.

Boggy held up the conch shell with both hands.

"*Cohobo!*" he said. "*Cohobo!*"

A hole had been cut into the spiny end of the conch shell and now Boggy brought it to his lips and blew. It began low, almost inaudible, like a hum from deep within. By the time it hit the height of the crescendo, it was like the whistle blaring on a freight train rolling around the bend.

It scared Shula. She put her hands over her ears. But she didn't cry.

Boggy gave three long blasts on the conch trumpet. He set it down and walked over to where we sat.

"That is how we call the zemis, little one," he said to Shula. "And to-night they come to give you your name."

He took Shula from Barbara's arms and made three more passes around the fire, dancing and chanting, holding Shula high above his head.

Boggy motioned for Barbara and me to stand and join them by the fire. He returned Shula to Barbara's arms. He picked up the leather pouch and held it in front of Shula.

"This now belongs to you," he said. "It contains three zemis. They will be your companions for all your days."

He opened the pouch and pulled out three of the carved objects he had found along the runway in Walker's Cay. The first one he held up was oblong, about the size of his thumb, and if you looked hard you could make out what looked like large, round eyes and a scowling mouth.

"This is Yúcahu, Supreme God and Spirit of the Sky. And this is his mother, Atabey," said Boggy, holding up a second carving. It wore a scowl, too, and had a big, protruding belly. "Atabey is the mother of all things and the Goddess of Fertility."

"Whoa, hold on," I said. "My daughter is six months old. She's got a long way to go before she needs to know anything about fertility. Heck, I'm not even going to let her date until she's twenty."

Boggy ignored me.

"And this is Guabancex, Goddess of the Winds," said Boggy, holding up the third carving. "See how her mouth is open? If it pleases her, she can create a gentle breeze. Or, if she is angry, she makes a hurricane."

"Or if she's just slightly ticked off she breaks wind," I said.

Barbara jabbed me in the ribs.

"Enough," she said.

Boggy returned the three carvings to the leather pouch. Barbara held it while he took Shula from her and danced around the fire again, whispering into Shula's ear. Shula wore a solemn expression, one that I'd never seen on her before, the look of an old soul.

They returned to where we stood and Boggy held Shula out to us.

"I present to you . . . Cohibici," he said.

"Hello, Cohibici," Barbara said.

"Cohibici," I said. "What does it mean?"

Boggy said, "Is Taino for 'precious shell.' "

Barbara took Shula from Boggy, rocked her in her arms.

"My little Cohibici. My precious little shell. I like it," she said. "It's pretty."

Shula was fading fast. Barbara said she better get her to bed. She gave Boggy a hug.

"Thank you for that. It was wonderful, quite moving. I got goose bumps," Barbara said. "It is good to know that our daughter will have spirits by her side to protect her."

After they were gone, Boggy and I sat by the fire. I studied the flames, lost in grim thought.

"What bothers you, Zachary?"

"Just trying to figure it all out."

"Ah," Boggy said. "The work of us all."

"The whole thing with the conch shells. Me finding one where none was supposed to be found. It just showed up. This beautiful shell that I forgot about and then it was there when I needed it. Only I used it for something ugly and horrible," I said. "Then tonight, you blowing a conch shell to call the zemis. And my daughter, her Taino name—precious little shell."

"Yes, what is it, Zachary?"

"Her name. Was that something you just pulled out of your hat?"

Boggy touched his head. He looked at me.

"I do not wear a hat, Zachary."

"You know what I mean, dammit. When did you decide what her Taino name was going to be?"

"I did not decide. It was spoken to me."

"When?"

"Many days ago."

"Before we left for the Bahamas?"

"Oh yes, long before that."

"So when I found the conch shell and you said, '*It bodes well that you found it*,' you meant because it related to my daughter's Taino name. Not because I would use that shell to kill someone."

Boggy shrugged.

"It meant what it meant," he said.

"A whole lot of coincidence," I said.

"And that troubles you, why?"

"It troubles me because I don't believe in coincidence."

"Perhaps then, it was no coincidence," Boggy said.

"But if it wasn't coincidence, then that means it just happened. Only, it's too weird, too coincidental, for all of it to just happen. Which means something *caused* it to happen. Some spirit, some force. That Yúcahu guy, or Atabey, or whoever, sitting up there in the sky."

"Yes, it would mean that."

"But see, that's the thing," I said. "I don't believe in any of that either."

Boggy looked at me. He put a hand on my shoulder.

"You need to work on it," he said.

56

Mickey Ryser hung in there for almost three months, until the end of July. I didn't make it back to Lady Cut Cay to visit him. We had made our peace and said our good-byes and I wanted him to have that time with his daughter.

It was Jen who called with the news.

"Yesterday at sunset," she said. "He'd had a good day. He was weak, but we went out on *Radiance* and he was as happy as I had seen him. When we got back to the house, he rested for a while. And then we went out to watch the sunset on the upstairs porch. He had been telling me about the flash of green and how he had seen it several times from there on the island. Have you ever seen it, Zack?"

"Once or twice."

"So, it's real? He wasn't just pulling my leg?"

"Oh no, it's real alright. When you see it, you'll know it."

"Maybe someday," she said. "Anyway, the sun went down, and it was just this orange speck on the water and he said, 'There, there, do you see it?' I squinted and squinted, but I didn't see a thing. Then I turned and looked at him. He was gone."

57

We waited a few weeks to throw Mickey's wake. He was cremated in Nassau. And just before Labor Day, Jen set out from Lady Cut Cay aboard *Radiance*, bound for Miami. Curtis, Edwin, and Miss Rose accompanied her. Along the way, they tossed out some of Mickey's ashes at some of his favorite spots, with a healthy dusting going into the Gulf Stream.

We held the wake at Vizcaya Mansion, just like Mickey planned. He had set aside money to rent it for an evening, after it was closed to the public.

The crowd that came to honor him filled the place and spilled out into the gardens. All kinds of people—business associates, bankers and lawyers, politicians of every stripe. Two former governors of Florida, the senior U.S. Senator, presidents of three universities. Mickey had been generous in spreading around his donations and the gratitude that evening was genuine.

A lot of folks came down from Minorca Beach, part of the surf crowd who grew up with Mickey or used to hang out at his shop back in the day. There were charter boat captains from Key West, bartenders from South Beach, biker dudes from all over, models and musicians, artists and designers, and a few young women who represented the elite talent from Fort Lauderdale's better strip clubs. Mickey got around.

Some of my teammates with the Gators and the Dolphins were there. Coach Shula showed up, too. I let him hold his namesake.

"She's got my dimples," he said.

I didn't argue. You never argued with the Coach.

There was a ton of food, three bars, and two bands. One called themselves the Spam All-Stars and had an Afro-Cuban jazz groove going. The other one, the Kronics, played old rock 'n' roll.

About an hour into the evening, Jen Ryser welcomed everyone and read a poem she'd written to honor her father. I gave the eulogy and only had to stop twice to wipe my eyes, which I thought was pretty good, considering.

Plenty of people stood up to tell favorite stories about Mickey. There were lots of laughs, lots of tears. The way it's supposed to be.

The ceremony ended with Edwin singing an a cappella version of "Redemption Song." He sang it with his eyes closed. His voice was strong and true. When it was over the silence hung heavy. And then everyone headed for the bars.

I fetched a chardonnay for Barbara, a beer for myself, and some water for Shula. We were sitting at a table in a side garden when Jen Ryser joined us.

"Could I steal your husband for a few minutes?"

"I certainly won't press charges," Barbara said.

I walked with Jen behind the mansion down to the bay. *Radiance* was anchored out near the channel, its dinghy tied up at the mansion's concrete dock.

"I need to show you something," Jen said.

We hopped in the dinghy and she motored us out to *Radiance*. She stepped aboard and I followed her to the main salon. She gestured to the couch. I sat.

A thick accordion file sat atop the coffee table. Beside it a slim manila folder.

"For you," she said, passing the accordion file to me.

I flipped through the file. It contained *Radiance*'s complete maintenance record from its launch in 1971, through three successive owners, all the way to Mickey Ryser. Tens of thousands of dollars' worth of work: rebuilt seacocks, remounted rudders, new cutlass bearings and exhaust hoses, upgraded electronics and gauges, new holding tanks, water pumps, batteries and generators, right down to a new compressor for the air horn. And that didn't even get into any of the engine work or replacing the furnishings.

I put the file on the table.

"OK," I said, "you showed me this, why?"

"Because my father wanted to be sure you saw that before you saw this."

She handed me the manila folder. I opened it. It contained *Radiance*'s registration and all its official paperwork.

"What does this mean, Jen?"

She smiled.

"It means *Radiance* is yours," she said. "If you want it, that is. Otherwise, my father's will states that it should be sold, with the proceeds dispersed among his charities."

I didn't know what to say. So I didn't say anything.

"He wanted *Radiance* to stay in the family. It's too much boat for me. Plus, I'm more about sailboats," Jen said. "You're the closest thing he ever had to a brother, Zack. He was really hoping that you would accept the boat."

"I accept," I said. "I'm overwhelmed, but I accept."

"Good," she said. "Because in that case, there's one more thing."

She got up from the couch and went to a closet. She pulled out the two duffel bags I'd seen on the dock that day back in April.

"I was a little nervous about bringing all this back into the country, but it went without a hitch," she said. "Guess I'm now officially a smuggler."

"Worse things to be," I said.

She plopped the bags down at my feet. An envelope was taped to the top of one of the bags. My name was on it.

"Open it," Jen said.

The handwriting was Mickey's.

"Dear Zack-o,

"Before you start drooling I want you to know something: The money inside these bags isn't for you. So don't start feeling too goddam grateful.

"I want you to take some of it—you decide how much—and give it to Abel Delgado's wife. Pay off her house or something. She deserves it. Spend some money on her kids. The fact that they don't have a father is my fault, and I want to make sure they are taken care of.

"The rest of the money is for *Radiance*. Treat her right. Keep her in the family. Stay in touch with Jen and take her for a ride on it every now and then, even though she's a goddam sailor and looks upon *Radiance* as a stinkpot. Jen's a good girl, but she's not all grown-up yet, and she'll need you from time to time."

I looked at Jen.

She said, "Don't worry. I read it already. I'm not at all offended."

I returned my attention to the note.

"*Radiance* is not a cheap date. That day when you asked me what it cost to maintain her? I was lying my ass off. Because upkeep," Mickey wrote, "really *is* a bitch.

"You'll notice the ceramic urn sitting on the end table by the couch . . ."

I stopped reading and looked at the end table. The urn bore an intricate blue and white design, Mexican pottery with a stopper in the top.

I looked at Jen. She smiled.

"That's me inside," the note went on. "Or what's left of me anyway. Dust to dust, ashes to ashes, and all that good stuff.

"What, you thought I wasn't going to hang around? I'll be watching, Zack-o, I'll be watching. But don't let it creep you out. I won't pull any weird shit.

"And if you drop anchor someplace really cool, someplace where the water is blue and the horizon is clear, where there's good music playing and the moment is magical, then sprinkle a little bit of me off the transom, so I can enjoy it, too.

"Yer bro, Mickey."